MAGIC OR DIE

Inner Demons, Book One

J.P. Jackson

A NineStar Press Publication

Published by NineStar Press
P.O. Box 91792,
Albuquerque, New Mexico, 87199 USA.
www.ninestarpress.com

Magic or Die

Printed in the USA
First Edition
July, 2018
Print ISBN: 978-1-949340-02-0

Also available in eBook, ISBN: 978-1-948608-99-2

Warning: This book contains sexually explicit content, which may only be suitable for mature readers, and depictions of violence, homophobia, imprisonment, mental illness, character death, and religious topics.

James Martin is a teacher, a powerful Psychic, and an alcoholic. He used to work for the Center for Magical Research and Development, a facility that houses people who can't control their supernatural abilities, but left after one of his students was killed, turning to vodka to soothe his emotional pain. The problem is he still has one year left on his contract.

When James is forced to return to the CMRD, he finds himself confronting the demons of his past and attempting to protect his new class from a possible death sentence, because if they don't pass their final exams, they'll be euthanized.

James also discovers that his class isn't bringing in enough sponsors, the agencies and world governments who supply grants and ultimately purchase graduates of the CMRD, and that means no profit for the facility. James and his students face impossible odds—measure up to the facility's unreachable standards or escape.

Dedication

To Lonny. Everything I do is so much richer when shared with you. Love you always.

To the Magicals who helped make this a much better tale: David, Rachel, Katherine, Brandon, Kim, James, Kari, Amy, and Mike. I can't begin to tell you how much all your time, thoughts, and ideas made me rethink everything about this story! You guys are the best darn beta-readers any author could hope to have.

To my editor Jason, damn you and your plot bunnies! This is all your fault. You're the bestest.

To the fantastic people at NineStar Press, and particularly Raevyn, thank you for continued support.

The CMRD is the acronym for the Canadian Centre for Magical Research and Development, but those who have had dealings with the corporation refer to it in whispers as Control Magic or Die.

One: Call Back

"YES, MIRIAM. YES, I know. I know it's been over a year. I'm not sure I'm ready."

The knuckles on my hand cramped from clasping my cell phone in a death grip. I glanced at my watch. This conversation had gone on too long. In the span of two minutes, Miriam had managed to exhume memories and history I wanted buried and forgotten. I sucked in a short breath as nausea surged like a tsunami of fear. Its behemoth wave washed bile against the back of my throat.

I slumped down the stained and weathered wall of the coffin-sized studio apartment I reluctantly called a home. It wasn't a bad place to live, except for the cockroaches I found on a daily basis. I'm sure they considered it a veritable paradise. Absentmindedly, I toed an old pizza box near my foot while listening to Miriam. One of the insects scampered across the matted Berber carpet.

Gross.

Cody. A pale ghostlike face flashed before me. His hair, the exact colour of fall fallowed fields, hung listlessly over one eye, as blood trickled out of the corner of his mouth. His chapped lips parted, asking me, "Why?"

I ignored the vision. Well, ignored wasn't the right word, more like boxed it up with a heavy rock and pitched it into the abyss of my mind with all the other terrifying nightmares.

"I know. I owe you, yes. I'm just not sure—" I crawled over to the upended crate being used as a coffee table, grasping for my last pack of smokes. I lit one, enjoying the soothing crackle of the tobacco as it ignited, and then inhaled deeply.

Ah, yes. Hello, nicotine, my demon friend.

Miriam continued blithering while I half-heartedly listened to her soul-sucking voice. She was demanding my presence.

"What? You mean, tomorrow? Miriam, I don't think it's a good idea." I drew in another steady stream of the toxic smoke. It burned my lungs as the addictive chemicals flooded through my body. *I really need to quit.*

Scraping together the smallest ounce of courage, I attempted to defy her. "No, I can't."

A wraithlike hand, desiccated and fragile, inched its way across my shoulder and gripped my tense neck muscle. Its sharp nails dug into my flesh. Its bite, a warning.

Cody's lifeless lips brushed my ear, sending cold shivers skittering across my back. Eruptions of goose flesh covered my neck and shoulders. His voice was a memory and a sound I would never forget.

"Don't do this. You'll kill me again." His icy breath whispered to me.

Another box, a bigger rock, another addition to the pit of despair in my head.

"No," I replied to one of Miriam's inane questions. "There's an Arcane too? I've never been good with them. They creep me out. No, I don't think I've *ever* seen that. Shit." Miriam had just described a scene for me. My flesh turned buggy, as if I had chiggers nesting and burrowing deep into my skin. "Oh god that's gross. It's also not a good sign." I pointed uselessly at the wall, waving my finger, trying to make a point to the caller. "I never took the exam for the third class." Miriam had asked if I'd kept up my licensing. I instantly felt guilty. I should have done it years ago. One thing was becoming evident from the conversation—she needed my help. Help only I could give.

"All right, maybe, I think I can. Consult only. Do you hear me, Miriam? Just a consult." I had tried desperately to stay the hell out of this. I wasn't ready. I didn't want to go back there. "What time? Yes. I'm pretty sure. Miriam—" A thousand reservations ran through my mind, a wild stampede, unbridled, laced with dread and fear. "How many? How many in this class?"

The question sat like the world perched on my shoulders. The higher the number, the bigger the world, the more responsibility, an undeniable possibility of...

"Five! Are you kidding me? I can't do five. No. No! It's not possible."

She was out of her mind.

"Yes, my sister is still on the streets. You know that's close to blackmail, right?" I stubbed out the cigarette. The lacquer of smoke in my mouth tasted like I had just licked the bottom of an ashtray, and it was suddenly very hard to breathe. *Why do I smoke again?*

"Fine. Tomorrow. Yes. Ten a.m. Yes, I'll be there. What do you mean dress appropriately?"

I looked at my cell phone, disgusted as the call ended.

I flipped the device onto the floor as if it had burst into flame and branded the conversation into my hand. I snorted. Like, I'd forget.

Stretching around to the other side of the crate, I grabbed blindly for a bottle I hoped was there. By all the gods' great divine gifts, it was. And it still had liquid in it. In fact, it was surprisingly half-full.

I tipped the vodka bottle back, allowing its burn to strip away the cancer stick's smoky film inside my mouth.

Swaying back and forth with my eyes closed, I tried to drown out the endless voices in my head. The words inundated my impending thoughts of doom and failure, and I could feel the chaos and panic mounting. Steadying myself and regaining my mental capacities, I gazed out the window. It was dark already and only six, early evening at best. Yay for daylight-savings time and late fall in Canada. Lights from the downtown cityscape lazily twinkled and danced before me. It should have been a pretty sight, but the darkness always seemed too oppressive, like a shroud. And I knew better. Things lived in the shadows.

I took another swig from the clear glass bottle. The burn hit my throat and disintegrated the bile that had crept up there.

Five very gifted students.

I rubbed the stubble covering my face and took yet another nip. Except it wasn't a quick sip, it was a good one. A long one.

The window acted like a mirror, and my image reflected against the backdrop of the city skyline. I looked like shit. My short brown hair had cowlicks; thank god I kept it close. But the rest? No wonder Miriam instructed me to clean it up. The shirt I was sort of wearing was only half buttoned and stained in several spots. I had no pants on, but the pair of tighty-whities, which weren't exactly white anymore, or tight, were ripped and showed more flesh than they were supposed to. Jesus.

How did my life get here?

Five young people had no control of their gifts.

And I had a sister who was lost out in the sparkle-light of downtown's darkness, up to who knew what, and doing it with god only knew who, mired in her own addictions.

I glanced around my shit-hole apartment, wondering what the fuck I was going to do.

Two: The Interview

MORNING CAME WAY too early.

The cell phone's alarm sounded off, penetrating my brain like a crystalline spike driving into my skull over and over and over.

Reaching across the bed, I grabbed my phone and tapped the button, ending the assault.

There were no less than a dozen texts from Miriam. All were variations of *don't be late.*

Rolling out of bed hurt. My head was dead weight and the throbbing pulse of my heartbeat pounded a steady rhythm. All I could picture was a sadistic garden gnome smashing my brain with a little war hammer. As my foot hit the floor, I inadvertently kicked an empty vodka bottle, sending it spinning against the wall. The resulting racket was like the tap-dancing of a hundred steel-plated shoes with my forehead as their stage.

I stretched out my back and vertebrae popped in succession all the way down my spine. Instant relief. But the clothes that were still stuck to me from the previous night pulled me back to reality, along with sharp stabs of pain from my hangover headache. I ripped off the holey underwear, scrunched them into a ball, and as I was about to pitch them into the corner with the rest of the to-do laundry, I realized the pile was just a little too big. Betcha there wasn't another clean pair. My balls were stuck to the inside of my thighs from the sweat of an alcohol-induced sleep.

I gave my bunched-up gotch a quick whiff. *Whoa.*

They sailed through the air and landed on top of the mountain of used clothes.

"Commando it is," I mumbled and then added the shirt to the growing mound after giving my pits the sniff test.

The shirt unwadded as it flew and a trailing sleeve caught the neck of another empty glass bottle which was precariously perched on my creative crate of a coffee table. The resulting bang and clank of the bottle hitting the floor and rolling made me grab my head as that little monster inside smashed its weapon a little harder.

How much did you drink last night, you idiot?

I shuffled my way down the hall to the bathroom and flicked on the light, instantly regretting the decision. Fumbling through the darkness would have been easier on my eyes. I dug through the vanity's only drawer, found the bottle of Tylenol, and fought with the lid, then eventually tapped out a couple of little promissory gems of pain relief. I swallowed them and a couple of ibuprofen without water. Water would only make me spew at this point.

Next step, get wet.

The shower wasn't exactly hot or well pressurized, but it was better than showing up to Miriam's party smelling like a day-old martini. I was not shaving. Screw her.

With a bit of luck and a little scrounging, I came up with a pair of gray slacks and a light-blue dress shirt. Both were tight. Dammit.

My middle had a jiggle.

When the fuck did that happen?

The pack of cigarettes was empty. I'd have to pick up another on the way. After snagging my wallet, a coat, the car keys, and my cell, I launched myself out into the world and headed across the street to where my rusted-out 90s Corolla sat. It was champagne beige. Champagne. That was fuckin' humorous. Champagne would imply luxury or class. This poor machine hadn't had either in a long time. My breath hung in front of me. The damp and cold autumn air hurt my face. But as much as it stung, it was oddly soothing against my dehydrated existence.

The car required a little coaxing and a few salty words in order to get going, but as soon as the engine revved to life, a belt somewhere under the hood started squealing. A nice old lady, dragging one of those two-wheeler shopping carts behind her, gave me a dirty look. I took back the *nice* part.

Embarrassed by my car's lack of silence, I slammed it into drive and pulled away. Only then did I notice the parking ticket flapping itself violently against the windshield.

"For fuck's sake." I was in a mood. I turned the windshield wipers on and the ticket dislodged and flew away like a little bird.

The car's heat didn't work well, even though I cranked it to the hottest it would possibly go and hoped for tropical ferns to sprout from the dash. A glance to my phone told me it was already nine thirty. Despite Miriam's numerous texts, I was going to be late.

THE FACILITY WAS out of town.

Which was smart. If something were ever to happen, at least it could be contained.

The car's brakes squealed as I approached the guard's booth. The vehicle's interior hadn't warmed, and my lips were tinged blue from the long drive without heat. I rolled down the window.

"James Martin here to see Miriam van Allen," I said unemotionally and blew a lungful of smoke out the open window and stamped out the cig in the car's overflowing ashtray. I'd driven up to this checkpoint a hundred times before, but oddly, the same person was never stationed there.

The guard, who didn't look like puberty had come to visit yet, checked his logs. Then his eyebrows flew halfway up his scalp as he returned his glare to me, judging.

"Mr. Martin, you're already twenty minutes late. Mrs. van Allen won't be pleased. Proceed in, park in section C spot 42, and then report at the security desk."

I rolled up the window without a word of acknowledgement. What a snot. They wanted me, not the other way around. They could bloody well wait.

The front doors to the facility reminded me of a school, which was funny, because by trade, I was a teacher. But no school district was going to hire one of us.

"James Martin here to see Miriam van Allen," I said as I walked up to the second guard sitting behind an imposing security desk in front of the walk-through metal scanner. He got the same enthusiasm from me as the gatekeeper did.

He too checked his logs. The bureaucracy and red tape there ran deep. Streamers of red. Spools and spools of it. I tapped my foot impatiently, waiting for him to find my invitation. I flicked my wrist towards me and stole another glance at my watch—*Jesus*—I was almost thirty minutes late. Miriam was going to lose her shit if she hadn't lost it already.

"He's with me," Miriam said. Speak of the devil. The devil was decked out in a starched black dress, which was rather form-fitting for a lady of her age, sporting six layers of pearls and a white updo with so much hairspray I could smell it from where I stood.

"Miriam, you look lovely." I feigned an I'm-happy-to-see-you face.

"Shut up, James." She smiled evilly at me and then nodded at the guard. Her voice had more rasp to it than I remembered. "You're late. I told you not to be. And I also said dress appropriately. The least you could have done was wear underwear."

She linked her arm into mine and gently guided me through the security gates. I chanced a peek down to my crotch. It wasn't *that* noticeable.

"This isn't a game, James. I need you, and what's more, these kids need you."

"Believe me, I know. That's why I haven't come back, Miriam. I'm not suitable or capable for this job."

"Nonsense. You're a stubborn idiot. One of the most talented Psyches I've ever met, as well. And today, I'm going to make you use it." She turned us down a metal corridor. The odd door peppered the long hallway. Portals to hell, I was sure of it.

We made several turns on our walk, and it didn't take long before I was completely screwed around. Here I was again, lost in the bowels of the CMRD.

An armed guard passed us and then cut sharply away down another intersecting hallway.

"That's new," I said, staring after the uniformed man with an assault weapon strapped over his shoulder. He disappeared as he made his way to another destination. This place was massive.

"We've had to make a few adjustments. They're getting stronger."

"Who? The five you mentioned?"

"No, James. All of them."

"How many are here?" I asked, shocked.

"Enough. But that's not for you to worry about. Here," she said and then turned a doorknob and pushed the door open.

I followed in behind her, but then she stepped aside and I found myself front and center in a long room with a huge oval stone slab. There were at least twenty people sitting around the tabletop, mostly men, a few in uniforms unrecognizable to me. But I could tell from the smell in the room, every last one of them was some type of high-ranking powered official.

"Ladies and gentlemen." Miriam nodded her head towards the executive crowd and then turned towards me. "Meet Mr. James Martin."

There was nothing but blank stares boring holes through me. I could feel a big round globe settling on top of my shoulders again, just like Atlas. Stress is a very heavy thing.

I gave them a wave, then looked at Miriam and shrugged, not sure what to expect next.

Miriam rolled her eyes. "Honestly, James."

A uniformed toad stood up and glared at the two of us. He didn't seem particularly pleased, and his jowls wobbled as he started to speak.

"We waited a half hour for this?" He pointed in my direction.

"I assure you, Major Harris, James is the best candidate for what we need."

"You'll forgive me if I'm not impressed." His short sausage fingers rummaged through files and papers in front of him as he sat back down, dismissing me in the process.

"James, if you would, please?" Miriam nudged me.

"Really, Miriam? I said a consult. That was the only reason I was coming."

"Just do it, James." She smiled at me, but her teeth were firmly planted together. She was not happy. One thing I had learned from my last stint with the CMRD—when Miriam gets pissed, ragingly angry, she gets mean.

"Fine."

I took a deep breath. I hated doing this.

I closed my eyes and searched for the spot. It was up front in my head. Fishing, looking for it—sometimes, it was just right there other times, I had to go on an expedition but...ah...there it was. I could feel my brain tense— yeah, I know, that's not possible, but that's what it felt like. And then I pushed it forward.

It was like a bubble expanded and enveloped the entire room, and I loved to watch as people noticed a subtle change in themselves as soon as I'd touched them with that amorphous shimmer. The magic is an energy only other *Magicals*—people like me—can see. The regular folks, *Norms* can't see it, but they can feel it. The sensation I get when I'm about to take them over is all-consuming, addictive even. It's a tingling, a pull, a trigger that sets off the hunt within me, a primal stalker instinct as soon as I see that glint in their eyes. It's their shock. A surprise, but an unpleasant one.

Laugh.

The entire room of high-powered La-Di-Das all started giggling and chuckling, a few even bellowed out a good hearty guffaw.

But even as they were laughing, there were looks of complete confusion on their faces. Questioning glances, gazes shot across the table to the others around the room that said, "I'm not doing this. What the hell is happening?"

Stand up.

The entire room immediately came to attention.

Grab the person's hand next to you.

Everyone grabbed the person's hand next them, forming a ring made from grasped hands. It appeared as if they were all first graders about to go on a school trip.

Grab the person to your right and...

"James, let go. I think that's enough." Miriam's bony claw gripped my bicep.

There was a snap, a sharp sting, like a rubber band flicked back and smacked my flesh as I released the entire room, all twenty-plus of them. There were a few stunned faces, pallid in colour, knowing I could control them utterly. A couple of sighs as I released them, and one lady who started crying.

"Ladies and gentlemen, may I reintroduce Mr. James Martin. James belongs to the Psyche class and is one of the most powerful Empaths we've ever had the privilege of hiring."

There was a collective uncomfortableness as the uppity snots came to the realization of the extent of my abilities.

Suck on that, you assholes.

Three: Class List

"ALL RIGHT." MIRIAM tried to assuage the small crowd and waited until the side banter in the room dissipated. "I understand James's abilities are rather unsettling and somewhat forceful."

"Exactly how many others have abilities like him? He controlled every single one of us. What's to prevent him from controlling an army?" Major Harris said. He was shaking, and his fat stuffy face formed angry red blotches that bled together. From the way his jowls hung over his tight shirt collar, you'd swear he was swelling with rage at my takeover.

"I couldn't sustain large numbers of people for any lengthy period of time, and frankly, you weren't actively resisting me. You were just sitting there," I said. It was true. My abilities also had a physical cost and other limitations. "If you fought the impulses I had sent, you wouldn't have succumbed. It works best on the element of surprise." I gave them little morsels of information. That certainly wasn't the total extent of my restrictions, but I'll be damned if I was going to give it all away.

"Feel better, Major?" Miriam asked. "Perhaps you'll agree James is the most qualified for the job, then." She looked around the room, presumably waiting for anyone to disagree. "Very good, let's proceed. We are here today to review prospective candidates. These are the five students James will be taking on."

The participants in the room nervously shifted the dossiers in front of them.

"I didn't agree to take on any class. I said consult—" I hissed from the corner of my mouth while my hackles rose and panic stirred in my gut.

"Need I remind you about your sister?" she whispered to me through tightly pursed lips and gritted teeth.

"I hate you," I retorted back just as quietly.

"In front of each of you are dossier reports. Let's start with the first." A hidden movie screen descended, filling up the front of the room. Lights around the periphery of the stone table dimmed as spotlights above each seat turned on, creating an eerie halo around the executives' heads.

"The first is twenty-four-year-old Ning Chiu," Miriam started, as I grabbed the file on the girl. A picture of Ning appeared on the screen. She was pretty, bright, perky, and looked like she was all of sixteen in her schoolgirl uniform. "Ning is an exchange student from Beijing, China. She speaks Mandarin, Cantonese, English, German, and Italian. She's incredibly gifted with languages and came to Canada to study the North American prairie indigenous tongues."

Miriam held up a remote and pushed a few buttons. The picture on the screen flickered, disappeared, and then returned. She clicked the remote again and *poof*, the image was gone, blinding the audience with a pure white screen.

"Goddamn thing..." She pushed more buttons and waved the remote with unsuccessful results in the direction of where Ning's picture had been. People around the table held their hands over their eyes, trying to shy away from the blinding light.

An underling who had been standing against the back wall rushed forward.

"May I," he inquired as his hands flailed in an attempt to wrestle the remote away from her.

"Just make it work," Miriam barked.

With the click of a few buttons, the tech guy had a movie clip playing with Ning and an unknown male interviewer who was off-screen.

"Ning, can you make the wind blow?"

"Yes," Ning said softly. She closed her eyes as her long black hair swooped and swayed as if she was outside in a gentle autumn breeze.

"More?" the interviewer asked.

"Are you sure?" she said tentatively.

"Yes, please."

A whirlwind began, and a desk behind Ning jerked and shifted and then lifted off the floor, spinning in a clockwise motion, pivoting on one desk leg. Papers, books, an assortment of odd items were violently sucked into the vortex Ning had created. A spiralling tunnel of wind, akin to a mini tornado, twirled behind her. Objects caught up in its rotation flew out at random intervals, but oddly, as items were ejected from the small twister, none of them came anywhere near Ning.

"Now the ice?" the interviewer asked.

"No, please..." Ning's eyes seemed to plead with the unseen requestor.

"Yes, Ning. Do it."

She grimaced and brought her shoulders close in to her neck. It was obvious Ning was uncomfortable with the request, perhaps even a little scared. She opened her eyes to reveal her dark-chocolate irises had morphed into shimmering ice blue. Her face had changed too. It was sterner, a touch angry as her eye twitched. Ice crystals erupted on the surface of her skin and raced across the side of her face encapsulating it within a glassy surface. It was smooth but opaque, and it reminded me of Chinese Opera masks.

Behind her, the whirling dust devil took on a bluish tinge as the tornado filled with ice crystals. From within the windstorm, a skeletal face made out of hoarfrost formed, its maw opened and long fangs grew.

With a sudden burst, the frozen creature flung itself forward, escaping the whirlwind and sailing towards the camera as its long skeletal body, seemingly made of icicles, stretched forward with clawed hands.

A garbled scream erupted, presumably the male interviewer, as blood sprayed across the room. Droplets of spatter dotted Ning's cheek. Within seconds, the ice guise disappeared from her face, melting into dripping water, while Ning's bottom lip trembled and her eyes filled with tears. The camera panned down as if whoever was holding it had lost control. Streaks of blood were splattered across the room and Ning's clothes, painting a stark contrast against her light-blue top. Her wide eyes, which had obviously seen a horrific scene, shut tight, and she broke down sobbing.

The video stopped, and Miriam heaved a deep sigh. She made a *tsk* noise and shook her head.

"Ning, such a lovely girl, can control wind and ice, which would make her an Elemental, but the appearance of the ice demon would suggest she has some abilities in the Arcane realm as well. Her talents showed up unexpectedly after a minor car accident. However, if she doesn't manifest her magical energy each hour, she loses control. We've now had three guards killed in the line of duty, frozen in various methods when Ning forgets to use her talents."

"What happened to the interviewer?" a woman in the back asked, somewhat startled at what she'd just witnessed.

"We've learned not to push our subjects, and since that incident, we've implemented segregation protocols so the students are never physically able to come into contact with our staff. With one exception of course." Miriam looked towards me. "Our teachers are exposed, but then we are now attempting to ensure that the instructors are as gifted as our students."

"Wait," I said, confused. "She's Elemental and Arcane?"

"Doesn't that go against what we know?" Major Harris asked. "I thought each person exhibits an ability from one class and one class only."

"That's what we had originally thought, yes." She paused, her mouth forming just the slightest of frowns. "These five...well—" She stopped, inhaled and fidgeted. She cast a quick glance in my direction. "—they are vastly more powerful than anything we've seen, and each of them have scored at least at a Cat Five level." There was a slight tremble to Miriam's voice. Perhaps the others in the room hadn't taken note of it, or even suspected that her normally raspy voice was like that.

I knew better. She was concerned. That made me even less eager to take on any new projects with the CMRD. If they didn't know what they had gotten themselves into...

"That's impossible," Major Harris scoffed. For the most part, I couldn't argue with him, as much as I wanted to. He was right. Folks who displayed a magical talent only ever belonged to one group, from the Elemental, Psyche, or Arcane classes. This was the first time I had ever heard of anyone having abilities in more than one class.

Cats, or categories, were a way of ranking how powerful a person was. Cat One was the weakest, displaying their ability only in high-emotion situations. They generally weren't trainable. Anyone classified into a Cat Five was dangerous and rare. People who scored that high had an extraordinary level of control over most spells or abilities within a particular class. I was just barely a Cat Five, and that was arguable, as there were certain things within the Psyche class I'd never been able to do. I'd been told once that Cat Five individuals were so rare that out of the entire human population we numbered less than one hundred thousand. That might seem like a lot, but in comparison to the billions of people on the planet, it's a very small percentage.

Miriam ignored Major Harris.

"Moving on, we have Chris Sanderhill." She pushed more buttons on the remote, and nothing happened on the screen. The underling returned and offered assistance. There was a thrashing of hands and more awkwardness in the room as she gave the tech support guy a truly dirty look. He took the remote and stood near her, taking control over the audio-visual equipment.

"As I was saying, Chris Sanderhill, twenty-one, from Mississauga, Ontario. A very angry youth, but that rage and ire fuels his fire. Literally.

Chris is easily the most powerful Earth and Fire Elemental we've ever seen. But he is also a shapeshifter."

"Does he incorporate both in the shifted form?" I asked.

"As a matter of fact, his favourite form is a fire wolf. Correctly guessed, James. As you might imagine, not only is Chris powerful as his animal, a *large* wolf at that, but his paw prints leave embers, stoking fires wherever he treads. His bite similarly cuts and cauterizes at the same time.

"Chris's problem, however, is that, once his anger takes over, there's little anyone can do to calm him down until he drops from exhaustion. If he's allowed to continue in this state, our physicians estimate his life expectancy is less than two years."

The movie clip showed a gigantic wolf, black as night, with the edges of its fur sparking and glowing like live campfire cinders. It trotted off into a grass clearing, leaving behind glowing footprints that ignited the dry prairie scrub. Within seconds of the wolf's passing, a raging fire burned, with CMRD employees in full fire gear attempting to douse the bonfire.

Before the wolf completely disappeared off the movie screen, there was a burst of smoke that surrounded and concealed the beast. I tilted my head, staring at the film. That wasn't quite right. It was more like the eruption was the wolf exploding, but then the cloud coalesced back into a human. The camera panned in, and the humanoid form turned to face the lens. It was Chris, and he snarled as tiny embers of fire flickered and burned just under the surface of his dark skin.

"Why is he so angry?" I asked.

"Chris had a twin brother who was killed. We understand it was gang-related, but we haven't pursued the matter with Chris. He gets too emotional and, well, this happens. Apparently, they were mirror twins. Rare. As much as Chris is Earth and Fire, his brother was Water and Air. Shame, really," Miriam said. She glanced at me sideways, as if to indicate that this was where I should start with Chris's anger issues.

I am not taking another class...but who else is going to help them?

A few of the bigwigs fidgeted uncomfortably in their seats. Chris was damaged goods. Powerful and destructive damaged goods. But there was more than one person in the room dashing out notes in secret files.

"And then we have Camila Rodriguez. Camila's talents are primarily within the Psyche realm. She's capable of creating Astral Projections to anywhere she's ever personally been, regardless of distance, and physically able to manipulate her environment through her projections. That is not a talent we see often. We believe she can also explore short distances while in Astral form, something that is also quite unusual. She's an Elanchu, capable of glamour and illusions, and she's quite the gifted liar." As Miriam frowned, the little old lady lines around her mouth were prominent, making her look very aged.

"What's an Elanchu?" a man in a navy pinstripe suit asked.

"It's a soothsayer, of sorts," I replied. "A person who is able to identify truth from lies when someone speaks."

"Yes, correct, thank you, James. Except Camila can also see illusions for what they are as well. She sees what's really in front of her. Truly an all-around detection of actuality from falsehoods," Miriam said. "We've put her up against a handful of our most talented illusionists and she sees through everything."

The screen flickered as a video showed Camila in a testing cell from deep within the walls of the CMRD, and then the video screen split, showing several CMRD employees in what looked like a staff area or break room. Within seconds, ghostlike apparitions materialized, perfect copies of Camila, albeit transparent and ethereal. The spectral Camilas grabbed objects—a coffee mug, the toaster, a broom—and hurled them at the employees. One fellow, taken completely by surprise, received a toaster to the head, which slashed his forehead open, spraying blood across the table where he sat. Chaos erupted as the employees battled inanimate objects and apparitions while the guy who got hit with the toaster held his head, trying to stop the bleeding.

The room where Camila sat grew dark. She straightened her spine as the activity in the break room continued, and then slowly, she sneered while arching an eyebrow.

"Camila has a bit of a mean-spirited streak in her, which we find difficult to control. She gets bored easily." Miriam spat out the words. It's fairly clear she didn't like her. "However, the girl sometimes loses control of her projections. Twice now, her projections have attempted murder, and we've had one death on campus that we haven't been able to explain. We suspect it was Camila, but she denies it. Furthermore, in rare cases her projections freeze and stutter. We're not sure what is happening to them, and on those occasions, Camila becomes distant and reclusive. We wonder if there isn't a degree of time manipulation happening, but we're just not sure." She gave me another side-glance as if to say *are you getting this?*

I sighed. *I can't help you, Miriam, or these students.*

I turned away from her, fed up with her insistence of me being her saviour teacher and studied the muckety-mucks in the room. I let my extra-sensory perceptions do the work. It was another trick of mine, but it wasn't always reliable when there were so many individuals in a small space. I sent out a wave. A ripple. A boomerang that would net the emotional landscape in the room. I watched it undulate through the air, hit the back wall, and slowly slink its way back to me. No one had any clue what I'd just done.

As the wave washed over me I could sense the random feelings of others.

Responsibility.

Frivolousness.

Fear but coupled with that, excitement and pride.

More pride, accomplishment, and superiority.

And then I understood. So that was who these people were. Military, intelligence agencies, multinational corporate bigwigs who wanted to have a stake in these individuals. Jobs for the talented, so to speak. I hated Miriam a little more. She was selling us. Controlling us and then using young people as commodities.

"We have two more to review. I'm going to ask...if there are any among us who have strong religious beliefs, you may wish to leave the room—you will be targeted. Our next subject is Annabelle Smith, nineteen, raised in a staunch religious environment until an incident occurred during one of the congregation's worship services. Her parents contacted us shortly thereafter. Annabelle has been with us ever since. She does not exist with her entities very well. In fact, she's terrified of them."

"I'm sorry, what do you mean, exist with?" A lady wearing a small gold cross on a chain hanging around her neck raised her hand and asked the question.

"She's an Arcane," I said. The minute she mentioned the religious thing, I could tell what the next student was all about. And it made me nervous. "There's some dispute as to whether or not Arcanes truly have magical abilities or if the magic emanates from the creatures that have chosen them. Are the demons simply manifesting their own abilities and using the human host as a conduit? We don't know."

"Are you telling me she's possessed?" the woman asked.

"Yes," I responded, looking her dead in the eye.

She smirked and looked around the table as if to say that's not possible, but she pulled her hand up and clasped her gold chain and the little religious icon closely.

One person got up and left.

Those all around the table watched as the man, whose skin had turned ashen white, walked out of the room with all of his belongings. The door closed loudly behind him.

"Very well. You've been warned. This is Annabelle." The IT guy pressed a button. From the look on his face, you'd think he had just started a horror movie, scared but excited at the same time.

Annabelle was petite. A waif of a human who had taken to the darkness like a shadow. Her clothes were all black and Victorian with lace trim. Her hair was jet, and as she emerged from the shadows of an unknown room, her voluminous hair billowed out behind her in a writhing mass.

That can't all be hair.

She jerked her head awkwardly to one side, like a spasmodic marionette, and then she simply vanished, only to reappear in another corner of the room, facing away from the camera. Trailing black tendrils of mist ebbed and flowed out from her back and head. Within the writhing mist, faces appeared and disappeared.

Annabelle blinked out again. The screen returned to black.

In a flash, the monitor was filled with her alabaster face. Her eyes were snake slits and glowed a phosphorescent orange, her face was a roadmap of black veins.

In a tiny shrill voice, she whispered, "I see you..."

Black mist apparated in the middle of the stone table where we were all sitting, its tentacles writhing and swirling. The occasional wisp lashed out at various participants around the room, including Miriam. She flinched. People around the table jumped back in complete shock. Others were in awe.

"Jesus Christ," Miriam swore. "James, do something."

"With what? That's nothing more than an apparition."

"If anything happens," she said as I shook my head and put my hand up to stop Miriam from muttering any more nonsense.

Fuck Arcanes. They were so damn creepy. Regardless, I watched everything, carefully.

The amorphous blob of jet smoke spiralled and churned and then inched itself in front of the woman with the gold cross.

A face formed in the mist. At first, it looked like Annabelle.

"I see you..." the shrill voice repeated. Its echo seemed to hang in the air like a contagious disease.

The woman screamed as Annabelle's face shifted and morphed into a gruesome visage. Presumably this was one of the demons that lived inside of her. The beast's eyes were covered in scarred flesh, and the skin around the mouth peeled away, exposing rows and rows of jagged and razor-like teeth.

A tongue lashed out and licked the cheek of the religious woman.

She scrunched up her face in disgust and let out a mousy whimper. If I was a betting man, I would have laid a large sum of money that this woman was going directly to her priest for confession and to bathe herself in the holy water at the baptismal font after this brush with the dark side.

The demon laughed. The chuckle turned into an aggressive growl.

"Oh shit," I said and launched myself around Miriam to stand behind the woman who was still clutching her cross tightly.

Extending out towards the demon, I pushed with my mind, creating a force field, another bubble of sorts that sheathed the demon head and the swirling mist.

The captured fiend shifted its attention towards me. The head grew and expanded within the bubble's confines.

As it filled my sphere, a slick, oily sensation flooded through my brain and washed down my back. Demons—always dirty. The flesh of the demon face squished up against the margins of my psychic balloon until the sound of ripping flesh could be heard.

With a loud *bang,* the head exploded and blood filled the inside of my bubble.

The force field gurgled with red gelatinous goo, which floated and churned. It steamed with a loud *hiss,* and then it all just disappeared.

Except the demon's laughter. That soul-harrowing sound filled the room.

The woman with the gold chain stood up. Her skin was pallid and clammy as beads of sweat dotted her forehead. She looked a little green around the edges. She grabbed her purse and ushered herself out of the room. The door banged loudly behind her, causing several people to jump at the sound.

"Despite this show, Annabelle is terrified of her demons and clearly has no control over them. They torment her daily, and she has told us on numerous occasions what the creatures would like to do to her. It's not very pleasant."

I looked at Miriam as she said this, and shook my head.

"What the hell am I supposed to do with that?" I whispered to her as I passed by to resume my seat. I felt dirty, unclean. Demons always made me feel like I had three days' worth of sweat and grime clinging to my skin.

She gave me yet another contemptible look. If I could have gotten away with it, I would have wrapped my hands around her thin neck. Or I could have just grazed her shoulder and made her feel like walking out into traffic.

"Lastly, we have Isaiah Dannenberg, twenty-five years old," Miriam said as the technician clicked more buttons. Isaiah's picture took over the front of the room.

He was a stern-looking guy, heavily bearded, pointed nose with deep-set brown eyes. But brown didn't do it justice. There were flecks of amber and gold too. His eyes were stunning. He was hunched over slightly, a posture that said "I'm tired."

Who's that spent at twenty-five?

With a click, the audio-visual equipment switched modes to a movie clip. The screen was fuzzy and erratic. The picture veered and wobbled and then flashed into crystal clarity, only to return to static again.

"We have a hard time getting any video of Isaiah. His abilities continually run high enough to create interference with our recording devices." Miriam said.

Isaiah was floating in a dark barren room. IV tubing ran out of each arm as he hung suspended from...

"Is he levitating?" I asked, my brows furrowed together.

"Yes."

"Why the IVs?" My question was slow, and I put emphasis on each word.

"He's being kept in a medical coma," she quipped.

"What—" I started and then asked, "Why?" There was hesitation in my voice. Levitation was a scarcity, kind of like healing. It was a talent that was unbelievably rare. Prevailing thought was that gravity was the hardest of all scientific forces to contradict, and the amount of energy required to counteract it wasn't found in individuals very often. Even for those who could perform levitation, it was usually short lived and executed under heavy concentration. That level of attentiveness would not have been possible while being kept in a medically induced coma.

"Isaiah is perhaps our most special case. He has absolutely no control over any of his abilities."

I squinted and studied her. "What's the catch? Spit it out. There's no way anyone can perform that kind of levitation under sedation. What gives?"

She shot me another one of her death stares but knew she had to tell me. "Isaiah is everything."

"What do you mean?"

"I mean, James, he has exhibited talents over each of the elements, he has successfully passed every Psyche test we can throw at him, and the demon who has chosen him is perhaps the most ancient creature we've been able to research."

"Are you telling me he has all three classes?"

"Yes. It's a first in a number of ways. Most of the young people we have here at the CMRD are found by us through news reports or tips phoned in by the general public. Isaiah came to us. He had been living on the streets for the last three years, and for a majority of that time kept himself high on whatever street drug he could find. That numbed him enough to maintain a subdued state of his abilities so they didn't overtake him and destroy him, or others.

"The magical power within him is enough to rip anything apart with just the sheer force alone. His Elemental abilities are uncharted. Luckily, the demon keeps him whole so Isaiah's body isn't damaged. After all, a dead body can't be a host to the demon. Isaiah's Psyche talents allow him to sense what others are experiencing around him through telepathy, but we've also witnessed him having conversations—which we can only assume is with his demon. Basically, this state is the easiest way for him to exist, currently. We'd like to change that.

"And James that is where you come in. We want you. You need to help Ning get into the habit of releasing her ability regularly enough so she doesn't kill anyone else. With Chris, develop anger-management techniques and extend his life expectancy, figure out why Camila is losing control of her astrals, and instruct Annabelle in the use of magical script so she can confront her demons. Isaiah, well, if we can just get him to a point where he can exist in a conscious state without disrupting everything around him, that will be a win.

"The time limit has been set at six months," Miriam said.

"You're a bitch. You know that, right?"

Her cheeks flushed red the minute I said that, but I cared very little about Miriam's feelings. She was crazy if she thought I could fix these kids in that amount of time. "Someone in Chris's shoes could require years of therapy to control that level of anger and you're giving me six months? I'm not even trained in psychology. And then there's four others. And you and I both know what's going to happen at the end of six months if they don't come through your tests with flying colours." I shook with anger, heat radiating off my face. How dare she put me on the spot like this!

"What happens?" Major Harris asked.

"The CMRD likes to 'put down' those who are uncontrollable," I spat through clenched teeth. I shook my head and looked towards the wall.

"You mean—exterminate?" the major asked.

"That's exactly what I mean."

The collective stirred in the room. Most would be uncomfortable with killing a human being, but clearly there were those who believed otherwise.

"If we can't teach them to control the gifts they have, they are a danger to all of us. Those dangers need to be eliminated." Miriam was steadfast in the CMRD rhetoric. She didn't see these five as lost young people with lives and fears and blood coursing through their veins just like everyone else.

"Agreed," Major Harris stated plain as day. "A threat to the population should be contained. Very well. I think Mr. Martin here has the ability to make progress with each of the potential candidates. I want evaluations, progress reports, and in-person viewing opportunities every month. I also want to claim Christopher Sanderhill. We'll put him to good use."

"Very well," she started with a pleased expression plastered on her face.

"What do you mean claim?" I asked, but Miriam ignored me.

"Major Harris, you know the process. Let's begin the bidding, shall we?"

"The bidding?" I asked as I stood up. My psyche energy was humming, collecting. I was pissed.

"Jason, Rodney, would you please show Mr. Martin to the waiting room?" Miriam flicked her evil harpy talon towards two of her muscle-heads and then pointed at me with one long corpse-like digit. "Don't go anywhere, James. We have a lot to discuss."

Rodney and Jason took up residence on either side of me, two towers of intimidating muscle, and began shepherding me towards the meeting room's closed door. They'd be escorting my ill-behaved self to said "waiting room." Like I had the ability to go anywhere other than where *she* had directed.

Fuck you, Miriam, and your waiting room.

God, I need a cigarette.

Four: Job Offer

ALTHOUGH THE TYPICAL steroid-filled gym rats, Jason and Rodney were nice enough, I could have just looped my hands through their arms and *made* them take me to the front door of the CMRD, but the videos I had just seen of the kids weighed heavily on me. Each one needed help desperately. It hadn't been that many years since I was in their shoes. I was a full-fledged graduate from the CMRD, but back then, they hadn't begun their extermination policy.

The kids would falter without instruction and assistance... They would never pass the CMRD final exam. They were basically sitting on death row.

So instead of escorting myself out of the building, I let the muscle-heads steer me through the various hallways and corridors leading on to Miriam's waiting room.

My god, this place is huge. How did I ever forget that?

Our scenic tour gave me the time to think back to the recordings I had just seen. Ning seemed so frightened, and I don't think I've ever seen anyone as irate as Chris. His raging fire was visible in the veins that ran underneath the skin, like little rivers of lava. Annabelle terrified the hell out of me. I couldn't imagine what she had to deal with mentally hosting multiple demons inside of her, and Camila was most definitely a problem. But how do you cure a mean girl?

And then there was Isaiah. There was a warm spot of familiarity spreading through my chest for Isaiah. I could relate to his past. There was a draw to being so stoned and numb the abilities within didn't consume you. And sometimes, they did that anyway. They took over and wiped out who you were, or who you thought you were. Even in his levitating state of medically induced coma, Isaiah's face was so drawn and tired. He should have appeared at peace, restful. Instead, his face said "I'm finished." At twenty-five, no one should already be that consumed. But then, I too had been that tired. I had a connection to Isaiah. I was pretty sure I understood him.

Her evil tricks were working. The clutching desire to help these kids with their wayward talents was worming itself under my skin.

Rodney opened a random door down the hallway they had led me, another one of the CMRD's portals to hell. It was one of many I had seen frequently sprinkled throughout the vast networking system of corridors in the CMRD complex. I glanced through the open door. It was a nice enough room, not exactly a gateway to the underworld, and furnished tastefully. Although there wasn't a single window anywhere.

I sat on the large overstuffed blue sofa that sported a faint floral pattern. As my butt hit the cushion, it enveloped me, cradling my body. Damn, it was comfortable, and soft. I ran my hand over the velvety microfiber upholstery as I closed my eyes and simply enjoyed the sensation. It was a rarity for me to be able to experience anything this luxurious. The cockroaches in my apartment would have simply died if they'd had this to run over all day long.

Stroking the furniture lasted about two minutes, and then I found myself glancing at the clock. Constantly. Another twenty minutes ticked by. Okay, so whatever Miriam was doing, it was going to take a while. There were magazines on the coffee table, so I flicked through them and found a *National Geographic*. That's always good for at least an article or two. I flipped to the list of expositions in the issue and found one on Ice Age Hyenas and another on Coffin Flies and Corpse Eating Beetles. *Goodie! I'm all set.*

Bidding. What the hell is she doing? Auctioning off these kids? I don't remember any bidding when I was here. Most of us attended university after, except Ronald, he …

Dammit. Ronald enlisted into the army and nobody knew where Drew had disappeared. Had the CMRD had been culling those students who didn't pass all along? Fuck.

I kicked off my shoes, threw my feet up onto the coffee table, and tucked into the magazine. But it wasn't like I was really reading it. I wished I had something to drink. I glanced around the room. Sadly, there was no refrigerator or vending machine. Not like I had a bunch of money to buy anything anyway.

At least another hour passed by, and I had paged my way through pretty much every magazine in front of me. I was sitting there twiddling my thumbs and fidgeting when Jason opened the door and escorted the Crypt Keeper, Miriam, into my hostage cell, toting several large folders stuffed with papers. As she walked past the muscle-head guardians, she handed the stack of files to Rodney.

"I'm so glad you decided to show up. I was just about to go home," I said with a snarl.

"Shut up, James. Despite your idiocy, you put your talents on display well enough. Our benefactors have agreed that you offer up abilities that are well suited to assist the candidates we reviewed today."

"Really, wow. That's so awesome! I was so sure I didn't get the job." I gave Miriam a look that said *go fuck yourself*, and if I hadn't known any better, I would have sworn that she was telepathic.

"Jesus Christ, James. What's the matter with you? This is an incredible opportunity for you. Don't you get it? If you get these kids in line and ready for their next phase, you'll have their sponsors lining up to give you much easier assignments with their own people. This could make it for you, and then you won't have to live life in that shit hole of an apartment anymore."

"You think that's what's important to me? An apartment?"

"James, I've seen it."

My head swivelled to her direction. *What do you mean, you've seen it?*

"It's a horrifying little hovel of a studio. Look at this." She waved her hand like Vanna White. "You could call this home."

"Call what home? This? Mind you, the sofa is really comfy, but still. No. I'm good."

"We could help you with your sister too. Last I heard, she was hanging out in that wretched place on Stephen Avenue. What's it called?" She tapped her finger against her lips as she thought. "Clementine's, I think. Dreadful place. You know, word on the street is she's hanging out with Raven Nightshade."

I rolled my eyes into the back of my head, where they stayed, for a long time. Raven was rumoured to dabble in the fourth class of magic. The dirty class no one talked about.

"The police have investigated him now, what, three times for being involved in missing persons cases. Each one of those cases, the victims were underage. You know that, right? Minors, James. Missing minors. Bloody shame none of the charges ever seemed to stick. And if that weren't enough, Raven's been suspected of recruiting for Damien Scarslor."

Great, the two names in the magic world no one wanted to be associated with. Rumour had it Damien liked them young and liked to engage in rather perverted activities and wasn't particular on anything other than age. And both of these monsters had at one point been through the CMRD.

"My connections have seen Shawna with both of these people."

"Holy shit, Miriam, you just come out swinging, don't you? How did you manage to get a hold of *this* kind of information? Who'd you have to bribe or, worse, manipulate with magic to get this? This is beneath you. You're trying way too hard. Why?"

Miriam looked at me with disgust and a whole overflowing wheelbarrow of hate.

"I abhor dealing with you people. You're all way too perceptive."

"Oh my god. Really? Anyone with half a brain would have caught on to your schemes."

Miriam looked over at Rodney and Jason, then back at me and cocked an eyebrow.

"I said *half* a brain."

"Here's the deal. You help me, and I will help you. You get those five kids to a point where they won't kill themselves or each other and at least capable of taking baby steps out in the real world, and I will make sure your sister is found, put into treatment, and gets herself back onto stable footing. And for you, a hefty payday, a nicer set of wheels than the rust rocket you have outside, and some better clothes. Maybe even underwear."

I knew she added in that last one as a dig.

"No."

"Well then, let me put it to you another way." Miriam snapped her fingers and Rodney came to life. He hauled over the large manila folders and passed them all to the Devil.

She opened the top file folder, carefully fingered the numerous number of pages contained within, and then pulled out several sheets that were all stapled together.

"Remember this?"

"Yes," I said as my heart sunk.

"Let me add to it."

Miriam got up and took several steps over to a panel that was next to the door. After having spent one long and boring hour in this room, one would think I'd have spied out the device while waiting for her. She placed a palm on it and it glowed slightly.

Biometrics—impressive. And expensive.

Across the room, another compartment opened, revealing a rather sophisticated-looking electronic board with a number of backlit buttons. She walked casually over to the control panel and pressed a few of the keys.

The wall behind me retracted, revealing a huge bedroom, with a four-poster king bed, very nice bedroom furniture, and a closet with its door slightly ajar, filled with clothes.

Another wall slid open, this time a bathroom. That at least had a door for privacy, but it was open, and I could see a rather impressive tile shower.

Miriam stood at the panel, her arms crossed, and tapped her foot in a steady, plodding, impatient rhythm. At her age, she should have been wearing more sensible shoes. Spiked heels on a lady of her maturity...that's just dangerous.

Think of your hips, Miriam. A broken hip would be disastrous.

She closed one eye and arched the eyebrow of the other while pursing her lips, as if she attempted to discern what was going on in my mind.

"Now, if that wasn't enough..." She pressed one more button on the control panel.

One entire side of the apartment disappeared. Well, no, that wasn't right. The wall became clear. I would have thought at first glance that it was a solid wall, made from concrete, but it was in fact glass. Frosted glass. And in the corner, there was a door that let out a soft *psst*, as if it was decompressing. On the other side of the glass wall stood a huge empty room. Huge was a misnomer. Gargantuan. Warehouse big, airport-hangar mammoth, and in the middle of that vast emptiness were five plexiglass cubes. There was a spotlight on each one, and I knew immediately what they were.

They were the cells containing the five students I had seen with Major Harris and his cronies.

"This is how you're keeping them? They are not zoo animals! For Christ's sake, Miriam."

"They are a danger to society, to each other, and to themselves. At least this way, they are contained."

Isaiah floated in the center of his cube. Even from this distance, I could tell it was him. He looked like a puppet with strings coming out of his arms. I knew better. Those were the IVs that kept him in a perpetual state of catatonia.

Ning was glaring right at me from within her cube. She placed a hand on the plexiglass, as if by doing so she was waving or saying hello. She didn't look happy, and it appeared as if she was pleading with me to release her from a nightmare. Then she pulled away from the front of her cell as ice crystals formed a palm print. They multiplied until the wall was covered in ice.

"You will be their teacher, their mentor, their coach. I don't care what you want to call it, but that's who you are as of right now. Frankly, I don't care what your thoughts are on this. I need you to get this done. We've been lenient with you after what happened in your last class. But you have a contract to fulfil with us," Miriam said as she pointed to the piece of paper that lay on the coffee table. "That incident happened over a year ago, and now, we're coming to collect on the rest of the time you signed up for. Remember what I told you, James. A payout. A salary. You need the money. We'll also help you find Shawna."

"My sister can be difficult to find," I said, which was true. I had spent many days in the past tracking her down, trying to get her into rehab or at least a shelter. Most of the time, it was a wasted effort. But what was I supposed to do? She was *my sister*.

Miriam took a long black piece of plastic out of the control panel and walked it over to the coffee table and gingerly placed it on the surface.

"That will allow you to open the students' cells. Once you think you have control over them and want to start practicing, they'll need to come out of their rooms. Under no circumstances are you to push the red set. If you let the students out, use the white buttons at the bottom." Miriam walked back to the biometric pad and placed her skeletal hand over it. It pulsed for the second time. The electronic panel slid shut.

"The least you could do is leave me with a carton of smokes and a bottle of vodka." I raised my voice slightly.

Holy shit, I'm trapped.

"Vodka?" she said with a derisive little chuckle. "That's the last thing you need. Clean it up, James. I believe I've told you that once already. Classes start when you're able to stand. Good luck."

Rodney escorted her out of the waiting room. Scratch that—my apartment—and as the door closed, the locks clinked into their final resting place.

"Shit." I rubbed my face, hard.

I was stuck there, fulfilling the last year of my contract.

Already I felt jittery, just thinking about there not being anything to drink or smoke.

There was a pile of papers and files left on the coffee table next to the remote control. Miriam was tricky that way, always leaving things. Maybe it had been Rodney. He looked shifty. I walked over and glanced at the folders. The dossiers on the students. I picked the first one up—Isaiah's.

Looking at his picture, I got lost in the sharp lines of his face. So rugged. And furry. I snorted a little. Furry had not been "my type" in the past, but...he was kinda cute.

Stop that. He's one of your goddamn students. I traced the outline of his nose with my finger. *Yeah, he's definitely cute.*

I looked around my tiny little room. This isn't going to go well. The air seemed suddenly too hot, stifling. I was stuck there. I needed something to do, anything to take my mind off...vodka and smokes.

I sifted through the files, just another form of fiddling. I got lost for a long time, drawn in by the reports and pictures of each student, skimming each of the files and the histories of these kids. After all, they were now mine, and my responsibility. But it didn't take long before a headache started, a nagging throb that began behind my eyes, and within a short period of time, it became a vice grip squishing my brain tighter and tighter. I swore my eyes were going to pop out of my head.

My stomach lurched. This wasn't going to end well. I ran to the toilet but didn't quite make it.

I don't know how many times I puked, but when I finally stopped, my abs were shredded and sore and the bile stung the back of my throat. My mouth had that nasty pasty film in it from the constant retching.

I lay on the cold tile of the bathroom floor, which was oddly soothing considering how freaking hot and sweaty I was. The clinical surface was cold, and I rolled over and put my cheek against the floor.

I noticed my head was right next to the toilet, but I honestly didn't care. That's when the shaking started. I could feel my limbs tense up and then vibrate, like I had spent too long outside in a Canadian blizzard. Even my torso clenched and shook.

Then the vomiting continued. And that's how I spent the vast majority of the night. Cold tile floor, shivering and shaking and puking.

Welcome back to the CMRD, James. We're here to help you.

Help me through alcohol withdrawal. *Yeah, great. Thanks.*

I DON'T REMEMBER when, but I vaguely recall spending an inordinate amount of time in the shower, lying next to the drain as hot water blasted me from above. The water never got cold; that much I could recall.

But despite blacking out for periods, I was now resting in bed. There were several glasses with water on the bedside table, and I still felt like shit.

Shakes would rattle through my body occasionally, but they didn't last long. The headache I had was still there, but not as prevalent.

It had been a shitty night. Literally and figuratively. That was another unpleasant memory; a lot of time spent on the can.

I rolled over, pulled the blankets around me, and tried to get some sleep.

White dead hands pulled the covers back, exposing my nakedness as his milky-eyed gaze studied me carefully. "Go home. Leave here. You can't help them. You promised me, and you left me to die!" Cody growled at me.

I pulled the covers back up and then held them over my head.

The next time I woke up, I was in scrubs and in the hospital wing of the CMRD. An IV in my arm yanked as I rolled over, which pulled the skin tight.

"Careful, Mr. Martin. That IV line is going to make this transition a little easier for you."

"Oh shit." My head thumped and banged as I squinted, trying to focus. It didn't help.

"Yes. It's gonna be like this for a while, but thankfully, we can mitigate your symptoms a little." She walked over to the IV line and stuck a needle in it.

The next few days were hazy.

SITTING ON THE big comfy blue couch in my apartment, I lounged in sweat pants and a T-shirt. Having gotten past the worst of the DTs, but still a little shaky, I was laying low. Doctor's orders. Miriam stopped by occasionally to "check on my well-being," which was bullshit. I knew she took great delight in my torture and discomfort. I had so much hate for that woman.

At least she gave me a few packs of cigarettes.

One addiction at a time, and at least now, I'm not going to kill everyone.

There was nothing to do in this boring, sterile living area of the facility. The only thing that had been left for me were the student files, the ones I had started with before my body decided to rage against me.

I picked them up and perused them.

I was still jittery and constantly stressed out, thinking about the kids who were so close to me and yet felt like a million miles away. Random violent thoughts regarding Miriam crept into my head on a regular basis as well. My hands or my legs still shook occasionally.

Each file on the kids was extensive, an example of the CMRD's thoroughness. The amount of detail in each manila folder was nothing short of spine tingling. Chris was left-handed, Camila's brother had attempted suicide several times, eventually succeeding, and Ning's student visa would run out in April of the following year. Every bloody little detail.

Overhead, a very loud *thunk* sounded as the spotlights on the cubes in the airport hangar shut off, leaving the space in pitch darkness. The glass wall in my apartment slowly returned to its opaque state, concealing the hangar from view and shutting me off from the five cubes.

I glanced at my watch. Where had the time gone?

I walked over to the glass wall and got a last peek into the darkness of the arena as the frosting climbed up from the floor, obscuring my view.

Whether I wanted it or not, I guess I was the fucking teacher. *I am not ready for this. I can't do this.* I took a few steps into the center of my new digs.

I grabbed the cigarette pack off the table, pulled a smoke out, and lit it, then sucked in the poison, finding it calming. My body still felt like crap, and my nerves rang out at any little thought that made me cringe or think negatively.

Despite the extravagance of my new surroundings and the continual gnawing in my brain from the DTs, the videos from that first meeting, which was already days ago, replayed in my head.

Ning and her trembling lip with a cheek splattered with blood. Chris and eruptions of fire. Camila smiling devilishly into the camera, looking as if she caused the world's chaos. Annabelle and her creepy voice with the slimy demons. Isaiah. Such a handsome creature, numb and incapable of dealing with the world. And my own guilt, which was invoking dread and fear that always led me to my bottles of vodka.

And then thoughts of Cody, pasty and white. Haunting eyes begging me to help him. I don't know how long I stood there, thinking, but the ash from my cigarette was long and about to fall onto the floor. One thing was for sure, I was trapped. And these kids didn't stand a chance with me as their instructor.

Welcome to your first day of hell, class. My name is Mr. Martin, and I'm here to make sure you don't kill yourselves.

Five: First Period

I SLEPT HORRIBLY, tossing and turning all night long. The need for booze gnawed at my brain as disturbing thoughts fought back in the form of twisted dreams. Anxiety and nerves chewed on my guts. I was quite sure that at one point my stomach was actually trying to leave my body and begin its own search for vodka. At least, I *assumed* that's what it would be after. Lord knew, that's all my brain was focusing on the past week—a tall glass with ice and that clear, numbing liquid.

Regardless of the fitful night's sleep, part of my emotional duress was the uncertainty of how to best approach the kids in their holding cells, the other part was a realization that Miriam would not be providing me with any liquor.

I had a cigarette for breakfast, which was glorious. But it would have been so much better with a cup of coffee.

I wanted a quick shower, but that turned into a longer-than-expected adventure. There was seemingly no end to the amount of available hot water, and it was the nicest bathroom I'd ever been in. But there were things to do. I shut the water off as billows of steam ebbed and flowed within the shower stall.

The fluffy towels were first-rate as well, soft and plush. They felt good against all the body parts. I wrapped the towel around my waist as the bottom of my feet slapped across the clinically cold tiled floor, reminding me where I was, lost in the bowels of the CMRD, not a penthouse apartment. The ostentatious surroundings might have let me believe otherwise.

I searched the clothes in the closet and found an outfit that fit me well enough, but the style was arguable, and everything was tighter than I preferred. Although they hugged my body in the right spots, except for the belly.

I grabbed the extra inches around my middle and wiggled them. *Ugh.*

The apartment was not equipped with either a kitchen or a TV. This was not going to be a good morning if I couldn't get a cup of coffee, and soon. I was missing too many elements of my regular morning. I might end up with my own demons manifesting themselves if I didn't manage to regain a little familiarity.

Coffee. I need coffee. Baileys would be good.

Thinking about it, though, was only torture, and I was contemplating having another smoke but figured I might as well venture out and see if the kids were up.

They're not kids. They're all adults.

It was time to meet them.

I returned to the spot where Miriam had left the remote, picked it up, and studied the device. This shouldn't be too hard to operate. All the buttons were labelled rather nicely. Open Classroom Wall. Open Cell One. Open Cell Two, etc.

I pushed the button that would allow me access to the titanic space where their cells were, and the familiar *psst* sounded as the door on the far side opened up to the hanger and the glass wall slowly defrosted itself. The spotlights over each cube beamed brightly, reminding me of renaissance paintings depicting halos around divinity.

As I walked out into the vast arena, I noted the difference in the environment. The air was cooler and fresher, which was a nice change, but it was also damp, reminding me of a cemetery or a mausoleum. Annabelle sprang to mind, along with her horde of demons. I walked a little quicker towards Ning.

Ning was watching me as I approached. She waved tentatively, and I waved back. She seemed like a good place to start.

The space between us was longer than I expected, but as I got closer to her, it also became apparent that the individual cells were spaced well away from each other. Which really, was probably a smart choice. If shit went sideways, at least the students would be safely out of harm's way.

Most magical abilities had a radius; a maximum effect area. Mine was pretty close, force fields and energy shields were only viable up to ten feet or so, and then they seemed to fizzle out. As an Empath, skin-to-skin contact was the best, but that wasn't information I let just anyone know.

"Hi," I said to Ning. It was always hard to start off the first contact. Was she outgoing? Easy to get along with?

"Hello," she responded politely, casting her gaze downward. Her voice was muffled from the thick barrier between us.

"My name is James. You're Ning, right?"

"Yes. Nice to meet you, Mr. James. You work for Ms. Miriam?" She was hesitant, appearing cautious as she said Miriam's name.

"Not by choice." I rolled my eyes.

Ning giggled. I liked her already, and I could tell she'd be easy to get along with.

"Have you met the others?" I asked her.

"No. They tell us we are too dangerous." Ning looked sideways, as if she was expecting someone to appear from the shadows. She was apprehensive, as if she would be punished for talking to me. Made me wonder how closely they had been watched. "Aren't you afraid of us?" she whispered.

"No, not yet, but then I'm like you." I gave Ning a wink and smiled as her eyes widened. "This is kind of silly, talking through glass." Teleportation was not my most developed skill, but as long as I could see where I needed to end up, a short hop wasn't usually too hard. There was a nice spot in the middle of Ning's room that had no clutter or items.

"Mind if I come in?" I pointed towards the center of her room.

Ning's face instantly changed and became round and happy. "No, company would be nice!"

I focused on the spot in the middle of her rather tidy room.

It always started in my feet. Tiny pinpricks dotted the underside of my toes, like I'd crossed my legs for too long. That sensation slithered up the backs of my calves, across my butt, and then once it hit my spine, the jump happened so fast I needed to be homed in on where I wanted to go.

I've been told that an onlooker sees what appears to be a string or hook pulling me and then I disappear in a blur. Which is interesting because people who don't have any abilities, *Norms*, can't see my force fields, and yet they see the beginning of my 'port. Magic had its own rules, which I struggled to understand. And I was "the teacher." Sometimes, you had to accept what was put in front of you and go with the flow.

There was a rush in my ears. Then there I was, standing in the middle of Ning's cell.

She squealed with delight and ran over to me faster than I could rebalance myself. After throwing her arms around me, she gave me a huge hug.

"Mr. James! That was amazing!" She smelled like coconut oil and lime. It was pleasant but a little overwhelming. Ning pulled back, untangling her arms from me, and then she blushed, hard. Her head dropped as she stared at the floor. "I'm sorry. I shouldn't have hugged you without asking."

"That's okay." I chuckled as I reached out and gently touched her shoulder. I gave her a gentle pat. I didn't have much of a personal-space bubble, unless I could tell someone was an asshole. Then they needed to keep a good distance. She seemed like a sweet girl. Her room was far more organized than mine ever would have been. There were stacks of books and art supplies.

"Are you going to test us like the others? I will probably fail." She chanced a quick glance towards me.

"No. Well, I suppose I might test you later, but not right now. I guess I'm your new teacher?" I said with furrowed brows but also a half-assed smile. It didn't feel right having that word falling out of my face. *Teacher*.

"Oh!" Ning smiled at me, beaming. "I would like that." Her voice was soft and had a slight lilt to it.

"They told me you have to use your abilities at least once an hour, right?"

"Yes, but I forget, other times, *she* stops me."

"She?"

"Yuki-onna. The snow woman."

"Wait, that's Japanese folklore, right? I thought a Yuki-onna was more of a ghost, not a demon."

"Well, you're correct. It is Japanese in origin. She doesn't seem to care that I am Chinese. As to what she is, I can't say. I would call it a demon."

"Well, demons don't care too much for human ethnicities. They have roots buried in lost cultures and civilizations, so if you think about it, they were born in cultures that are so forgotten to us, that they don't care where each of us have come from. They'll attach themselves to anyone who'll have them." Ning was wringing her hands and decidedly uncomfortable as she sat down at her desk.

Her room had lots of stuffed animals and cute things with large eyes scattered along shelves hung over her bed. A big pink bed with lots of fluffy pillows and a big duvet with a huge red heart on it sat off to one side of the room.

I could tell she liked her pretty things.

In one corner, there was a small stereo and a TV.

"Hmph, I don't even have one of those," I said, pointing to the electronics.

"They are rewards for good behaviour. I am told I have more things than the others." She smiled.

"No doubt." I chortled. Okay, so this was another one of Miriam's games. That pretty much meant I was stuck with what I had and getting anything of luxury like a bottle of vodka would be beyond impossible.

That's the last thing you need. Remember the past week?

I wasn't known around these parts for good behaviour. There also wasn't a lot of love between Miriam and me, at least, not after the last time I had a class with the CMRD.

"How about meals? When do those come around?" I asked.

"Soon." Ning smiled as she glanced at the clock on her bedside table. "Breakfast is at eight, lunch at noon, and dinner at six, and again, if we're good, they bring us snacks or leave goodies in our rooms for us when we go to the labs."

"Good to know." I didn't want to show too much disdain for the CMRD in front of Ning, but seriously? These were adults and they were being treated like children.

"Ning, Ms. Miriam hired me to help out all five of you. So, this once-an-hour thing, have you done anything yet this morning?"

"No." Ning's head dropped.

"Oh, maybe we should then?"

"Now?"

"Why not?"

"Do you think you should be on the other side of the glass?" She pointed towards the darkened area of the hangar.

"I think I'll be okay. I can protect myself," I said, trying to alleviate her concerns.

Ning gasped. "Oh, you could just teleport away!"

"Well, sure, I could do that. Go on..."

Ning bit her bottom lip, then closed her eyes and opened her arms.

A shiver ran down my spine as the air suddenly got very cold.

Snowflakes formed right in front of my eyes and then floated on the air currents down to the floor.

"Very cool!" I said to Ning, as she smiled.

The wind suddenly picked up, jostling and moving the stuffed animals within the room, and as the gusts blew past, the amount of snow increased as well.

"You should stop. Before we're buried in snow?" I raised my voice at her to be heard over the wind.

Ning's eyes had clouded over with a milky film and ice crystals were forming on the surface of the skin. She didn't move and made no motion that she had heard me.

I had to fight the wind a little in order to get near enough to Ning, but when I finally did, I grabbed her shoulders and gave her a good shake.

"Ning! You can make it stop now!"

Her eyes reverted back to their deep-chestnut colour, and she looked at me with shock and surprise on her face.

"I'm so sorry," she said, her lip quivering as her head dropped, her gaze focused around my feet.

"Hey, it's all good." I lifted her chin so that her eyes met mine. "Most of us have little idiosyncrasies with our talents. It's no biggie. Do you have a cell phone?"

"I did. But..."

"Really? For Pete's sake. Okay. I'll see what I can do about that. We just need to set a reminder for you once an hour—get you into the habit. Once that happens, you should be good on that front. Unless *she* stops you—we'll have to figure that one out. Are you all right at night? Do you have to wake up at night to let off a little steam?"

"No, thankfully. I would be very tired if that was the case."

I chuckled at her response. "No doubt. Okay. Well, it's almost eight, breakfast should be here shortly. I want to go see the others. We'll talk later?"

"Yes, please, Mr. James." Ning smiled.

Such a nice kid.

I popped out of her room and then walked the length of the hangar, past Camila who was thankfully still asleep. Honestly, I wasn't sure how to tackle her, even though she was Psyche just like me. There was something about her that worried me, and I couldn't put my finger on it. Chris was in his wolf form, pacing in front of the glass. Smoke rose from his fur. There was a slick of slobber and nose prints along the length of the plexiglass cube, just about at the same height as his wolf's head. The wolf glared at me, fire burning in its eyes. I kept walking.

Annabelle's room was full of the same dark mist that had appeared above the oval table—creepy. It ebbed and swirled within the glass cell. I swore I saw things in it, but I couldn't see her. Going out to meet the students had been a bit of a bust so far. There was only one cube left, so I continued my trek over to see Isaiah.

He was there, still floating, levitating with his arms out to his sides and his feet dangling. He looked like he'd been crucified on an invisible cross. As much as Annabelle's mist gave me the heebie-jeebies, there was a thickness in the atmosphere surrounding Isaiah's cube. Every step closer was akin to wading through sludge.

He was dressed in nothing but hospital-issued scrubs, just the pants, and even those hung loose around his waist. His wiry frame was too thin, I suspected a result of the drugs he'd been on for too long. Other than that, he seemed to be in good shape, a little muscular, but tough, lithe. Furry little beast too. Dark circles drooped heavily around his eyes. His thick beard was grown out and unmanaged. He should've been the shapeshifter, not Chris.

He reminded me of the classic werewolf but in human form. Rough and hairy.

"God, you look awful. Too bad too, 'cause you're definitely a cutie. We gotta get you outta there," I said aloud to no one in particular.

I can't believe you just said that. Jesus, what's the matter with you?

I put my hand on his see-through cell wall and leaned in closer, studying him as he gently rocked back and forth.

"Hey there. And you might be?"

I spun around to face the voice that came from behind me, scaring the shit out of me. I was totally unaware that anyone else was in the massive black hole that was the holding area for my five students.

It was Isaiah?

I dashed a quick glance back over my shoulder to the cube where Isaiah was held. He was still there, suspended, still swaying.

I looked again towards the other Isaiah, with my head canted to one side and an eyebrow raised.

What the hell?

"Not hell. Not yet anyway. Astral Projection I believe it's called—if you're wondering how I'm here and there at the same time."

I was stunned. Attempting to croak out a clever phrase or perhaps even an intelligent retort, it dawned on me, he'd also read my mind. That was a lot of abilities being used all at once.

"Yes, I can do all of those things." Another voice came from behind me. I spun to my left, and there was Isaiah again, a third copy. "And here too." A fourth.

"That's…" Wow. I'd never seen this, ever. "Isaiah, that's very impressive. I don't think I've ever seen anyone levitate, read minds, and create Astrals all at once. Never mind the fact that you're under sedation. And your Astrals…" I tentatively extended a hand and touched the nearest Isaiah's shoulder. It was solid. Flesh and bone with a body temperature. "Wow, dude, just wow. You know most Astrals are see-through, right?"

Isaiah smiled at me with a twinkle in his crystal-blue eyes. His grin was more beguiling, but it just made him all the more endearing.

"So, you like them furry, huh?" Isaiah winked at me, then ran a hand over his chest. His fingers moved and glided through the thick hair that covered his torso and abdomen.

"Ah…yeah?" If the guy was a telepath, there was absolutely no point in lying. But at the same time, this was one of my students! I couldn't think like this. "Sure, furry is nice. Sorry…hard to keep some thoughts bottled up." Note to self, compartmentalize around Isaiah. "How are you…I thought you were being kept sedated."

"I am. But I still know everything that's going on around me. In fact, the sedation keeps parts of me numb and stilled so the rest of my mind can function. By the way, I like 'em burly. You'll do." He winked again at me.

Cody appeared, ghostly and ethereal behind Isaiah's shoulder. He was chalky in appearance, a true see-through specter. His hair hung across his face.

Black rotted lips cracked open. "Don't do this. You'll kill him too. It's not fair. You promised you'd keep me safe. Don't make the same promises to him. You'll kill him. You'll kill them all."

I shook my head, destroying the vision of a memory.

Isaiah shot a glance over his shoulder. "Seeing ghosts?"

"Exactly."

"Ghosts aren't really there. Don't let it bother you too much. I'm Isaiah." He stuck out his hand, offering a handshake.

I reached to grab it, glancing back over my shoulder just to confirm. Yup. Isaiah was currently in two spots at the same time.

"I'm James." I took his hand. It was warm, and his grip was good, firm, but not stupid tight. And his hands were rough. "Nice to meet you." I squinted my eyes, sizing him up. This was so incredible. "And thanks for the advice. Ghosts are one thing, memories, however, have a tendency to stick with you for a while."

"Ah, a haunted mind. We're all a little broken and scarred, huh? I like you. You're one of us too. I can smell it. That's probably a better move. The last two 'teachers' they gave us were Norms. They didn't last long. Ning killed one of them by accident. He was a bit of a fucker anyway. If Ning's snow woman hadn't got him, Annabelle's demons were itching to play in his entrails." Isaiah gave me a side glance and one of those smirks that already had me melting.

Stop it! No melting allowed.

Those blue eyes of his were cold enough to freeze me, yet I was tingly warm inside. It was too easy to gaze into them and forget about everything else, something I was currently guilty of doing.

Wait, how does he know the others? Ning said she hadn't met anyone.

He grabbed my bicep and gave it a good squeeze, then ran his hand down my arm. His touch was light, sensual, almost soothing. "You work out? You know, you could show me a few things." Isaiah cocked an eyebrow as he studied me closely. "Yup, this is gonna be fun. I can tell already. Say, you got a cigarette?"

My brain put together an image of Isaiah and me sharing a cigarette after a romping session of...

Oh, fuck my life.

Six: Administrative Control

"CAN YOU GET them to untangle me here? I think I might like it better meeting you in person, while I'm not drugged out of my mind. Whaddya say?" Isaiah asked with a wink. He glanced at me sheepishly. I could tell he was flirting, his eyes darting in my direction every few seconds when he looked up from where he was more focused on the floor.

Not subtle. Not even a little. Still...so damn cute.

"Well, I can certainly do my best to make that happen, but in truth, it won't be up to me entirely." As I spoke, I peered into his crystal-blue eyes, if for no other reason than to try to get him to stay focused on me.

Holy shit, he's beautiful. No! I can't do this, not again. I'm not ready for another class. And I just can't...not with Isaiah...

"You'll make it happen. I have faith in you." Isaiah smiled, and I swooned.

"No pressure." I shook my head slightly as I said it. I wasn't convinced Miriam would just roll over and give in to my requests. Not on day one and especially not after spending a week in Medical getting sober.

Isaiah's Astral inched towards me, closing the small distance between us, wearing a look of "come and get it." Isaiah had flirting mastered, and he was much too close.

But before I could reason out the best course of action, Isaiah was standing almost nose to chest—he was considerably shorter than me—and I could feel his hot breath through my shirt. He glanced up and held me steadfast with his icy-blue stare. It was the most mischievous smile I'd ever seen. He placed his hand in the middle of my chest just below my throat, then let it slide over my pecs, over my dad bod of a belly and down to the top of my jeans. His gaze never wavered, and the look he gave me was plump full of confidence and sensuality. Isaiah was too skilled at this seduction game. The emotions he was emitting were almost tangible, especially to an empath like myself. His smile got bigger. He winked, and I swore I saw a twinkle from his mesmerizing blue eyes. From above us, a buzzer sounded and a light flashed. That broke the moment.

"Ah, breakfast. You should go eat. Come back later, 'kay?" And with that, Isaiah was gone.

A voice boomed from overhead. "James, have you released the kids from their cells?" It was Miriam.

I rolled my eyes and shook my head. "Just talking to them, Miriam," I called out in a huff. I swore. Dealing with her this regularly was going to take everything out of me.

"Come back to your apartment," she said, cold and monotone, as a click sounded indicating the intercom system had switched off. There was silence for a few seconds as I sighed and looked at the dangling Isaiah, then shrugged. The system's audible click sounded again. "Please," she added. *She has never said please to me like that. She wants something.*

Isaiah was still levitating with arms outstretched. He had asked to be unhooked and let loose. It was up to me to get him out of there. I had the briefest of inappropriate thoughts. I imagined helping an incapable lot of Miriam's muscle-heads unhook him from his IVs, my hand wrapped around his torso, trying to steady him while the workers dismantled the tubes. A tingly wave of arousal came over me. It was a nice thought, feeling his warm hairy body and his tight muscles, when I noticed a smile beginning to spread across the levitating Isaiah's face. There I was, thinking unsuitable thoughts again, and there he was in the real world, reading my mind, and reacting to it despite his sedation.

Isaiah's head drooped to one side and his eyes were closed, but as he gently swayed back and forth on his invisible crucifix, I would have sworn he was staring right at me. And that smile...

That was going to be the first thing we worked on. Respect and boundaries. I couldn't have him digging away in my head. Eventually, I would think of something other than how cute he was.

And you have to stop thinking about those *things!*

I turned away from him and started walking back to my "apartment" when I heard him in my head, *Inappropriate thoughts are welcome!*

Yup, first lesson. Boundaries.

My teeth gnashed together. We were both adults, but if I was going to be responsible for him, the last thing I would do was start a tryst. First day on my own, relatively pain free, sober, and capable of standing on my own, and this is how it begins? Glancing at the row of cubes, I decided my impending task had devolved from difficult to impossible.

Upon entering the apartment, I found Miriam sitting at the dining table with an assortment of various breakfast dishes. Another wall had disappeared revealing—surprise, surprise—a kitchen.

Well, geez. Look at that. Oh woman, I hate you.

The scent of freshly brewed coffee saturated the air. I inhaled the welcoming aroma.

"You didn't think to do this any time over the past week?" I gestured to the stainless fridge while glaring at her. "A snack or a glass of water in the middle of the night would have been nice instead of having to drink from the bathroom sink. That's kind of nasty." I studied the kitchen. It was sleek, blacks and whites with stainless-steel appliances, black granite countertops, and a rather cool-looking metallic silver backsplash made up of thousands of mosaic tiles. "But the coffee smells amazing."

"I see you're playing nice with your class already, getting to know them. This is good, James. They need to trust you," Miriam said, ignoring my rant. She grabbed an empty plate from the stack that had been piled on the table and proceeded to scoop out small helpings of what looked like scrambled eggs. "So, initial thoughts?"

Your expectations about how you want this class to go are way out of line?

I was stuck there, thanks to the damn contract I had signed years before under duress, so I *best* make this bearable and play her game.

I sighed. A small piece of me gave in, resigning myself to my role in Miriam's master plan. I slipped into teacher mode, which brought back familiar skills.

Assess and evaluate.

"Ning is immature but sweet. I think she'll be fairly easy to assist. But she needs her mobile device back. We need to set up an hourly alarm for her, a reminder to let off a bit of built-up energy. Chris was in wolf form, pacing. Not much evaluation going to happen with that. Is that normal for him?" I snagged my own plate, discovering I was terribly hungry, which I hadn't been in days. In short order, the plate was full of food.

"Usually." Miriam got up and returned with two coffee mugs and a pot of freshly brewed coffee for our breakfast meeting.

"Great. No idea what to make of a pacing wolf, other than I might be considered dinner if I get too close. Annabelle's cell was filled with Arcane mist. I couldn't even see her. Are you sure you shouldn't be calling in someone who's better suited to deal with her? I'm honestly a little out of my league with such intense demonic abilities."

"Well, now that you mention it, there's a coven we've contacted. Supposedly the most powerful one, but they are located in eastern Bulgaria, a small city called Varna on the coast of the Black Sea. It will be a while until we see them here." She stirred the sugar she had dumped into her coffee. Funny, for as vile as she could be, I was surprised she liked sugar. I would have thought strychnine straight up would have been her drink of choice.

"I have to say, that's a relief. Honestly, I'm not sure what I can do with her." I shrugged slightly as I took a sip of my own mug, brimming with dark liquid goodness, and immediately, the world seemed like a nicer place. I leaned back in my chair as I took another swig of the earthy-brown goodness.

I closed my eyes briefly and enjoyed its delightfulness.

"Well, you'll have to start the instruction for at least a little while, so best you get to know her. We don't expect the Varna coven for at least another couple of days. The leader's response was that they would come, in time. She was rather cryptic about it all. But they made it very clear they weren't going to take in a novice who was completely untrained. Apparently, they are beyond that." Miriam gave a slight shrug, as if she didn't care either way.

The coven's response didn't surprise me. Arcanes and their demons were just that, cryptic, and they had protocols for dealing with their own. Levels of tutoring coupled with years of study was standard, but most of it was done steeped in secrecy.

"Camila was asleep, so nothing from her. But she concerns me as well."

"She should."

"You're not helping, Miriam."

"And I see Isaiah came out to meet you?" Again, she ignored me.

"Yes. He wants to be unmedicated."

Upon hearing that, she stopped eating her breakfast, looked me dead in the eye while raising an eyebrow. "I don't think that's wise."

"He's an adult. I don't think we can keep him sedated forever, especially if he's telling me he wants to be off the drugs."

"I really don't care what his wishes are. I have to think about the safety of my employees here, and anyone else he'd come into contact with. You haven't seen what he's capable of."

"I never will if he's sedated the entire time."

Miriam sighed. She knew I was right on this. "If we do this, James, you're entirely responsible. And no one else is present, just my team, you, and Isaiah. Having the other students there too would be an unnecessary risk."

"All right. Let's do it this afternoon." A quick thought of me, alone, with Isaiah and those loose hospital scrub pants flashed through my mind.

No, no, no. Stop thinking about Isaiah like that!

Miriam studied me carefully. She nodded curtly and then politely chewed on a forkful of eggs. She was quiet as she munched on breakfast. She put the cutlery down on the plate, which made little clinking noises that seemed to hang rather heavy in the air in a space otherwise eerily quiet.

From where I sat, I could tell she was putting together a list of everything that would be required for this afternoon's adventure. She was calculating and planning and thinking of every permutation of "things going wrong" she possibly could. Brushing her heavily lipsticked lips with a white napkin (I instantly felt sorry for the housekeeping staff—that stain was never coming out), she placed the used serviette on her plate and leaned back in the chair, folding her hands together and placing them in her lap.

"Fine. I'll arrange it. But I'm warning you. Be hypervigilant."

"Good. Now, let's talk about this 'bidding' thing. What the hell? We're not commodities."

"I'd like to think you're intelligent and capable, James—but then you say stupid things like this. Look around you. These facilities do not come cheap and don't think for a minute that the government gives us nearly enough funds to run this place." She waved one of her bony fingers, complete with a long manicured red talon, towards the student cubes. "Their sponsors pay for all of this."

"Who are they? The sponsors," I asked, already knowing the answer, but I wanted confirmation.

"The usual. Military, the Intelligence community, larger corporations. Chris will be going to the Army. They are quite protective of their investment in him. All you have to do is calm him down. I think the structure of the armed forces will do him a world of good."

"Not if he can't respect authority," I added.

"Well now, that's your job to teach him, isn't it?"

"Great. This is all new since I was here last," I said.

"Yes, well, funding isn't what it once was. We are having to get creative to keep enough money coming into the CMRD so that we can continue our work."

"What about Ning? If Chris is army bound, what about her?"

"She's an interesting one. Believe it or not, the United Nations have expressed an interest in her, and not for her talents. At least, not her *unusual* talents. They want her because of her exceptional linguistic abilities."

"That's wonderful!" I felt my face expand with happiness. Each of them deserved a good life, a happy existence. Not being stuck in a cube. To think, despite the magical crap, Ning would have a shot at a normal life. There was a lot of stigma attached to us. I would never be hired as a regular teacher, ever again. At one point, I had been pretty good at it too. "What about the other three?"

"Camila is wanted by the Canadian Security Intelligence Service for obvious reasons. Annabelle, well, to be honest, no one was going to claim her after that display. I'll confide this to you. I'm hoping this Bulgarian coven comes through and, despite their rules, claim her as one of their own. Some of the stunts she's done to our staff have scared my people half to death."

"What about Isaiah?"

"Yes. Well. Why don't you see what you can do with him first? I have a personal interest in him and his extraordinary talents. But, he's dangerous. And you know what happened last time."

Cody, dressed all in clinical white clothes, was strapped to a table. He begged and cried for help, while several people held him down. A needle, lodged in his arm, wobbled. Objects around the room started to fly rapidly...

"Yeah, I'm well aware." I pushed my plate forward. I'd lost my appetite.

"Do what you can. No one is expecting them to be perfectly functioning, well-adjusted people. They just want the threat level knocked down several notches. I know you can do that. Don't get in your head either. You'll ruminate on this and destroy any chance of success. You know the expression. You are your own worst enemy."

"Yeah, well, thanks for that." It was true, though. I couldn't argue with her. "Knocking the threat level down—that's easier said than done."

"I'm hard on you because you're capable of great things. Giving you higher than normal expectations is for your own good. You'll stretch yourself to get there. I've seen you do it. Now, I want you to relax for the rest of the morning. I've expanded your apartment. There's a gym over there with equipment in it. I know you used to enjoy the activity. You should think about starting again. We've also installed a TV as well." Miriam reached across the table and grabbed my wrist. Her hand was ice cold, but her bony fingers wrapped around my arm and she squeezed me. "You can do this. I have faith in you. And we're here if you need anything, but we're also keeping all of you isolated. We need to make sure they'll be okay. At the other end of the hangar, there's a classroom. If you can get them all settled and collected, we'll raise the glass partitions and you can have them in a regular class setting.

"In the classroom, there are the usual assortment of magical reference books available, too, but if you need anything more specific..."

"Well, Annabelle will need them. She'll have to start studying the protection wards and circle glyphs in order to protect herself."

Miriam stared at me while still clasping my wrist. She said with a smirk, "See. You can do this."

I sighed. My chest felt heavy, most likely from guilt. There seemed to be a mountain-sized portion of the useless emotion now squarely settled onto my shoulders. It did not feel good.

"If you really loved me, you'd make sure there's a few bottles of vodka in my apartment too."

Miriam got up from the table, walked over to the kitchen, and opened one of the cupboards, "I know you too well. You can't handle alcohol, and we just got you sober. You're over the worst hump to getting clean. No, none for you. But I've left you with a carton of cigarettes and a few nicotine patches. I want you to quit this as well."

She closed the cupboard and walked towards the door that led into the bowels of the CMRD, but stopped and turned to glare at me. "Don't mess this up, James."

She spun, her heels clicking on the cold sterile floor. She opened the thick metal door and then disappeared beyond it. The metal closed with a *thud* behind her as the locks *slinked* into place.

What could possibly go wrong?

Seven: Lunch Break

I DIDN'T WASTE any time going to the cupboard to rip open one of the cartons of smokes. Thankfully, Miriam had also left a lighter. I pulled the first pack out and clenched it tightly. Not too hard, mind you. I didn't want to damage them. But I held them snug enough to know they were there, and to claim them all as mine.

Well, maybe I'd give one to Isaiah.

Stop it already. Thinking fondly of Mr. Furry is not allowed!

I sat down at the messy kitchen table, still clutching the lighter and cigarettes, pushed my plate away, and gently rapped my forehead against the tabletop several times.

I had to get over this little infatuation with Isaiah and the gnawing thoughts that this insurmountable task of teaching the kids would end up in a fiery disaster.

I sat back up and peeled the plastic off the pack of smokes. As the cellophane came off, the rich, sweet smell of tobacco filled the air. I licked my lips and pulled a cigarette out, rolled it between my fingers for a few seconds, and then tapped the end on the hard surface of the table. I lit it. The warmth of the flame and the wisp of smoke that twirled off the end of the cigarette instantly gratified and calmed me. As much as I hated to admit it, the devil with the white updo was right. I needed to quit. This addiction would kill me. Damn it all, that woman knew me too well—hence the nicotine patches.

I shoved the opened pack of smokes into my shirt pocket.

Inhale. Just breathe.

Glancing over to the extra opened rooms that Miriam had graciously granted me access to, I spied the gym. Yes! That was the answer. I hadn't had a decent workout in months. Too much time had passed since the last time I'd seen the inside of one. Lifting weights might be the perfect way to refocus. I used to do it pretty damn regularly. Maybe Miriam was right: time to start again.

I snuffed out the half-burned cigarette in the ashtray, careful not to mangle it. I could have the rest later. The smell of ashes hung in the air as I twirled the end of the smoke around the bottom of the ashtray, smothering out any possible embers.

After a quick rummage around my bedroom to find out where the appropriate workout clothes might have been stashed, I finally found an assortment of active-wear. I pulled them out and held them up in front of me as I looked into the mirror.

But with no other choices, I snorted derisively and rolled my eyes as I slipped out of the professional teacher clothes and laid them out on the bed. I would need them for this afternoon when we got to take Isaiah off his meds.

The gym clothes slid on like a second skin, way too tight for what I normally would have worn. I checked out the style and look of the CMRD's choice of athletic clothing in the mirror. I looked like a pimped-out racing car for all the decals and fancy pin-striping adorning my outfit.

A sharp pain stabbed and penetrated deep into my temple.

Billowing vapours of chalky smoke blew and huffed as a pale face emerged from the smoulder. The very dead body of my ex-boyfriend walked out of the spectral cloud and wrapped his cold rotting arms around my middle. The white fabric of his tracksuit hung in tattered shreds from his body, exposing a sickening vision of decay.

Cody, who was just a little taller than I was, nuzzled his iced skin into the back of my neck.

"You like him, don't you?"

"Leave me. You're not really here."

"But I'll always be here, and I can't let you do this again. You won't succeed. He's too out of control. You will kill him, just like you killed me."

Cody tilted his head to the side, unnaturally far as if his neck had been snapped. His maw opened, exposing a rotting mouth; then his blackened teeth bit down on my earlobe. An action that once turned me on now repulsed me.

I could feel his teeth. Shivering, I shut my eyes and pushed him away. He wasn't there. He couldn't be there. This was my magic getting the best of me. It was my subconscious.

And none of this is real.

The icy fingers slithered away and dissipated.

As my eyelids broke open, the remains of Cody slowly evaporated. My breath formed a cloud in front of me, the air chilled, and suddenly, I was nauseated.

I ran to the bathroom and made it just as I vomited the eggs I had stuffed into my face for breakfast.

THE CLANK AND rattle of metal against steel bars filled the room as I pushed the barbell up and down. Repeat times ten.

Oddly enough, this actually felt good. It felt right, normal.

Why did I quit doing this again?

Placing the bar and weights on their resting spot, I slithered down the bench, sat up, and grabbed the water bottle to take a good swig.

Sweat ran down my forehead, off my cheek, and dripped onto the mat.

God love the cleaning staff. They don't pay them enough.

When I lay back down and placed myself under the bar, the cool leather of the bench felt good against my hot skin. I gripped the bar with both hands, putting them firmly into position, and hoisted up.

Muscles complained and argued, but I ignored them.

"Come on, bro. Give me five more."

A shot of adrenaline rushed through my body and the barbell dropped. After balancing it quickly, so it didn't land on my head, I glanced above me. Isaiah was standing right behind my head, in just his bottom scrubs.

Lord, give me strength.

"Come on, James. Push it." He cocked an eyebrow at me as a wicked smile spread across his face. His hands were outstretched as if he would catch the barbell if I slipped.

"I don't need you to spot me," I huffed out as a pushed the weight up.

Isaiah grabbed the bar on either side of my hands, then slid his hands so that they were overtop of mine. I could feel the heat emanating from him, but I knew he wasn't there.

"Come on, James. Don't ruin the fun." He winked. "I want you hot and sweaty."

This can't be happening.

Isaiah shuffled in a little closer to the barbell, with his legs planted on each side of the bench, which meant his crotch was right above my nose. He chuckled.

I finished my set with a couple quick frustrated pushes of the barbell, angst and sexual tension fuelling me to completion. Isaiah made sure the bar was safely placed back on its rest.

After shimmying down the bench and away from Isaiah, I sat up and twisted so that I could face him.

"Isaiah, we need to talk about boundaries, dude."

"Oh come on. Look at you." Isaiah took the two steps towards me so he was standing right in front and his furry, delicious chest was directly in my line of sight. He placed his hand on my sweaty torso. I could feel my heart skip a beat. "Ha! Feel that?" Isaiah smirked. He grabbed my hand and placed it on his bare chest, forcing my hand over his pecs and down his abs. His stomach muscles twitched. "I feel it too." He winked at me. "So don't try to tell me that you're not attracted to me, because I know you are. Just so you know, that goes both ways." He put his palm on my chest again, cupped the muscle, and squeezed. "Betcha got just a dusting of fur there too, don't ya? Just the way I like it." He leered at me and licked his lips again.

"Isaiah, look, if I'm going to be your teacher, this can't happen. Even if I wanted it to, it just can't." I couldn't deny he was exciting me. And gym shorts, especially Lycra, weren't going to hide my excitement from him.

"Why not? It happened with Cody, right?"

"Okay, and this is exactly what I'm talking about. Boundaries, dude. You are not to go digging around in my head. Do you understand? Cody is off-limits to you. I need and want my privacy, and what happened with Cody, I vowed will never happen again. Ever. Period. So just let that settle into your head." Any excitement that had been there was gone.

"Hmmm. Well, I'm not going to let you go. That's not going to happen." Isaiah leaned forward, too close. In fact, he came in so close I was forced back. His gaze never wavered as he stared at me with those soul-catching blue irises. Before I knew it, I was lying on the bench, and he'd pressed his body on top of me and whispered in my ear, "I don't do boundaries very well. You intrigue me, and I like you too much." Isaiah canted his head to his side, and his crystalline blue eyes flashed. "I know you can and will help him. And I can smell how much you want him too." I could feel Isaiah's hardened dick against my leg.

Why the hell was he talking about himself like that? He was horny and crazy.

And then he was gone. Disappeared. The room was deathly quiet and the air still. I covered my face in my hands.

Jesus Christ, and fuck.

WITH MY WORKOUT completely ruined, I showered, put my teacher clothes back on, and walked out to the kitchen. Sitting on the table was a black DVD case.

I picked it up and read the label *Watch Me.*

Shaking my head, I wondered what on God's good green earth Miriam had conjured up this time and then turned around and studied the TV that had been installed earlier.

I inserted the disc into media player, turned on the TV, and (thank the gods for click and play) the disc automatically started playing. The screen came to life to a camera panning around the interior of a poorly lit warehouse. There was enough illumination to recognize the vastness of the room, with huge shipping containers stacked against each of the walls. In the center, a woman stood in a white gown surrounded by a circle of lit candles. Her head was tilted back and she was chanting with splayed arms and hands. At her feet and inside the circle lay a body in a rather awkward position.

The camera zoomed in, the picture momentarily blurry until the autofocus feature returned the image to crystal clarity.

The woman's face filled the TV screen.

It was Shawna. My sister.

She bent over, grabbed a large knife lying next to her feet, then raised her arm up and plunged the blade into the side of the body in front of her.

The unknown human jerked violently with each stab and screamed in concert with the assault. Shawna plunged the knife in several more times and then dropped the weapon. She pushed her hands into her victim's torso, extracted them and brought them up to her face to inspect them.

Long dripping strings of dark-red liquid slid and oozed over her fingers and fell out of her palms. In one of her hands, she held an organ. I had no idea which, but I was repulsed.

Shawna's eyes narrowed, and a smile stretched across her face, crinkling the corners of her eyes and creating deep creases around her nose.

I've never seen her so...

I shut off the DVD player and sunk into the sofa. I hung my head as I reached up to cradle my forehead.

What the hell have you got yourself into now, Shawna?

It couldn't have been her. It just couldn't. My thoughts raced back to our childhood, and Razzmouse. That had been our family cat, except he was huge and almost more like a dog. Razzmouse was a Maine Coon. Mom had found him as a stray in her last year of university and adopted him. So, when we were born, Razzmouse was more like an older sibling than a family pet. I was pretty sure he thought of us as his kids, and Shawna was particularly attached to him. When Razzmouse died, Shawna had just turned eleven, and it traumatized her for months. Granted, she was also the one who found the cat's dead body. He had decided to die in her closet amongst the piles of clothes she never put away or hung up.

But remembering that...Shawna couldn't handle the death of the family cat and was always particularly sensitive about death—to the point that even watching a character die on a TV show was often too much for her.

How did you go from that to this?

I stared at the DVD case in disbelief. It just couldn't have been Shawna.

The lights flashed above me, and the door opened as one of the housekeeping staff wheeled a cart with my lunch over to the table where I had found the DVD, then set up my meal.

I had no appetite whatsoever. Camila appeared as a transparent apparition sitting in the chair that Miriam had occupied earlier this morning. The attendant jumped back, startled at the apparition. She muttered something that sounded less than complimentary, finished her duties, and exited my apartment.

"Let's have lunch!" she said enthusiastically—she seemed chipper and perky, but there was an underlying feeling of mania to her emotions. I squinted at her, trying to determine her motivations. Distrust settled in.

She smiled and extended a hand towards my chair. It moved on its own, pulling itself out from the table.

"Have a seat. We can chat while you eat."

What the fuck did I do in my life to deserve this hell?

Eight: Third Period

RESIGNED TO MY fate, I walked over and had a seat at the kitchen table. But after looking at what appeared to be casserole noodle surprise, I couldn't do it. I just couldn't eat. Not after watching the Shawna video. Besides, the lumpy mess in a white ceramic dish seemed too much like institutional food.

Camila started her chatter as soon as I sat down.

"I'm so happy you're here. At least this time, they gave us someone who's like us. I know you'll understand us better. What's the matter? Aren't you going to eat? I want out of this glass cube. I don't suppose you could make that happen? I'm sure you have to put us all through tests. Right? I'll pass them. I know I can. I don't know about the others, though—you know—they don't have the same self-control I do. But God, I hate this box. I want to see the sun again. I really need to see the sun again.

"So, how long have you worked for the CMRD? I think I'd like to do that too. I'm good enough—you know—right? Like, I can do this stuff. This magic 'n' shit. I can teach students how to do this.

"So, what are you going to do with us first? Are we getting advanced magic lessons? Like in Harry Potter and all that?"

Holy fuck a duck, this girl.

"Well," I said, putting the lid back on the lunch dish—looking at it was making my stomach queasy, "this afternoon, we're going to take Isaiah off the tubes and see if we can get him conscious, off the drugs, and not causing magical mayhem."

"Seriously not a good idea." She fidgeted, and while the Astral vibrated, the entire table shook. I chanced a quick glance under the table, and just as I had suspected, Camila was bouncing her leg up and down at a rapid rate.

"Why not?" I said, cocking an eyebrow.

"Dude, he's the worst. No control there at all, you know? Like, that's just asking for trouble. You should take me out first. I can show you everything I can do. It'll be fun! Hey, what about a field trip. Yeah! We could, like, go into the city or something. That'd be awesome!"

"No one's going anywhere," I said sternly.

"Oh, dude, come on. Seriously? No fun." She pouted her lips and glanced at me with an expression that implied you're-not-cool.

"True, but this afternoon, we're going to focus on Isaiah. If that goes well, then I'll come have a chat with you. How does that sound?"

"Shitty." Camila looked pissed. Great. First encounter with the girl and she's as much trouble as I originally thought, and now she's upset with me.

"Ning told me that she hadn't met everyone else. So, how is it you know what Isaiah is or isn't capable of?" I had to ask. Both Camila and Isaiah seemed to have knowledge of the others. Or was Ning not telling me the truth?

"Dude, come on, really? Ah, Astrals? I can just walk down the way and have a look."

"So you spy on them?" Wow, this chick was something else. She was going to be fun to teach.

She frowned at me and was about to speak, when the big metal door to the outside hallway opened up and in walked Miriam and several of her guards, all of whom were suited up with special matching black uniforms and utility belts full of an assortment of various items. It kind of reminded me of Batman's outfit.

"Ugh, her," Camila said and then vanished.

"That girl is nothing but trouble," Miriam said, pointing at the now-empty space.

"Miriam, it's not nice to treat the students like shit," I said. "Who are these guys and why are they here?"

"You want to get Isaiah. Let's go get him. But I'll tell you right now, I don't think this is a good idea."

"How am I supposed to know what I'm dealing with or make an assessment of any kind if you've got the kid so drugged up and strung out that all I get are astral projections? That's hardly going to give me an accurate picture of what I'm up against."

"All right then, let's go." Miriam shrugged and then gestured towards the door on the far side of the apartment that granted access to the hangar where the kids lived.

I didn't move a muscle, and Miriam gave me another of her famous unhappy faces.

"What do you want me to do? I'm not a doctor. I have no idea how to remove an IV."

Miriam screwed up her face at me. Pretty sure she threw in a snarl as well. She and her brigade of minions strode past me and out into the hangar. Her heels made a *click, click, click* as she walked her way out of my confines and towards the students.

Shaking my head, I followed, unsure of what was going to happen, and if I was being completely honest with myself, I had a tingling in my stomach, which might have been nervousness. Was it a warning? Hard to tell.

What if Isaiah really couldn't control his shit?

Miriam and I stood elbow to elbow as her minions entered in through the side of Isaiah's cube, where a door lay open. They spent an exorbitant amount of time putzing and chatting amongst themselves. Nothing much was getting accomplished and I was about to lose my patience and just go over to Isaiah and yank the damn tubes out myself when, as if my thoughts had directed them, they started propping up step ladders in order to position themselves at the right height to Isaiah's arms.

I looked away. Last thing I can stomach is watching needles go in or out of flesh.

"Just tell me when he's unhooked." I covered my eyes.

"Good God, James, really?" Miriam's crew banged around while doing things, but I refused to look, and eventually Miriam said, "He's done."

Except she had lied and they were still sliding the last and largest needle out of his arm. Blood welled up on the surface of his skin. Bile rose into the back of my throat.

When the last IV had come out, the tubes that had pushed a slow drip of catatonia-inducing meds hung lifelessly from the ceiling.

A shiver ran down my back.

The intensity of the workers, their constant movement and coordinated effort was overwhelming. Within seconds, the team swarmed within Isaiah's cube, like rainforest ants overtaking an enemy. One of the workers broke away, looked towards Miriam, and nodded.

She walked up to the cube where, on the side panel, there was a keypad. She entered in a few numbers and the entire front of the cell lifted itself up like the trunk of a car.

Isaiah was out in the open for the first time in God only knew how long. More importantly, we were exposed to him.

A hospital-like bed was situated a few feet away from where Isaiah was still levitating. It looked rather similar to the one I had spent time in while sobering up in the medical wing.

Isaiah, with no change in his state, continued to levitate and sway gently despite the brouhaha occurring beneath him. The raw talent this guy displayed was stupefying. And damn, yes, he was still too freakin' cute.

The cast of thousands that had attended to Isaiah, slowly backed away, removed the step ladders, and waited. No one made a sound.

Silence enveloped us, and it was as if no one even breathed. We were waiting for the other shoe to drop.

A couple of the bigger muscle-heads remained next to Isaiah, I assumed to catch him should he simply fall out of the air.

Miriam tapped her feet with impatience.

The seconds ticked by, which crawled into minutes.

Miriam glanced towards me. "I certainly hope you know what you're doing."

"Well, right now, I'm waiting."

There was movement from Isaiah as his outstretched arms slowly descended and came to rest at his sides. His shoulders slumped forward, and the distance between his feet and the floor of the hangar decreased considerably.

His naked toes grazed the cold cement, as his head lolled to one side.

A string of drool seeped out of the corner of his mouth.

Well, that's not attractive.

Isaiah dropped suddenly, to his knees, then nose-dived forward and did a face-plant. A sickening *crack* sounded from his forehead hitting concrete. Miriam's people tentatively stepped forward, but Miriam held her hand out and they all took a big collective step back.

"For fuck's sake," I said, then walked over to Isaiah. I bent over, grabbed him under his arms, and started to lift him up.

"James," Miriam warned, but I gave her this look, and in my head, all I could think is *God, you're such a bitch.*

Isaiah stirred as I helped him up to his feet. His lip was split and a small trickle of blood ran over his chin.

He tugged his head up, opened his eyelids hesitantly, and studied me closely with light brown eyes, edged in a deep ring of black. The look he was giving me was one of confusion, as if he had no idea who I was.

Wait...what? Isaiah's eyes were blue, ice crystal blue, weren't they?

"Who....who are you?" he croaked.

His legs gave out from underneath him as he stumbled and lost his balance. Rickety limbs from the months of being sedated had no muscle strength to keep him standing, like a fawn that was hours old. I hugged him to my chest to prevent another tumble.

Isaiah weighed way less than he should, but a tingle started in my stomach as I looked right into his teddy-bear brown eyes. The heat from his body permeated my clothes. Isaiah, pressed so close to me, was exhilarating. I wanted this to go well.

"Hi," I said very quietly and cautiously.

"Who the hell are you?" he asked with a tone in his voice that signalled alarm bells in my head. He really had no idea who I was?

"We've already met, Isaiah. I'm James, you're new...teacher."

From behind Isaiah, I could see dark mist swirling about, emanating from his back and forming a large cloud behind us.

Everyone stopped dead as if movement would give away their position as the haze churned and swirled. Miriam's mob took another collective step backward, looks of panic darting between them.

"Shit," I mistakenly said out loud.

"What? Whaddya mean, shit?" Isaiah glanced at me with panic and then pushed himself off me, as a shadowy form rose behind him, half concealed in the demon mist. Several pointed and curved horns jutted out from the top of the beast's head and a loud growl rumbled through the hangar.

"Goddammit, James." Miriam's face scrunched up like a wadded piece of paper. She did an about-face and marched back to my apartment.

The growl evolved into a bellow, like the sound of wild beasts, and the temperature in the room became very cold and dank. A thick musky scent saturated the air, enough to make me gag. Isaiah's face was a mask of terror.

A large whip-like tail lashed out at me from the horned figure. The appendage was covered with razor-sharp spikes along a crested ridge, and a barb on the end narrowly missed my face as I dodged to the side. The tail slithered back, coiling itself around Isaiah's leg.

"Mine..." a subhuman voice rolled through the hangar. It was filled with gravel and so hollow, it felt like my soul was shrinking into the deepest corners of my body. "No, no...not again," Isaiah whispered. A frown formed on his face and tears fell from his eyes. The front of his scrubs suddenly darkened as he started to piss himself. The taint of rot that filled the air was overcome by a new odour, a smell of ozone and urine. The hairs on my arms and the back of my neck stood straight up.

An alarm blared. Miriam had obviously sounded for the sentinels.

"Oh shit." I ducked as a bolt of lightning zapped past me and forked its way around the room. Energy was palpable within the hangar, and from the briefest of glances, the immediate vicinity around Isaiah had become one big lightning storm. I motioned for the guards to exit, making rapid movements with my arm. I chanced a glance towards the other cubes. Each student was facing us and watching as if we were a sci-fi TV show. But none of them seemed to be enjoying themselves...except Camila. She was smiling and mouthing "Told you" over and over. I hoped their cubes would keep them safe.

"Run!" I screamed, but the muscle-heads had already plowed past me. I was the last one left, and that saying about the zombie apocalypse ran through my head. *You don't have to run the fastest. You just have to run faster than the slowest person.* Except at the moment, I was the slowest person.

The dimly lit hangar had lost any luminescence and was cast into the depths of night. Shadows from the corners of the room deepened and lengthened. I couldn't see anything except the glow from my apartment and even that was hazy. Another bolt of electricity zapped past me and hit the far wall, illuminating it with a sharp burst of blue light. The fork of lightning splintered and little tails of energy zigzagged off in various directions.

The air around me rapidly picked up into gale-force winds, and within seconds, I was struggling against air currents in an attempt to move forward. I pushed with all my might against the steady current, but I wasn't getting very far.

The demon tail lashed out again and wrapped around my feet, then yanked me towards Isaiah.

I fell forward but threw my hands out ahead of me, narrowly missing my face being smacked open on the concrete like Isaiah's had. A deep chuckle filled the air as the tail dragged me backward.

Panic coursed through me as I clawed at the polished concrete floors. There was nothing to grasp or cling to, and as I was slogged backward, the demonic tail gripped my legs tighter and tighter.

I flipped over. There was only one thing I could do—get Isaiah to take control of his abilities. But with one glance, I could tell he was in no condition to take over anything. Isaiah's eyes were rolled back and showing nothing but whites as little jolts of electricity sparked from his shoulder to his waist, others from his hand to his leg. Sparks ignited and burst. The circular gales in the student hangar had to be the equivalent to a hurricane. The flashing light of Miriam's warning system blinded me with its epileptic pulse and the ear-splitting klaxon. It wasn't helping. It was only adding to the mayhem.

"Isaiah!" I screamed at him, trying to get his attention. Nothing.

Another tail lashed out and slapped me across the head. It stung, and then a warm wet feeling took over. I was bleeding.

I was out of options. Focusing in on Isaiah, or more accurately, the space right beside him, I imagined myself standing right there. The tingly feeling in my feet started, the pins and needles, and then—

Woosh...

I bounced right beside Isaiah, and placed my hand against his warm and hairy chest, and then pushed with all the mental strength I could muster.

Calm the fuck down.

A warmth spread throughout my chest, over my shoulders, running down my arm and into the meat of the palm of my hand. The soothing energy surged out through my fingertips.

As it hit Isaiah's flesh, his body instantly absorbed the empathic command. He sucked in a deep breath and shivered. His outstretched arms relaxed and his eyes rolled forward, appearing normal. The blustery gales diminished as the mist slowly evaporated and the demon within it shrunk away.

Isaiah was hyperventilating, but I continued to push quiet and peaceful thoughts into him.

I registered the heat that was wafting off of Isaiah. It was intense, as if he had a fever. I rubbed his torso to calm him down, and his heaving chest returned to normal breathing. He fell into me and nuzzled his head into my chest.

Doors on the other side of the massive arena, which I had no idea existed, slammed open with metal clanging against metal. I expected an army of Miriam's henchmen, toting guns with a sundry of ammunitions to control the magical chaos. Instead, a massive cloud of black mist flowed forward and slithered into the hangar. An ethereal glow radiated from the inside the amorphous mass, pulsating like a heartbeat with an eerie green tinge.

The mist waned and then parted as four forms appeared, all decked out in black clothes with silver chains dangling from various pockets. Rivets adorned the outfits, lining cuffs and hems. Piercings through lips and eyebrows decorated each of the individuals, two women and two men.

They were the perfect-looking Goth children of the night, and I had no idea who the fuck they were.

Nine: School Nurse

"BOGDAN, DIETER, ENCAPSULATE the beast." A woman with black lipstick barked off a command. Her accent was thick, distinctive, but one I couldn't place. She carried herself with a formidable presence. The swirling black robe, complete with a cowl, was reminiscent of most depictions of the Angel of Death.

Isaiah was still breathing steadily, but there was no way I was removing my hands from him and breaking the empathic connection I had created.

"Siren, come with me," the leader said to a larger woman dressed in a garment resembling a black wedding dress. Then it hit me—this was the coven from Varna. Earlier than expected, but thank every god and demon they had arrived.

"You." She pointed at me. "Whatever you're doing, Empath, stop it. I need this demon contained so I know what we are dealing with."

I didn't want to break my connection, and clearly that thought ran across my face, but at the same time, I couldn't remain connected to Isaiah forever. I was going to have to sever the connection.

Arcane shit was creepier than hell, and I knew next to nothing about it. Time to let the professionals take over.

Just as I raised my hand from Isaiah's chest, his eyes, which had been closed, popped open, displaying those sparkling blue irises, which stared right at me. The body that had relaxed under my touch suddenly stiffened.

Isaiah grabbed my hand and growled, "You are not allowed to touch him without permission."

A sudden burst of energy, like a wave from an explosion sent me hurtling back, spinning through the air, out of control, until my head came into contact with something hard and unyielding.

Blinding white light flashed through my skull. The crystalline spike I had felt the morning I had agreed to come back to this god forsaken facility to consult on Miriam's latest project, pierced itself through my head again. But this time, a hangover and vodka had nothing to do with it.

I sat up, trying to focus, worried about Isaiah and where the members from the coven were. My eyesight blurred and I couldn't focus.

Then it all went black.

THE NEXT TIME my eyes opened, all I could see was white, and it hurt like glass stabbing me right through my irises.

I closed my eyes and tried to roll over, except an ache in my arm stopped me, and there was a tugging at the surface of my skin, preventing me from changing position.

Waves of grogginess and clouds of fog enshrouded me. Throbbing pain pounded out a steady beat deep within my brain. A mouthful of cotton bunged up my mouth and every muscle in my body refused to respond.

I needed to throw up.

Except I couldn't move, so the barf just rolled out and spilled down my front.

Suddenly, there were arms all over the place, and people manhandling me roughly. None of it felt any good.

And then my eyelids were a hundred pounds and I dropped back into the blackness and it was lights out.

MY EYES FLUTTERED open. It took a moment for the heavy burden of sleep to lift before I could grasp my immediate surroundings.

I was in a hospital. Wait...no, I was back in the medical wing of the CMRD.

Oh shit, Miriam's gonna go psycho-bitch on me.

My head still had a percussive rhythm and my forehead itched. I touched my brow only to find the unmistakable prickliness of surgical thread used for stitches. Shit.

Then, the crap-storm that happened in the student hangar came flooding back and the confusion of my surroundings and current bodily state changed, yielding to grief and misery. My shoulders felt very heavy and a tight knot formed in my stomach.

I've failed.

From my periphery, a hand appeared and covered the top of mine. It was warm and comforting, but the contact was gingerly made, tentative in its motion.

Still trying to get all my bearings, I glanced over to where the rest of the hand should have a body attached to it. There in the chair beside me was Isaiah. My eyes opened wide.

"Hi, I'm Isaiah."

"Yeah, I know who you are." My throat felt like sawdust and gravel had been lodged into it and the voice that came out didn't sound like me at all. I coughed out, "Could you get me some water?"

"Sure!" Isaiah jumped up and grabbed a pitcher, then poured a little liquid into a tiny plastic glass. "You want a straw too?"

"No, that's fine. Thank you." I took a sip, studying Isaiah. He seemed real enough, but there was no way to know for sure if this was an Astral or not. Isaiah could make solid copies, unlike Camila. "Look at me?"

Isaiah leaned forward with a smile buried in his scruffy beard, attempting friendliness. Although again, the actions were hesitant.

He cast a sorrowful gaze in my direction. "I'm sorry about what I did to you. It wasn't very nice. But in my defence, it wasn't really me. I've never seen *it* come out like that before. You pissed *him* off. I don't think I've ever felt that much anger coming from him." He looked away.

Aha. So, light-blue crystal eyes belong to the demon. Isaiah has rich chocolate brown.

"Isaiah, you don't have control over yourself," I said as I shifted in the hospital bed, wincing in pain.

"Careful, you're bruised all the way down your left side."

"Yeah, feels like it. So, brown eyes is you? How often do they turn blue?"

Isaiah closed his eyes and shook his head slowly. "Yeah, sorry. Whatever *it* did, I'm so sorry." Isaiah blushed hard, crimson rising under the skin into his cheekbones. His thick beard covered up most of his embarrassment, but just above the beard line, the skin burned a deep crimson. I wanted to run my fingers through his scruff. I'd never seen a beard so thick.

"Sorry?" I asked, with a bit of a lilt, trying to sound nonchalant. "Well, I wouldn't be. Before *it* put me here, *it* was rather...um...well, flirty. Let's call it flirty." I gave Isaiah a bit of a playful wink.

"Oh fuck. Oh my god. What did I do?" He placed his hands over his face, covering his shame and his now burning-red forehead. He was so flushed, I swore I could feel the heat from where I was lying.

"Nothing to be ashamed of," I reassured him.

"I am sorry Mr. Martin. Mrs. Van Allen told me what you did for me. I wanted to be the first person you saw when you woke up. Whatever you did...I haven't...I—" He stumbled hard. "I haven't been in control of anything in years. Whatever you did finally gave me enough serenity to pull my shit together. I can't begin to thank you enough. I can still feel it. What did you do?"

Despite my current condition, nothing could make me happier, and it created a warm ripple that washed through my chest as a smile spread across my face. I chuckled a little. That made a few things hurt, and the spasm of pain cut short my amusement.

"I used my Empath abilities and forced you to feel calm. It wasn't that hard, and I did it completely on instinct. I needed you to suppress everything that was going on and I was pretty sure the chaos was a result of you being scared."

"Yeah. Nail on head, dude. I've been terrified in suspended animation since I came here and they trussed me up."

"You've been in perpetual fear mode?"

"Well, I sorta came into the CMRD like that. I mean, after I sobered up. The demon likes to show me things, some violent things, some inappropriate things." Crimson cheeks burst into being once again. Goddamn, I wished he wasn't so freaking cute. Everything about him just came off as a nice guy caught in a shitty out-of-control situation.

"I've been there. Same place. Don't feel bad."

"What? With a demon?"

"No, no, definitely not that. I mean the sober thing. I haven't been sober until very recently." I smiled in his direction, and when he saw me staring at him, he returned the smile. He shifted his gaze to the side. Seemed I had a talent for making him do that.

Then he got serious again.

"This monster," he said, while poking himself in the chest with his finger. "That thing that's inside of me, I'd do just about anything to get rid of it. Tonka says I have to make peace with it."

"What's a Tonka?"

"Oh, sorry, I forgot. You've been out of it for a couple of days. Tonka, the high priestess of the Bulgarian Coven." Isaiah leaned forward, his hairy arm brushing up against mine, which sent my heart a-fluttering. He whispered, his breath hot on my neck, "She scares the shit out of me."

"I don't think she can hear you in here."

"Actually, I can." Tonka, draped in jet flowing robes appeared in the middle of the hospital room without either of us knowing it.

Isaiah and I both jumped at her words.

"Shit," Isaiah whispered.

"Don't swear, boy." Tonka's mantle billowed, and the giant silver chain wrapped around her waist jingled slightly as she approached my convalescence bed. Black mist wafted out behind her. Her eyes were shadowed in dark colours, with just a hint of sparkle.

God, she's playing this darkness shit up a bit.

Tonka raised an eyebrow as she cast a rather disapproving look in our direction. "Mr. Martin, I would suggest that you keep your thoughts in line; I am here, after all, at your institution's request."

"Shit," I whispered, mimicking Isaiah.

A corpse-like hand stretched out from behind Tonka's back, gripped her shoulder, then another appeared. It wrapped itself around her waist. Tonka's eyes rolled into the back of her head as she mumbled indecipherable words.

Isaiah and I looked at each other, with a what-the-fuck expression.

As the ghoulish limbs receded, Tonka's eyes returned to normal. "My imps tell me that your broken body will heal, but there are wounds in you that are deep and no healing performed by any of my kin will help you. You have ghosts of your own to deal with," she said and then cocked an eyebrow. "How can you expect to help these young *fokusnitsi* if you are the one who needs help?"

"What? Sorry? What's a fork-usnitti?" I said.

Tonka let out a low chuckle, then patted my leg. A shiver erupted from where she touched me. The thin hospital sheets were no match for her cold deathly touch. "You have so much to learn, but when you do, you will be remarkable. Watching you with Isaiah, you were formidable. I applaud your bravery. Not many would have gone up against an Asmodeus demon. Ancient creatures, mean, tailed with wicked horns."

Tonka shifted her gaze towards Isaiah. "Watch, young one." She waggled a long clawed finger that was adorned with a massive silver ring topped in an amber stone. "If you wake one morning and find you've grown a barbed tail, it will mean your beast has taken over."

"Jesus, nothing like a little subtlety." I gave Tonka a scowl.

"Mr. Martin, your little group of students is plagued with three different demons, each as monstrous as the other. Your people need to know how to deal with them, how to call to them, and ultimately how to control them, otherwise they themselves will be consumed and the demons will gain provenance."

"And how do you propose that we 'deal' with them," I asked. Isaiah looked terrified.

"By learning about them, who they are, what strengths they carry, but more importantly, what weakens them. You have the option of making contracts with them as well, but I find that rarely goes well. Siren is the only one I know who's clever binding agreement has worked, but then, Siren is not always herself after sunset."

"That's disconcerting. Thanks for sharing that." Isaiah gave me a look, a face that said *help me*. The fear he showed over the conversation appeared to be beyond what he was willing to bear.

Tonka saw the disheartened expression as much as I did and turned to Isaiah. "My boy, one thing you must remember, the demon chose you. There's something he wants from you. Find out what that is and you'll be able to negotiate. Once that happens, you'll be able to borrow his powers for your own. The abilities of an ancient Asmodeus are nothing to turn away.

"We cannot stay. We have pressing matters elsewhere that must be attended to, but when a plea for help is received, we don't take it lightly, and we aim to claim our own.

"I've had Siren enthral all your demons, but that won't last. You have a short period of time to get your students ready to be able to take on their darker counterparts. Each of the Arcane students will have to complete the Binding Ritual. It should be the first step in any human-demon relationship. Annabelle will be a challenge, as she needs to learn the most. Lucky girl, she is. It is rare indeed that a Legion will attach themselves to a human. Most people couldn't contain a horde. Annabelle can, but again, she needs tutelage."

"Well, you know, on that note, it would be grand if you could have a chat with the kids. They might take a different perspective if they heard the information coming from someone who's lived the experience."

Tonka took in the request, nodding slowly.

"There is merit in that request. I will remain here long enough to talk to them all. We have also left you scrolls and tomes. Basic study materials for new Arcanes. Make sure they all learn from them. I will return when we have reconciled our other matters. At that point, they will have to complete their Binding Ritual in front of me. If they pass, it will begin their relationship with the demon. If they fail, we will exorcise the beast away from them."

"That sounds like the better option. Why not just do that?" I asked.

"Because most don't survive it." And with that, the dark Tonka gave a curt nod and turned to walk away. Her billowing cloak flared, creating a giant circle of swirling black material that enveloped her form, and in a breath, she was gone.

"That is one creepy woman," I said as memories of Cody on the execution table wriggled back to the forefront of my memory. I got lost in that thought as a wave of anxiety threatened to overwhelm me. Isaiah gripped my hand.

"James, please help me." Isaiah's mouth trembled, and his eyes filled with tears. There was no mistaking the look of panic and fear on his face. "I don't want to die."

Shit, here we go again.

Ten: Detention

IT TOOK SOME doing, but I eventually calmed Isaiah down, and then discovered that he had used rather supernatural ways of finding himself to my side. His visit hadn't been sanctioned, and that meant fire and brimstone would be raining down on my head.

It wasn't long after Isaiah had disappeared—literally seconds passed—that Miriam burst in through the door, entering the med ward and making her way towards me.

"Mrs. Van Allen, he's not well enough for visitors yet." A pretty lady in medical scrubs stood up at the nursing station and came out into the hallway to block Miriam's progress. Thank God for all the windows in this ward. I could see clear across the entire wing for all the glass.

Miriam stopped cold and flipped herself around to give the medical staff person the most gruesome look. The poor girl shrank into herself, politely excused her presence from the hallway, and returned back to her charts and papers at the desk.

Miriam spun around and glared at me. She didn't move a stitch until she heard the door close behind her, ensuring we were alone. This did not bode well for me.

"Jesus Christ, James, I told you. I told you this was not a good idea. What the hell is wrong with you, and where is he?" She flipped her hands into the air.

"Where is who?"

"Don't play dumb with me. Remember your sister." Miriam squinted hard in my direction.

"Yes, found the little movie you left for me. What the fuck was that all about?" I had attempted to block the bloody image of Shawna's hands without a lot of success.

"Your sister is into seriously degenerate things. Dangerous things, James. You want us to help her, then get your shit together and fix this! Now, where did Isaiah go?" She tilted her head to the side as she glared at me.

"Miriam, get your panties unknotted, will you?" I wasn't ready or willing to talk about Shawna. Not yet. "Isaiah has enough control currently to pop himself in and out of here—how he's doing that, I have no idea. It didn't look like teleportation. So, getting him off the drugs and the induced medical nightmare he was living *was* the right thing to do. Back off.

"By the way, he thanked me, Miriam. Thanked me. Not you. Because of you, he was living in a constant nightmare. With his consciousness dulled, the demon had control over his dream state. That medically induced coma was your idea, wasn't it? Did you realize that it was a fantastic way for the demon to torment him? Nice way to treat your *students*.

"And if you saw Isaiah in here, you must have also seen Tonka too then?"

"Tonka was here? No. We didn't see that. That woman definitely has mystical ways. What did she want?" Miriam shook her head as she put her hands on her scrawny hips.

"Want? She didn't want anything."

"Nonsense. Her kind always wants something."

"All she did was tell me that Ning, Annabelle, and Isaiah's demons have been, for the moment, controlled, but it won't last long. The wards they've put in place will eventually wear off. She's left us material that will hopefully help and she's agreed to talk to them. If the kids don't learn how to contain the beasts, the coven will perform an exorcism."

Miriam closed her eyes, and then she clenched, shrinking into herself slightly. "If I could, James, I'd have her send the goddamn things back to where they came from. I never thought I would see the day when demons were commonplace, and yet, here I am. As much as we are here to help these people, I find it hard to gather sponsors for these...these...Arcanes. The demand for them is terribly small, and I don't blame anyone. Their magic is horrifyingly disturbing. I have nightmares on a regular basis, James. They simply aren't natural. Exorcisms might be for the best."

"Except the exorcism potentially will kill them. That's why. You're a heartless bitch."

Miriam sneered at me, which made me feel better. But as much as I loved giving Miriam total hell, every ounce of effort and energy I had was going into this conversation, and my body hurt. I wanted to go back to sleep.

Miriam's mouth puckered into a tight ring. She took several steps towards me, threateningly wagging a finger in my direction at the same time. I rolled my eyes. "This entire institution was created to help them, because without our intervention they'd wander out into the general public, hurting themselves and everyone else they came into contact with. Is that what you want? Wanton death and destruction everywhere? Because that's exactly what would happen.

"Running this place requires sponsors, James. I can't get sponsors for Magicals that scare the wits out of everyone they come into contact with!" Miriam shook her head. "Honestly, I've just about had it with you. You were so promising, and you had three years of successful classes before…" She stopped. Obviously, she was addressing the unspeakable. Cody. "You've been moping and pouting for too long. Enough is enough. Cody is gone, and we're all safer because of it. You know those people he murdered were just the beginning. He had no idea how to control his abilities. You did everything you could."

I flinched. The thought of Cody's face as the needle poked into his arm, the room filled with flying objects as his telekinesis raged out of check. The walls in the execution room had actually buckled as he struggled. Thankfully, the injection acted quickly. Miriam had had no idea that Cody and I had started a relationship. She had no idea that when Cody was with me, his mind was still and calm. If I had told Miriam about our tryst, Cody might still have been alive. And it wasn't information I could tell her now.

Miriam wasn't the most understanding when it came to my sexual preferences.

"The doctors tell me you should be fit enough to go back to your room as soon as I sign the release papers, but you're still badly bruised. I want those kids trained up. More importantly, their benefactors need them, and I need their money. We need people who are willing to invest in our cause, James. So do what you have to do, but get those kids into suitable shape. And then as soon as we get them dealt with, we're going to have to deal with your sister."

Everything was about money and her goddamn institution.

"Fuck you, Miriam. I don't believe in your cause. And what do you mean, deal with Shawna? What the hell does that mean? You said you were going to get her off the streets, and instead, you show me sick footage of her stabbing another human being."

"Saving her may no longer be an option."

"Excuse me?"

"We're not entirely sure, but we think she's gotten involved with Sanguimancy."

"I don't believe that." The blood rushed out of my head and hands, immediately making me cold and clammy. Sanguimancy, the dirty fourth class of magic that no one talked about and wasn't recognized. It was underground, and unthinkable.

"But Shawna has abilities. Why would she get involved with *that*?"

"How am I supposed to know? All I can tell you is that reports have come in that she's using blood magic. And she might have turned."

I closed my eyes and hung my head. If Shawna had turned, then there would be no claiming her back.

Sanguimancy was the magic for the Norms. If you had the stomach for it, you could have your own brand of magic, but the price was blood, either yours or someone else's. But eventually it changed the physical body. Eventually, all blood-magic users turned. If the world was uncertain about having a part of its population able to wield magic, it certainly wasn't ready to discover that truly evil magic did exist.

And the result was practitioners that used sacrificial victims to cast spells.

Practitioners of Sanguimancy murdered both animals and humans in order to collect and use their blood, for both spell-casting and to quench the fire that burned within them after the cast was done. And the only thing that satiated that fire was the blood of their victims.

Half used for the spell, half used to staunch the burn.

The world had vampires.

And if Miriam was telling the truth, my sister was now one of them.

Eleven: Prep Time

THE VERY CAPABLE and pretty nurse from the medical ward pushed me back to my quarters in a wheelchair. Walking was too painful, even with the support of a cane. I was quite sure my left side would implode or, at the very least, crumple. I was given orders that walking about was expected and required, but that it was to be in short spurts at first, a little longer each day. By the end of the week, I should be moving about without assistance.

I didn't believe them.

Isaiah had done a number on me—or his demon had. I couldn't blame him. He was acting on instinct and panic. Not a good combination when you have powerful abilities, and after all, it had been at my insistence that Miriam let me release Isaiah.

After a long thirty-minute walk from the med ward to my couch, I sat still and quiet. The nurse had propped me up with throw pillows, the cane was within reach if I needed it, pain meds sat beside me with a glass of water, and the remotes to the entertainment center had been left in front of me. I was certain the doctor had given orders to the CMRD staff to ensure my recovery was easy and swift.

I closed my eyes and tried to settle into the plush velvety couch, while taking in as deep a breath as I possibly could without my ribs loudly complaining. That didn't happen, and I winced as searing pain arced its way across my chest.

Miriam's face appeared in my thoughts, which made me instantly mad. Funny how a spike of pain made me think of her.

But there was a truth to it. I didn't like her, and I no longer had any interest in ensuring her methods or causes were being carried out or not.

Fuck the CMRD.

But at the same time, I just couldn't get up and leave. For two reasons. Contractually, I did owe them. But I only owed them one more class. After this, I was done. Secondly, no matter how much I hated Miriam, those kids in the hangar needed me more.

Poor Ning. Just looking at her, I could tell she was terrified of her Yuki-onna. Camila, from what I had seen, was frenetic and out of control, and Isaiah, well, he needed a lot of help. They all needed help. I was pretty sure the kids had no idea what was at stake: get it together or get the needle.

I had to do this for them. I had to save them.

I still wasn't sure what I was going to do with Annabelle and her horde of demons, or Chris and his anger issues.

My mind reeled as images from my various meetings with the students flashed through my mind. I still had not spent any time with Chris or Annabelle. I had to rectify that, and soon. Of course, my mind kept wandering back to Isaiah. As much as I couldn't think about him in *that way*, it was hard not to acknowledge the attraction. Our last time together in the medical wing stuck with me. His comment, *"I don't want to die"* had hit me hard, and had made old memories resurface. But then I remembered something else he said. *"Whatever you did, finally gave me enough serenity to pull my shit together."*

What I had done was push Empathic emotions into him. I had done it on instinct. Reaction to a stressful situation. Just as he had done when throwing me across the hangar.

And that was it!

Why on earth had I not thought of this until now?

Without the demons in the way, I could easily get them all in a state where we could at least sit around, get to know each other, and maybe, just maybe figure out how to help them.

Empathic powers—push them all into a state of calm.

So, first lesson tomorrow morning, that's exactly what I was going to do. Get them calm and then start the journey in getting them stable.

I was going to save these kids and then get them the hell out of there in spite of Miriam. And then I needed to get out of there and find my damn sister.

Fuck you, Miriam.

Twelve: Guest Speaker

THE NEXT MORNING, I awoke to a knocking on the door to my apartment, the one that led to the hangar. With care not to aggravate my beaten body, I hoisted myself out of bed, wondering who the hell would be waking me at this hour, and from the hangar, no less.

Wrapping a robe around myself, I found the remote that would clear the frosted wall and open the door.

With a push of a button, the far wall became clear and the door let out its usual *psst*.

Tonka floated into my apartment, black mist trailing behind her, along with, I assumed, the lady known as Siren.

"Mr. Martin. I trust you slept well."

"I suppose. It's going to be a while before I get truly restful sleep," I replied, flinching as I shifted to watch her walk into my living room. "What can I do for you?"

"I'm here to collect you. You wanted me to address your Arcane students. This is the time I have, so we should talk to them now."

I glanced at the clock. It was six in the morning. Not really time for an instructional class.

"You realize that they are most likely still asleep?" I asked her, arching an eyebrow.

"Of course, but my time here is short. I've waited long enough to ensure that you could be present for this tête-à-tête. Please humour me in allowing me to have this session at an hour that is convenient for me."

"Fine. Give me a few minutes to put some clothes on and grab a cup of coffee. Would you like one?" I asked, trying to be hospitable.

Tonka and Siren both grimaced.

"Caffeine is not a suggested chemical for Arcanes. Hyperactivity makes our internal residents more aggressive than normal," Siren chirped. Her voice was rather positive and uplifting, unlike Tonka's ominous deadpan speech. "I don't believe we've formally met. My name is Siren."

I nodded at her and stuck my hand out for a handshake. "Nice to meet you. I'm James."

My hand was left hanging in air, unaddressed.

Siren looked at me awkwardly and performed a spasmodic curtsy.

"Forgive me, Mr. Martin. Contact with non-Arcanes has rather undesirable consequences."

I raised my eyebrows in surprise. "Um…yes, well. Very good, then." I needed to change the uncomfortable conversation and quickly. "You don't have an accent that I can pick up on. Are you from the Canadian Prairies or the American Midwest?"

"Omaha, Nebraska, Mr. Martin."

"That makes sense then. Give me a few minutes?"

Tonka waved in my general direction. I couldn't tell if the gesture was a denial or permission. I took it as the later, and unfortunately, a few minutes turned into almost a half an hour. My body wasn't going to go any faster than it had to.

With coffee cup in hand and an outfit that probably would have suited a physical education session more than a classroom, we made our way out into the hangar. I was happy to have found a loose pair of sweats and a hoodie to wear, even if Tonka gave my outfit a look of disapproval. She actually reminded me more of Miriam than I would have liked to tell her. Siren noticed the exchange and smirked.

"There is a classroom on the far side. I will wait there. Bring your three who are hosts," Tonka instructed and then melted into the darkness of the early morning. Siren looked at me, shrugged slightly, and wandered off in the direction of the classroom, the one Miriam had mentioned. I still hadn't seen it myself.

I stopped first at Ning's cube. She was still asleep. I rapped on the plexiglass, which didn't make a whole lot of noise, more of a series of dull thuds. It took a while, but finally, Ning stirred from her bed. The minute she saw me, her eyes lit up and a smile spread across her face.

"Morning, Ning. Can I come in?"

"Of course!" she said, then wrapped herself in her robe as well.

I put my coffee cup down on the floor and then popped into Ning's cube. "Sorry for getting you up so early, but Tonka, the high priestess from the coven that was sent for Annabelle, has asked that I gather the three of you who have demons. She's willing to talk to you all and give insights as to what it means to be Arcane. Would you like to come?" I reached out as I extended the invitation and gently touched her shoulder. In that instant and very gently as to not cause any notice, I implemented my formulated plan. Ning's shoulders drooped ever so slightly as I pushed an early-morning serenity into her body.

Mission accomplished.

"It is early, but I would very much like to hear what she has to say. So, of course." Ning stretched and yawned.

"I have to go gather the others. I'll be back to fetch you." I bounced out of her cell, grabbed my abandoned coffee and made my way down to Annabelle's cube. At this point, I had not had any contact with her, and in fact, had never met her in person. Her cube, as expected, was swirling with the demon fog, obscuring everything from view.

I leaned in close to the glass, hoping I would be able to see something should the mist part, when joltingly, Annabelle's face appeared on the other side of the see-through partition, staring directly back at me. I lurched back at the unexpected appearance. Her eyeballs were the colour of pitch.

She placed her hand in the same position mine was, mirroring my stance.

"Morning, Annabelle," I said, with a shiver running down my spine. "I know it's early, but Tonka, the high priestess from the Bulgarian coven has asked to see you, Ning, and Isaiah. Would you like to come?"

A tear rolled down her cheek. She nodded as a corpse hand wrapped itself around her neck and attempted to pull her back into the vapours. She fought it.

"Do you want me to come in and get you?" I asked.

Annabelle's eyes continued to shed tears, even though the rest of her face remained stoic. This was going to be a difficult teleport. I couldn't see anything.

"Annabelle, can you clear away any of the mist?"

She shook her head.

"Okay, then I'm coming in really close to you."

Once again, I placed my mug on the concrete floor of the hangar and focused on the spot right next to her. I felt the tingle and then the rush forward, but it was such a short hop that it happened in a blink. As soon as I was in the cell, Annabelle grabbed my hoodie, clenched it tight, and wound her hands into it. With the physical contact already in play, it was easy to give her a tender wave of calm.

Her sobbing lulled slightly and the black mist retreated a touch.

"We're going to go back outside the same way. Are you ready?"

She nodded almost imperceptibly, and I grabbed her shoulders and she clutched me. Then I bounced to the other side of the glass.

As soon as we were on the other side, Annabelle inhaled deeply and then slumped in towards my chest.

"Thank you." Annabelle inhaled again.

"Are you okay? What was going on?"

"One of the demons knew you were coming. He doesn't like you and didn't want me to go. He thought I might learn a trick or two to control him. He's one of the more violent beasts."

"I thought Tonka had contained all the demons?" I asked.

"That is contained. You should see what they're like unrestrained."

"Good god." My stomach churned in response. This poor girl. "Do we need to do anything? Or are you going to be okay?"

"Being around other people might help, for a while anyway. If for no other reason than just the distraction."

"Are you sure?" I put my arm around her to give her a hug. She seemed like she needed the comfort, and she accepted it and snuggled in close.

"Thank you. I'm Annabelle, but you already know that."

"You're welcome. I'm James, but you probably already knew that too." I tried to make a funny, anything to lighten the mood.

"I did." She sighed. "It's nice to meet you, James. If you're going to be our teacher, please, teach me how to get rid of them." She begged. Her voice cracked as she said it. The black mist that had been within her cube started to appear around us.

"Well, I think Tonka is going to have a good chat with the three of you."

"Oh! You're bringing Isaiah? I saw what happened the other day, but I haven't seen him since. I wasn't sure if he was okay or not. What about Camila? Is she coming too?"

"No, just the three of you who are Arcane. I asked Tonka to talk to you before she left."

"She's leaving?" Annabelle let go of me and looked shocked. "But I thought she was coming here to help me?" Her face instantly turned into a mess of worry lines and red stress blotches.

"I understand they have other tasks to attend to elsewhere but will return once they are done. Come on. Let's go get Isaiah."

Annabelle nodded, and I grabbed her shoulder, pushing another impulse of serenity. She was a tiny thing, and her white knuckles returned to the edge of my hoodie, continuing their death grip on my pullover. I suspected she was going to need a lot of emotional support.

I picked up my morning coffee—which was now lukewarm—and continued our walk towards Isaiah's cube. As we passed, Camila pressed up against the plexiglass. She waved to Annabelle. Annabelle waved back cautiously. Camila studied me very carefully and gave me a half smile.

"You two get along?" I asked.

Annabelle didn't respond right away, and then finally she nodded. "We've been here the longest. When things are calm in my cube, Camila sends an Astral and visits with me."

"How long have you been here?"

"I don't know, I've lost track. A year?"

Oh good lord, a year in a box.

"Well, it's nice you two had each other to talk to. Let's go get—" I started, but before I could finish, Isaiah was walking towards us.

"Hi, James." He waggled his eyebrows at me and then fell in on the other side, opposite to Annabelle, getting close enough that our shoulders touched.

My chest tightened and my stomach fluttered in response to Isaiah's touch.

"Okay then, off to the classroom?"

"You okay? Or do you need a little...you know, help?"

"Oh, you mean the hippie-feel-good vibe? If you're gonna touch me, then sure." Isaiah arched his brow and smirked.

I leaned in close and whispered, "You're awful."

He whispered back, "I know, but you like it." And with that, he winked and then slipped his hand through the crook of my elbow, careful not to spill my coffee. "Oh man, coffee! I could do with some of that. Okay, mister. Do your thing."

I shook my head.

I let a quick little pulse of feel-good slip between us. He sucked in a deep breath.

"Thanks, handsome." He smiled as we continued our way to the classroom.

Well, at least three of them seem to think I'm okay. And Camila hasn't been overly hostile yet. Hopefully, we can get Chris out of wolf form long enough to actually introduce ourselves.

TONKA WAS HANDING a rather-tattered large tome to Ning as we found the classroom and walked into it. It was old, dusty, and the desks were haphazardly scattered around the large room. At one point, it might have looked like a regular schoolroom, but now it was in such a state of disarray, dingy with boarded-up windows and layers of dust, that it was depressing, and a little creepy. The furniture was decades old.

I'd have to clean this up before trying to use it.

"Finally," Tonka said. "Sit. All of you." Siren hovered in the background, her attention aimed more toward the books that had been left in a piled heap. "I understand you have questions. I will try to answer what I can."

Isaiah raised his hand.

"You do not have to raise your hand. This is not primary school," she said harshly but factually.

Isaiah appeared a bit taken aback but continued with his question. "So, these demons, are they from hell? Where do they come from?"

"As far as we know, they are beings from a different reality than our own. They have the ability to exist within our own sphere, but only through us. They can physically animate for brief periods of time within short distances from their host. They are tethered to us, and we to them."

"So, they're not from hell?"

"What is hell? A Christian term for the underworld? Every culture has something similar. The Sumerians believe it was called Kur, and everyone was destined there, not just those deemed punishable or dastardly. Hinduism has no concept of a Christian-like hell where sinners are tortured, whereas ancient Egypt and Greece both had versions similar to what people refer to as Hell, today.

"Are our entities from there? I cannot say. It is true, a few demons are definitely aggressive and violent, but others are peaceful and passionate. Regardless of their characteristics or personality, they inhabit us and, in return, give us access to their abilities."

"That's sort of a non-answer, don't you think?" Isaiah questioned. "So, we don't know where they originate from?"

"No, nor do I care."

"But they are evil," Annabelle whispered, hanging her head and her ebony hair hiding her face.

"What is evil, child?" Tonka walked over to Annabelle, crouched down to be at her level, and lifted her chin with her delicate hand. Tonka wiped a tear as it fell from Annabelle's eye. "You carry a large responsibility. It is not often we see a human who is capable of containing the beasts you have within you. I know it seems an impossible task, but you will flourish."

"They want to do horrible things. I don't like them. I want them gone." Annabelle's cheeks were wet and her eyes red from crying again. "They terrorize my dreams and show me what they want to do to my body and to other people I love. They're horrible and I can't live any longer like this."

"Oh, my child. Listen to me carefully. You have aggressive entities, but I promise you that within your horde there will also be helpful ones. Even those that seem violent are less so once you understand them. Sometimes, our human brain has difficulty interpreting their needs and desires, and it comes across as disturbing and fierce. They are no more evil than you are."

"They want me dead."

"No, they do not. If you ceased to exist, then the life-forms within you would have nowhere else to be. I promise you. Listen to them and understand them. They will teach you what you need to know in order to live in harmony." Tonka had grabbed Annabelle's tiny hand and was rubbing her thumb over the back of it. It was the first time I had seen anything resembling compassion from Tonka.

"That's a lot of unhelpful advice for her now!" I raised my voice slightly. I wasn't willing to get into a confrontation with Tonka, but my heart ached for the wretched waif.

Tonka glared at me. "I'm not unfamiliar with how overwhelming the demands of a legion are, Mr. Martin. Annabelle has a difficult task ahead of her. Acquiescing to the needs of the demons residing within is a formidable chore. But it is doable. The creatures are not evil." She looked around the classroom. "What is evil?" She was expecting an answer.

"No, no thoughts? What is evil to you?" She pointedly stared at Isaiah.

He stumbled at first but then blurted out, "Being alone, isolated. Abandoning others."

"And do you think my demons would ever abandon me? Or I them? Never. They are part of me and we live together. What about you?" She looked at Ning.

"Death and murder of innocent people." Ning stared at Tonka, almost in a challenge.

"True. Taking a life could be considered evil. What if that life is taken out of self-preservation? Is it evil for one soldier to kill another? No. Unpleasant, yes. What about those who willingly sacrifice themselves? Is that not altruism? It is death, and often violently taken, but it is not evil.

"Evil is a perception. What appears to be wrong from one side is often the truth on the other. They call us Arcanes, but by definition, that word means 'understood by few.' And truly we are shown things others cannot understand or discern. People call us practitioners of the occult. That means we have access to hidden knowledge. People fear what they do not know or understand. Do not let your demons become your fears." Tonka was pointedly addressing Annabelle, but it was a good lesson for all of them. "Understand them. Open yourself up to their hidden knowledge and gain a different perspective, and I promise you, you will not see them as evil.

"They will be your fiercest protector, for without you, they no longer live. They will guide you through your life and show you secrets others will never see. Relish in that knowledge but choose wisely with whom you share it, for not all will understand or have the same insight you will.

"They live within you. You are part of them, and they are part of you. Become one with yourself. Become more than yourself." Tonka smiled at Annabelle who sat enraptured by the witch. I couldn't argue with her points, as cryptic as they might have been.

"I have a little token for you, dear. I hope you accept it and wear it with pride. You will need my help after here. Years of studying and perseverance will be required in order to learn all the secrets of your horde. If you wear it, I will always be able to find you." Tonka pulled out a slinky black metal chain holding a multifaceted peridot gemstone that glowed the same sickly green as the cloud that had brought the coven into the hangar. Sharp spikes radiated out from the center stone.

"But, just me? What about the others?" Annabelle looked at Isaiah and Ning.

"You are all special. In fact, Isaiah and Ning are unique in that I know no other who have abilities as Arcanes and talents in other classes. But because of your uniqueness, I'm not convinced that coven life is where you would fit in best. If you present yourselves to any other of the Arcane circles, you will not be turned away, but I doubt they would house you for long. Annabelle, you are distinctly one of us, and you will need us soon."

"But why can't you take me now?"

"There are things you must do here. Things you must discover first. My imps tell me that your path leads you to us, but not until you grow a little more on your own."

Annabelle sucked in a huge breath and sighed.

"Please forgive me," Tonka said, "but our time here is short, and there are things we must do. Annabelle, the necklace is yours."

Tonka and Siren turned to leave after Annabelle took the necklace and slipped it over her head. The pendant with the lime-green stone sat flush on her chest. I took a sip of my now-cold coffee.

And then Annabelle screamed.

The pendant's sharp spines contracted, digging into her flesh, anchoring the gemstone to her body. Blood wept out from the multiple punctures.

Tonka and Siren didn't turn, never stopped, and as they hit the door to the classroom, they vanished in a billow of demon mist.

I really hate Arcanes.

Thirteen: New Day, Fresh Start

AFTER THE BULGARIAN coven's visit, I made sure the kids got back to their cubes and encouraged them to go back to bed to get a little more rest. The housekeeping staff would be bringing the morning meal soon, and it was a good chance for me to return to my apartment and contemplate my next steps.

I settled onto my couch with a fresh cup of coffee and a smoke to ponder, scheme, and plot how I was going to do what needed to be done.

Gonna make 'em all chill the hell out.

Today was going to be different, and I was convinced what I had in mind was going to work.

When breakfast finally came, escorted in by the same nice housekeeping staffer, she studied me and smiled. But the dishes she placed rattled and clanked together as her hands shook. I watched her, in my best nonchalant manner possible, and allowed my abilities to taste the emotional energy she exuded. Static and fuzzy was what I got back. Poor thing was scared out of her mind. She glanced around the room, I assume searching for a spectral version of Camila. I returned her smile and gave her a friendly wink. She hurried out the door.

After hoisting myself off the couch, I made my way into the bedroom and found clothes to wear, then waltzed out to the kitchen.

I grabbed a piece of toast, stuffed it into my mouth, and polished it off. Once I finished swallowing the dry bread, I wished I could have another cup of coffee, but there was no time.

After buttoning up my light-blue dress shirt, I exited the door and began the long walk out into the student hangar with my cane in tow.

Starting off with the easiest one first, I walked right up to Ning's cell. She was already there, waiting for me and waving with a huge grin plastered across her face.

"Did you get anything from Tonka's talk this morning?" I asked.

"Not really. She was more focused on Annabelle, but then, she needs the most help."

I nodded at Ning's assessment. "Mind if I come in?"

"No, please do."

A *woosh* filled my ears as I teleported. Ning squealed with excitement as I bounced to a stop in the middle of her room. My ribs complained bitterly, but no time for pain today.

"Did they bring you a cell phone yet?"

"Yes, it showed up yesterday. Does it hurt?" she said, pointing to the cane and then to my side.

"A little, but I'll live. Have you set an hourly alarm?"

"I did. Thank you, Mr. James."

"Well, that's at least problem number one, right?" I said with a small measure of relief. One problem out of twenty with these kids. "Now, do you trust me?"

"Of course!" She said it too loudly.

"I understand Tonka and her crew have contained all of the various demons, yours included. So it's time to get together, but to do that, I'm going to use my abilities to ensure you stay calm. Are you okay with that?" Even though I had used them earlier that morning, there hadn't been time for permission or explanation. Now was the time for that.

"How will you make us stay calm?"

"I can make you feel anything I want. But if I touch you, make skin-on-skin contact, the emotional connection lingers, and we become connected."

"Oh! That would be very handy!"

"It doesn't always work. But I think it will between you and me because you're willing. Ready? It'll feel warm, like sunshine through an open window in summer."

"That sounds delightful! I haven't seen the sun in a long time."

I held my hand out, and she took it gladly. As she grasped my hand, I held hers tight while thinking of that warm ray of sunshine. Bright, cheery, relaxing, and most importantly, calm.

I could feel serenity wrap itself around my heart, then slowly bleed out through my chest, up and into my shoulder. Heat radiated down my arm, and then a tingle occurred where Ning's hand met mine. My energy, imbued for tranquillity and peacefulness, forced its way into Ning, and I smiled as her face registered the blossoming emotion within her.

The little stress lines of worry that had crinkled the corners of her eyes melted away as her mouth stretched into a large grin, complete with teeth. Her eyes opened, but the lids were heavy, as if she could have slept.

"Oh, Mr. James, that is the most amazing feeling—I..." Ning lost herself in her emotional state, clasped both her hands over her heart, and sighed. "I can't feel *her*." A tear formed in the corner of her eye and then rolled out, running over her plump cheek. I knew she meant her Yuki-onna.

"That's sort of the point." I gave her a wink and smirked a little. "Shall we get the others?"

"You mean, I get to finally meet Chris and Camila?"

"Ning, how long have you been here?"

"I wasn't entirely sure until the cell phone came back yesterday. I lost track, but if the date is right, then it's been four months and eighteen days." Ning's gaze was cast downward.

"And you haven't been out of your cell in that entire time?"

"A couple of times for testing!" She smiled.

You deserve what you put these kids through, Miriam.

"Well, Ning, today is going to be a little different. Shall we go see Annabelle?"

"With her demons?" Ning's eyes widened.

"Well, they *should* be contained for now. Come on. Let's go see."

"Okay," Ning said tentatively.

I held on to Ning's hand again and teleported the two of us out of her cell. I could do that, bring one other person with me, but that was all. Only one person at a time.

As we rematerialized outside of her glass cage, Ning sucked in the air.

"That was so cool!" She jumped up and down a few times. I turned to go see the others when Ning's excitement turned to reluctance. She grabbed the back of my shirt and tagged along behind me.

I took note as we passed by Chris and Camila's rooms. Chris was passed out on the floor of his room. Most likely he had dropped from exhaustion again. Camila was sitting cross-legged on the ceiling, reading a book, her long brown hair hanging down. She glanced at me as we passed. Shivers slithered down my spine.

Annabelle stood in the middle of her room, enveloped by the swirling black mist of the Arcane's demon world.

"Hi, Annabelle," I started to say.

"They told me you were coming back." Her voice was childlike and little more than a whisper.

"This is not my version of contained," I said.

"They still whisper to me." She scrunched up her eyebrows like it was painful for her to say.

"Anna, can I come in?"

"Annabelle, please call me Annabelle. And yes, of course."

Tingling started in my feet began and rushed up the spine, and then I was standing next to her. She was so small, a waif of a child, and fear was a constant on her face. In fact, I think being afraid was her demeanour.

A tentacle unfurled from the smoke behind her back and wrapped itself gingerly around her waist. Annabelle's eyes closed and she shivered. She moved her hands and arms out of the reach of the appendage—one of her demon's demonstrable actions.

"It says you should be wary of the spaces in between," she whispered.

"What?"

"When you jump from place to place," she said, her eyes darkening as she spoke, "there's the briefest of moments when you are in between. Be careful of what awaits you."

"Well, I've been doing it for many years and haven't run into any problems yet, so let's just hope that continues." That thought would permeate my dreams later, I was sure of it.

Annabelle stared at me, unmoving, the scaly appendage still wrapped around her waist. It glistened in the dim light of her mist-shrouded room. The smell was slightly sulfuric, but there was also a hint of saltwater, as if I were standing by the ocean.

"Where do you want to take me? They are asking. They want to know." Her voice squeaked.

"I'm just going to bring all the students together. I think it's time we all met and got to know one another. They are welcome to join if they'd like."

"Well, there's no choice there. They go wherever I do." She breathed heavily. "All right then. Let's go."

"Before we do, I'd like to do something that might help with making you and your demons a little more comfortable."

"Yes, they have shown me what you did with Isaiah and Ning. Please." Annabelle looked at me, her gaze and voice pleading as she whispered, "Get them away from me."

Not wanting to spend any more time caged in a small box with Annabelle, I pushed thoughts of serenity and harmony while gripping her shoulder. As soon as the emotion washed over her, Annabelle's eyes blinked a few times. Her eyes morphed from the colour of a moonless night to clear blue. The combination of the aqua colour with her pale skin and jet hair was stunning.

Annabelle sighed as a look of peace rested into her face.

"I can't...They aren't there! Thank you," she said, but she looked like she was going to cry.

Within seconds, Annabelle joined Ning on the outside. The two greeted each other as I stood in front of Isaiah's cube. Except he was already on the outside, beaming at me.

"Hi again," he said with a wink, which made all those warm fuzzies rise on the inside of my rib cage, making me feel all stupid.

"How do you get out? How do you do that? If you keep that up, you'll have Miriam on top of all of us."

"Nah, she won't come anywhere near me. Or Annabelle. She's terrified of the two of us. The others she has no use for." Isaiah shrugged and smirked. "Which doesn't bode well for any of us."

"No, it doesn't. All the more reason to behave. We don't want any uninvited guests popping in, now do we?"

"Speaking of unwanted visits..."

"What do you mean?"

Isaiah nodded his chin past my shoulder, and as I turned, Annabelle and Ning were hastily making their way towards us. Behind them came Miriam. *Click, click, click*, the spikes of her shoes tapped out on the floor like the hammering of nails into a coffin.

"James, what the hell is going on?" Miriam smiled in her best trying-hard-to-be-polite-in-front-of–the-students look.

It wasn't working. The three who I'd liberated stood behind me. Like I could protect them from the Grim Reaper.

"We're going to have class," I said while making air quotes, "and to do that, they have to actually sit in the classroom. We're going to talk, get to know each other, even learn some shit."

"You're still not healed up enough for this."

"Probably not, but you know what they say. No time like the present."

"You know what else they say," Miriam retorted. "Stupidity kills."

I grabbed Miriam by the elbow, which garnered me a vicious glare, and gently tugged her away from the little cluster of anxious students.

"Enough. Seriously. Ning tells me she's been here for four months, and Annabelle and Camila have been here at least a year. And not once have they been outside or even socialized with other people. What the hell's the matter with you?"

"Again, James, these are dangerous people. I have to protect my staff as much as I have to protect them from themselves."

"Well, not today. Do not try to stop this. Do you understand me? I am doing this, and if you don't like it, I walk out."

"You have a contract."

"What are you going to do? Sue me? Go for it. You can't get blood from a stone."

"Your sister, remember her?"

"Yes, well, you've already made it clear that this institute is no longer interested in rehabilitation. And we both know, if she is using Blood Magic, there's a good chance nothing you or I will do is going to help." I felt like the worst brother ever and a total traitor for giving up on my sister. At least that's what I wanted Miriam the Devil to think.

She'd had the upper hand for too long.

If Miriam was one of us, she might have sensed the flush that ran just under my skin. An excited rush of energy that was keeping a small glimmer of hope alive. Hope that Shawna wasn't as knee deep in sheep shit as I thought she might be. I had every intention of finding out for myself.

But first, I had kids who desperately needed help. "You want these kids made better? Then back off, Miriam."

She wrenched her arm free of my grasp and, while poking her clawed finger into my chest, said, "I'm watching everything you do."

"Fine." I cocked an eyebrow at her as I said it. She turned on her heel and disappeared into the darkness of the hangar.

As soon as she was out of sight, Ning put her hand over her mouth and giggled. Isaiah was giving me a look of total approval.

"All right. Let's get the others."

Here we go. God help me, here we go.

Fourteen: Health Class-Stop, Drop, and Roll

IF I WAS going to bring all of them together, that meant I had to confront Chris. He was the most dangerous out of all the students, not because of his ability but his unpredictability, and that scared the hell out of me. Even more so than Annabelle and her creepy demons. With Chris, I risked the chance of getting burned alive or eaten. Third-degree burns to most of my body or a chunk of me missing by a shapeshifter weren't experiences that ranked high on my list of things to do. That kind of risk wasn't exactly covered under hazard pay by the CMRD. But the last time I had walked past Chris's cell, he was passed out. I was hoping I would be lucky and he'd be in the same state.

"Ning, would you come with me? I might need you," I asked.

"Um...yes?" she asked hesitantly. "What for?"

"Getting everyone together in a classroom means I have to get Chris. I need a few minutes and the chance to push emotions into him before he goes all fire wolf on me. If I don't get that opportunity, I'm going to need you to subdue any fires, or the wolf on fire, or me on fire. Whichever happens your ice can do that." I hoped.

"I'll try, but I might freeze you both solid." Ning's eyes grew wide.

"Then don't do that."

"Ah, okay." Ning didn't look too sure about this plan and neither was I, but Ning was the best backup I could come up with.

"I know you can do this, Ning." I smiled at her. She half smiled. I could tell she wasn't as sure about her abilities. "Come on. Let's go get Chris."

Don't show fear, don't show fear, don't show fear.

If I kept saying it, maybe I'd start to believe it too.

We walked down the row until we got to Chris's cell. Just as my luck would have it, he wasn't passed out anymore. He was pacing—still human, mind you—but pacing. I've never known anyone who was calm and feeling stable who paced.

This wasn't good.

Well, shit. I inhaled a lungful of air, mindful of my healing body. *Here we go.*

Tight knots clenched in my stomach as I began my first contact with the fire wolf. I rapped on the outside cube wall, producing the same dull thuds that had woken Ning up, and Chris's head swivelled over to glare at me with fiery eyes.

"Oh man, this is not good," I huffed out.

"Mr. James, are you sure about this? He doesn't look happy," Ning asked from behind me.

I turned my head in her direction. "It's gotta be done." I glanced back at Chris, and his upper lip was curled as if he was snarling at me. "Shit. Okay."

"I'm here too." Isaiah appeared beside Ning. "I've got you if anything goes wrong."

"You guys are awesome. If this goes sideways, can you bring Ning in to ice the place down?"

Isaiah winked and nodded.

"Okay, here goes everything." I sucked in another deep breath, but my bruised and broken body was not having any of that. I winced in pain.

"Chris, I'm coming in. I just want to talk, okay?"

Chris had stopped his pacing and stood still, slightly crouched with his fists clenched. He made no acknowledgement that I had addressed him. He simply glared at me.

Sweat broke out along my back and the hair at the base of my neck rose.

That tingly feeling started, and I was focused on getting as close to Chris as possible. Surprise attack as it were. As long as he had no idea what was coming, this feebly hatched plan of mine just might actually work. 'Port in quick and close. Grab him, push emotions fast, and hope for the best.

Pins and needles tingled their way up the backs of my thighs...across the back...and *woosh.*

There I was, standing right next to Chris. The glare was gone and his face registered shock and surprise. I was almost standing on top of him. I grabbed him, already summoning the serenity from within and channelling it towards my intended target.

The heat wafting off Chris was almost too much to bear, but the minute my hand touched him, I knew I wasn't going to get out of this unscathed. With my palm planted on his neck just under his ear, I forced the empathic commands as fast as possible. Flames erupted from the surface of his skin and in between my fingers, and I could feel my hand growing hotter and hotter. Little embers were stoked under his dark skin as they flickered. I could hear the snap and pop, just like a campfire.

I kept imposing tranquillity and peacefulness into him, and the heat from our connection point kept getting stronger, as if I'd placed my hand on a radiator that had been running nonstop, or on a stove element that had been turned on and was slowly heating up, turning red.

I was about to pull away, the heat too much and the pain from my skin burning when the fire in his eyes died, snuffed out like a candle. He shoulders rounded slightly, losing the tension in them. The orange veins of fire, pulsing in time with his heartbeat, slowed. Perhaps I had won this battle of wills.

"Chris, are you okay?" I asked. He looked woozy. His knees gave out slightly and he stumbled.

"What did you do to me?" he asked, surprised and...what was that? Relief? Was I sensing a wave of exasperation and liberation from him?

"I'm sorry, Chris. I don't like to force emotions onto people unless they're willing, and they don't always work if the person is fighting my 'push,' but every time I've seen you, you're either pacing as a wolf or passed out from exhaustion. My name is James Martin. I've been assigned to the five of you, and I'm going to try to help you out with your abilities."

"Um, sure, nice to meet you? Look, I...I have to get out of here." His gaze suddenly darting back and forth, looking for an escape.

"That's why I'm here. I want to bring you out of this cell and let you meet the others."

"The others in prison next to me? No, I need to get out of here, this jail. I don't even know why I'm here."

"What?" Now it was my turn to be confused. "Why do you think you're in prison?"

"My brother and I took the day to go out into the rural areas. Next thing I knew, there were a whole bunch of dudes in uniforms coming at us. They shot at us. I watched Corey go down, and then I flipped to the wolf. I do that when I get angry. Next thing I remember, I'm waking up here."

"I'm confused, you mean you were captured and brought here?"

"I guess. I have no idea where *here* is! And I need to find out if my brother is alive or dead."

This was not the information I had been told about Chris and not the information that was in his file. The report had said that his brother had died in a gang-related shooting, and Chris, who had been lost in anger and guilt from the murder, wasn't able to remain in his family's home as fires kept erupting and the wolf would take over.

Did Miriam lie to me?

"Okay, so, you're at a facility called the CMRD," I said, my eyebrows furrowed, trying to placate Chris, give him information, and figure out what the hell had actually happened. "It's short for the Centre of Magical Research and Development. I was told you were brought here to help get your abilities under control. And that's why I was brought in. To help you and four others. Are you telling me you were brought here against your will?"

"I have no fucking idea what this place is or why I am being held here!"

Oh, Miriam, you're gonna get it with both barrels from me.

"I have to get home and find my brother," Chris said.

He looked at me, unsure of what was going on.

"Why do you look like you know something and you're not telling me?" Chris asked.

"Because what I was told about you and what you've just told me doesn't mesh or add up."

"Why was I brought here?"

"Most people who are here can't control their abilities."

"Ha. I can control them just fine. Just don't piss me off."

"What?" Every time Chris spoke, the situation was getting more confusing. "You can control your fire and your shapeshifting?"

"Well, yeah." He looked at me like I had rocks in my head. "If I get angry, then the wolf takes over and I pace till I drop. When that happened back home, I would go for a run, in either form. It would help me chill out. I know I have a short fuse. I got that from my father. What the fuck is going on?"

"I don't honestly know." I needed to talk to Miriam. This didn't make any sense. The reports and briefs in Chris's dossier did not match his story. Miriam had to know that I would find out what had happened the minute I talked to Chris, so why would she lie and fake reports? "How long have you been in here?"

"I have no fucking clue. But I'd guess about a month."

"Okay, I'm gonna get to the bottom of this and find out what the hell is going on. Until then, can you keep your shit together long enough to not be a danger to me or any of the others?"

"Get out of this box? Hell yes."

"Cool. Sorry about forcing emotions on you. I don't like to do that, but..." I let out short bark of a laugh. "You scared the shit out of me, man."

Chris studied me for a minute. Then lunged at me, hands stretched out, and fire erupting in little bursts from his fingertips.

"Jesus!" I jumped back, my heart thudding hard against my rib cage.

Chris laughed at me. "You're too easy."

"Holy fuck, man, don't do that!"

"I promise I'll behave, just get me out of here."

"Seriously, man, don't ever fucking do that again." My heart was still beating. Wish I could have pushed calmness and serenity into myself.

I bounced the two of us out of Chris's cell and stood with Ning and Isaiah.

Ning grabbed my hands, which were red and angry.

"You're burned. Look, they are starting to blister." Ning gave a side glance to Chris that was not friendly.

"Honestly, I'm fine. They'll be fine," I said. But they did sting. Now that I was out of harm's way and the endorphins were settling down, my hand was starting to hurt.

Ning glared at me with a face that said "I don't believe a word you're saying," then pulled both my hands close to her mouth.

She inhaled deeply and gently blew on my splayed-out hands.

Ice fog emanated from her mouth, rushing over my scorched skin, which had the most amazing soothing effect.

She took another breath and blew again. Then inspected my hands carefully.

"There. That should do it. But you're still gonna have blisters."

I pulled my hands back from her and inspected them.

"Wow, nice work!" I was impressed. Who said these kids didn't have control over their abilities? Oh right, Miriam did.

"Sorry about that, man," Chris said while looking at least a little sheepish.

"Well, let's just not have any repeat performances. Okay? Shall we go?"

"What about Camila?" Isaiah asked.

"I'll go get her. The rest of you can make your way to the classroom?" I asked.

They nodded in unison.

As I watched them walk away, they made their awkward introductions. Strangers thrown together in a bizarre situation. I couldn't help but notice the four of them didn't touch. They kept their distance from each other as they headed towards the classroom. We had work to do, but if Chris already had control of his abilities, then why was he here?

What the fuck are you up to, Miriam?

Fifteen: Magical Theory

"OKAY, SO WHO can tell me what the three generally accepted classes of magic are?" Collecting Camila turned out to be a simple task with no drama. She had been eager to leave her cell, and had given me no issues as we walked towards the others.

Chalk that up to pure luck.

The classroom, littered with desks and chairs, had three walls. It sort of stuck out from the hangar like a pimple. One side was wide open to the giant arena where the kids were housed, but the opposite side had several huge windows. Each one had been covered up with plywood. Chris and I spent fifteen minutes straining and groaning in an effort to pry the wooden panel off. Isaiah became impatient, shooed us out of his way, and with a flick of his hand, the covers flew off. The girls ducked as the sheets of wood flew over their heads, landing with a clatter in the darkness of the hangar. Sunlight spilled into the room, recharging everyone, despite the fact the windows were disgustingly dirty.

All five of them stood in front of the glass, peering into the inner courtyard of the CMRD, and although it was sunny, the ground was covered with a thick blanket of snow. Frost lined the outer rims of the glass panes. It had been late autumn the day I left my apartment to come back to the CMRD. I'd never guessed that several weeks later, I would still be here. Nor did I ever imagine that I would have gone so long without a window to look outside.

I had had personal contact with each of the kids that morning as I pushed a state of calm into their bodies. The emotional connection I fostered with them left me feeling a little drained. My experience in the past with empathic connections extended to singular contacts only. I had never attempted to maintain an empathic linking with five people at once.

"Anyone? Do any of you have an answer? I know the outside is interesting, but..."

Ning turned to look at me, then raised her hand to answer the question.

I glanced at her and nodded.

"Elemental, Psyche and Arcane. But Mr. James, you left one out."

"Yeah, on purpose," I grumbled.

Chris, still tired and worn from pacing as a wolf for hours on end, furrowed his eyebrows and turned to Ning, "What do you mean?"

"It's not polite to talk about it," Ning said as she took a seat in one of the empty desks.

Chris leaned against the windowsill, then scrunched his face up, "Who cares about polite. What's the fourth?"

"The hidden class is called Sanguimancy," I said. "We don't talk about it because no one wants to deal with it. It's an unthinkable means of garnering magical abilities."

"I still don't get it." Chris looked confused.

Camila rolled her eyes as she walked away from the windows and plopped herself into a chair. She hiked her boots up on another desk and crossed her ankles while lounging.

Annabelle spoke up. "It's also called blood magic, and it requires victims in order to cast spells—well, the bigger ones anyway." But as she said it, she dropped her head and studied her feet, as if she was expecting to be berated for answering.

"Are you shitting me? So, like human sacrifices?" Chris said, eyes wide.

"Nope. No shitting. Totally true. It's the magic sought by those obsessed with it, but who generally have no abilities of their own," I added. "How about we go back to the other three."

"Gladly. That's sick." Chris's face wrinkled in disgust, he sauntered over and took an empty chair.

"Ha!" Camila burst out in a short derisive laugh. "You'd think a big bad fire wolf would be able to handle a little blood and guts."

"How do you figure?" Chris whipped his head around and glared at Camila.

"You're a shapeshifting werewolf," she said while inspecting her cuticles, picking something out from under a nail. "Like, since when are werewolves prissy about a little blood? They're killing machines."

"I've never killed anyone," Chris said loudly and slammed his fist on the desktop. Flames erupted out from his clenched hand, scorching the laminated desk surface. A small fire danced its way across the surface, tiny flames at first, but they were getting larger by the second.

"Ning? Can you frost that out for me?"

She smiled, stood up, stepped over to the desk, and put one finger on the surface near the flames.

A soft crackling noise spread across the classroom as crystals formed a thin sheet of ice on the desk surface, snuffing out the fire.

But to ensure nothing else went wrong, I took a few steps over to Chris and gently placed my hand on his shoulder, pushing a renewed wave of relaxation into his body. His tense shoulders slumped forward, instantly melting, the spark of anger snuffed out.

My head spun a little. This continued effort was taking its toll.

Chris shivered. "Ooh, wow. Thanks, man. That was gonna go nuclear."

I nodded and gave him a little wink. If that's all it took to keep these five under control, then I would push emotions into them all day.

I turned to see Camila rolling her eyes again, to which I said, "Camila, it's not a good idea to tease a werewolf with anger issues." I smiled at her as I spoke gently. Last thing I wanted to do was prod her into more rebellion.

Walking back to the front of the class, I took a seat on the corner of the teacher's desk and continued. "Where were we?"

"Classes of magic," Isaiah volunteered.

"Right! You're correct, Ning. Elementals, Psyches, and Arcanes are the three generally accepted classes of current-day magic. Can anyone give me examples of the talents found in each class?"

Isaiah glanced up at me, from the desk he had commandeered in the front row—as close to me as possible, with his wanting stare—and smiled while wiggling his eyebrows. "Elementals control Earth, Air, Fire, and Water."

Oh man, that smile. And those eyes.

Such a flirt.

"But there's more," Ning said quietly.

"How can there be more?" Isaiah quipped, then spun and cast Ning an unbelieving frown.

"Metal, Stone, Ice, Smoke, Lightning. Just to name a few," she said and then smiled and raised an eyebrow. Her cockiness was refreshing and humorous, but after all, she did have control over Air and Ice, so she commanded one of the more unusual elements.

"Oh. I guess. Yeah. I never thought of those as elements," Isaiah said.

"Experts have conjectured that the more unusual elements are either blending of the basic four, or a more focused ability within an element. For instance, Lightning could be said to be Air and Fire, whereas Metal or Stone manipulation would be a focusing within the Earth Elemental," I explained.

Isaiah pursed his lips. He looked like he was contemplating an idea, but then stood up and raised his hands out in front of him. He closed his eyes and exhaled deeply.

Thick billows of charcoal smoke emanated from the palms of his hands and cascaded like a slow-motion waterfall to the floor. Swirls and waves of the black smoulder wound its way around his feet, obscuring everything from his knees down.

"That would be useful if you needed a smokescreen," Annabelle said, her eyes going wide. "I wish I could hide from my demons. I would like to do that."

"Huh, useless," Camila retorted. "I can see right through the smoke. It hides nothing."

"Well, true, it would be for you, Camila," I said. "But then, there are very few with an Elanchu ability. Another rare talent. You guys are quite the unusual bunch." I raised both my eyebrows and nodded my head to them all.

"What the hell is that? An Elean...what?" Chris looked confused. "Why hasn't anyone taught us this shit before? Like, why do I feel so dumb about all of this?"

"An Elanchu is a person who can see through illusions and magic spells. They are able to identify when people are telling lies or hiding truths. They are soothsayers, and Camila can do that." I gestured towards her.

Everyone looked at her with looks of shock.

"It's truly unusual, and many people would like to be able to have access to that talent. Imagine if you were in law enforcement or intelligence agencies. That ability would be very useful." I said.

Camila smiled and leaned back in her seat, looking as if she was the queen of them all.

"But that's a great example of the second class of magic, Psyches. Isaiah, what else can a Psyche do?"

"Telekinesis," he said, then smiled and held out his hand. A book from the other side of the room wiggled and then flung itself into his waiting grip.

"Astral Projection," Camila said, not wanting to be dethroned or outdone. Suddenly, there were several ghosts like Camila standing within the classroom.

"Teleportation too." I let myself pop over to the other side of the room.

Chris and Annabelle looked on in wonder. Ning just smiled and giggled.

An alarm sounded. It was Ning's phone going off.

"Ha—your hourly alarm! Well, you've already put out the fire, but, Ning, would you care to show off a little? How about some fun Ice Elemental stuff?"

"I can try," she said.

Ning closed her eyes and held her hands, cupped in front of her.

The air in the room suddenly became chilly. My breath fogged.

In Ning's hand, crystals formed and grew. Little branches of icicles at first, and then within seconds, it lengthened like a tree branch.

Except that wasn't right either, it was tinier, more delicate. Like a stem, and at the tip, delicate petals of a flower formed, and then the thin layers of ice peeled away as the crystal rose bloomed.

Ning took the sculpture, walked over to Camila, and handed it to her, although her gaze was focused more on the floor than its recipient.

Camila took it cautiously and then examined it.

"Wow, not bad." Camila said with a complimentary tone. First time I hadn't heard her be snarky or judgmental.

"So, Ning's dominion over Ice may very well be an aptitude of wind with water?" Annabelle asked.

"That's one theory, yes," I said.

Ning smiled and then returned to her chair and sat down.

"But what about the last class? The Arcanes?" I raised an eyebrow, my glance darting between Annabelle, Isaiah, and Ning. Three of them had their own demons. Any one of them should be able to answer.

Camila's projections, which had hung around the class, slowly disappeared.

"Depends on the relationship with the entity," Annabelle said. "Some say we don't have any magic of our own. We just channel and wield the powers of our parasites."

That made me stop. I'd never heard an Arcane describe their demon in such a way.

"Why would you call them parasites?"

"Because that's what I feel like they are. They suck the life out of me. They've destroyed everything I've ever cherished. They possess my body without permission and live off everything I do and experience. And they whisper things to me, and most of the time they are not nice." Annabelle's lip quivered as she spoke.

"Do you think it would be different if you had the knowledge to control them?"

"I'm not sure I'll ever have that. There are so many of them. And most are unkind." Her eyes welled up with tears. She was clearly in distress.

My heart tugged and ached. I walked over and placed my hand on her shoulder, gently pushing more calming and soothing emotions into her. As the emotions settled into her body, her sobs stilled.

The entire classroom swayed. I needed to sit down or lean up against something.

"Let's see if we can't get you three a little more skilled on these things. Tonka said she left books. Come on, everyone. Let's see what we've got." I gathered everyone around the pile of material clearly left by Tonka's crew. The books were various thicknesses and states of age, but all of them had the sigils and symbols of the Arcane etched into their front covers. I sat on the back of a chair that was closest to the book-covered table.

As Annabelle reached out for one of the books, an ominous growl ripped through the room and the black mist that had only emanated from her in gentle wisps suddenly exploded out from her in all directions.

Annabelle convulsed into a fit of sobs. The rest of the class immediately surrounded her and offered support, looking after her.

It was the first time they had all been together, but I was shocked that they cared and reacted to each other in a kind way.

We might actually get through this.

Another growl rumbled through the room, and I was pretty sure an underworld beastie slithered by my feet.

I hate demons.

Sixteen: Study Session-Annabelle

"LET'S TRY TO ignore the little monsters, shall we?"

Ning had her arm wrapped around Annabelle. Annabelle was hugging herself, and hyperventilating.

Chris leaned in close to her and said, "Get angry with them. Feel strong! We're all here. I'll set the wolf free and protect you." A flicker of flame sparked in Chris's eyes and veins of red ire flashed underneath his dark skin.

Annabelle's eyes grew wide at the display of personal pyrotechnics, and then a hesitant smile pulled up on the corners of her mouth.

She extended a hand, a gesture of thanks to the man of fire. "I'm afraid my demons are mine and mine alone to suffer."

I know she didn't mean to do it, but Annabelle was sucking the sunshine right out of the room. I had to deflect this and, hopefully, bolster Annabelle a little. "Shall we take a look at what Tonka left? Maybe there's something here that is going to help. Come on, step up. Let's have a look."

Isaiah grabbed Annabelle's free hand and Ning continued to hug her close.

As they stepped forward, the pile of esoteric books jostled and moved on their own. Piles rearranged themselves, and within seconds, each student had a mound of texts in front of them. A large tome skittered across the table and came to rest in front of me. The cover flipped open and, on the first page, writing began to appear. As it did, I read aloud the note.

"The volumes will sort themselves depending on their demons. There are journals each of them are to start. Once they learn a spell, invocation, or canticle, they are to inscribe it in their own handwriting into their *Book of Ways*. It will be their account on how to control and use their demons."

Ning, Isaiah, and Annabelle looked at each other. I could see they were uncomfortable with this.

"Look, I know this is all new, but I don't think you guys have any other choice. Remember Tonka is going to test you when she returns, and we have no idea when that is. You need to start. Come on. Pick up your books." I tried to encourage them. None of their faces looked as if they were convinced.

Finally, Annabelle, with decided determination, grabbed her pile, and headed to one of the corners. She put her homework on the desk, sighed deeply, then sat down and flipped open the first book.

Isaiah and Ning, seeing that nothing erupted or materialized out of the ancient-looking volumes, grabbed their respective stacks and settled in.

I turned to Camila and Chris. To be honest, I had no idea where to start. So I asked, "All right, you two, what are we going to do with you?"

"Oh, I know what I wanna do," Camila said. "So, wolf boy, you game for a little magic action?"

"What do you mean?" Chris and I said at the same time.

"A little magic, one-on-one, just you and me. See if you can block my projections."

"That's actually not a bad idea," I said.

Chris's abilities were obviously sparked by rage. If he learned how to use the Fire Elemental, and the wolf shapeshifting with more precision and practice, he might not lose his emotional control as easily. Practice makes perfect, after all.

"Just one thing, though, Camila. Don't tease. All right?" I added.

"Yeah, yeah, I'll be good. Come on. Let's go. This will be fun."

Chris nodded slowly, but I could tell from the look on his face he wasn't entirely convinced. I would be watching the two of them out the corner of my eye. But for now, I wanted to go check back in with Annabelle. She had ended up with an alarming tower of tomes to deal with, and her actions today had me concerned.

Turning towards my little group of Arcanes, I found them all engrossed in their studies. Ning was reading and Isaiah was practicing drawing sigils.

Good. I think I would call this getting somewhere with five impossible situations. See, Miriam, I can do this—and nothing has exploded, imploded, or died. So there.

In my mind, I was imagining sticking out my tongue at her as she frowned, the deep wrinkles became exaggerated with the facial expression—made by age and, at one point, I would have guessed, from smoking.

Annabelle was sitting in the corner of the classroom, unmoving, staring at the books in front of her. The black arcane mist drifted off the back of her head and dissipated a short ways from her.

I walked over and sat in the chair next to her.

"Daunting, isn't it," I said.

"Terrifying is more like it," she said softly.

"But if understanding them is the way to get control, why wouldn't you dive in, Annabelle?"

"Because I just want them gone. I don't know if I want or care to have control. I'm not you or Isaiah or Ning. I miss my family, and none of them want me anywhere near them with these things. I haven't seen my mom in two years. I miss her so much." A tear rolled down her cheek. She sniffed and wiped the watery streak with the back of her hand, the lace from her cuff catching the tear and clearing it away.

I took her pale, cold hand in mine.

"We are here for you. I can't force you to learn anything. But I will support you and give you the opportunity to gain control over the talents you have."

"I know, but—" Annabelle's hand stiffened and gripped me with ferocious strength. Her eyes clouded over and became milky.

"I see you..." she whispered in her mousey voice. It was eerie and sent a shiver down my spine.

Another hand emerged from her sleeve, one that was six fingered with black claws and emaciated flesh. Veins stuck out on the back of the hand, and the skin was patchy and red—it looked sickly. The demon appendage grabbed my wrist and held me tight.

"He wants you. He needs you," she rasped.

"Who does?" The hair on the back of my neck rose.

"The one who is everything. His demon wants you, and he will have you. Or he will ensure the human becomes his puppet. And then the beast will come for you." With her other arm, Annabelle was pointing directly at Isaiah. All the other students had stopped what they were doing and focused their rapt attention on Annabelle.

"Well, we'll have to see about that," I said defiantly.

Annabelle's head jerked awkwardly to one side, her blank white orbs peering over my shoulder.

"I see you," she said with the creepy expression again, looking off behind me. Her head swivelled back to rest her gaze to me. "I see him too. The white one. He is here."

I knew exactly who she was talking about. My stomach churned with nerves. It was my subconscious ghost of Cody.

"How can you see a memory?"

She laughed deeply and not in her own voice. It was one of her demons.

"He is no memory. Fool. You are haunted. He is always with you." The voice speaking was layered, Annabelle's soft girlish tones were there, but there was another discordant voice speaking through her at the same time. The air around us suddenly turned dank and rotten.

But her words hit home. The Cody I had seen was nothing more than a death that I had felt solely responsible for. "No, you're wrong. It's nothing more than my subconscious. A memory." I was raising my voice.

Her laughter continued, egging me on.

"You call that a memory? Memories don't have presence." As she said the last words, I went deathly cold, and I could feel Cody's hand grip my shoulder, his flaking chapped lips brush up against my earlobe.

"She sees me, why don't you believe that I'm here?" he whispered.

"Go away. You can't be here."

Cody laughed.

"Oh, but I am here, and I have always been here, watching you all the time. And I'm watching you with him. You cheap slut. Him! You can't have him. I won't let you. You are mine. Don't you remember? You said you'd protect me, you said you show me how to save myself. You broke your promise! You killed me just as you'll kill him."

Cody was angry as all hell, and his grasp on my neck clamped so tight the muscle spasmed.

"This isn't real!"

Annabelle hissed at me. "Oh, this is real, and he wants to tell everyone."

Camila stepped forward. "Shitballs, what the fuck, Teach?"

"You mean it's not an illusion?" Chris asked, his gaze darting between Camila and Cody.

Camila shook her head.

"It's absolutely fucking real!" she said.

Annabelle stood up and released me, then lifted her arms up towards the ceiling. The Arcane mist wafted off of her in giant waves until the floor was writhing and undulating like a sea of snakes.

All of my students were standing in a semicircle around me, knee deep in the Arcane fog.

Next to me, standing in the middle, was my Cody. Pale, rotting, cold, and dead.

"Holy shit," Isaiah said.

His voice shook me out of my disbelief. I whipped my head around to discover all the kids' stares were on Cody.

"You see him?" I asked, terrified of the response I knew deep down I was going to get.

"As clear as day," Isaiah said. His eyes were wide.

"Tell them who I am," Cody rasped.

"Can you all see and hear this?" I asked, my voice trembling.

The kids nodded in unison, eyes wide.

Cody sucked in a breath, his audible inhalation wet and sticky with fetid fluid. His smile was toothy, displaying what was left of his rotting mouth. And the expression wasn't anything borne out of happiness. It was pure evil.

"Tell them, James. Tell them or I will tell them myself."

"Cody, don't. That's not fair."

"Not fair? Not fair?" Cody screeched. "Fuck what's fair. My life ended. That wasn't fair."

"What is he talking about?" Isaiah asked. There were not-so-subtle tones of panic running through his words. I could feel the dread rising in all of them, my connection being tested, and their calmness evaporating.

"He hasn't told you?" Cody snapped back, then looked at me. "Oh, you vile bitch."

I knew right then, Cody was going to get revenge. The evil sneer that formed made me feel nauseous.

"Well, then. Let me ask you? Why do you think it's so important that you all learn how to control your powers? For whose benefit? Certainly not your own—it's for the humans, the Norms who are terrified of you. The CMRD imprisons you and shackles your abilities so that your deemed 'safe.' Okay to be let out into society. Right, James?" The acidic maliciousness dripping from his tongue was enough to burn holes in the tiled floor.

"What is he talking about, James?" Isaiah looked concerned.

"I..." My voice got stuck in my throat, as the sudden dryness swallowed the sound.

Isaiah's face changed from his flirty happiness to one of terrified panic. His fists were clenched at his side and little lightning bolts zapped out from them.

"It's true," Cody rasped. "You have a short amount of time to learn how to control the godlike talents you possess, and if you don't, they'll do to you what they did to me."

All eyes were on Cody. The temperature in the room plummeted. I shivered but wasn't sure if it was from the truth that was about to come out, the cold, or Cody's mal-intent.

"Spit it out, Ghost Boy. What the fuck do you mean?" Camila glared at Cody and then switched and focused all her rage on me with tunnel vision. She too was terrified.

"You won't have to worry about this, I swear. You'll all be fine!" I said loudly, halfway trying to convince myself.

They'll give you six months. If you don't learn to control yourself in that time, they'll stick a needle in your arm and kill you, just like they killed me. And James will sit there and watch them do it," Cody hissed and then laughed manically as his apparition disintegrated in wisps, leaving me standing alone, knee deep in swirling black Arcane mist.

Five young faces looked like the rug had just been pulled out from underneath them.

"They're going to kill us?" Ning asked. Her lip quivered.

Shit. Godammit. Fucking Arcanes.

I so need a cigarette.

Seventeen: History Lesson

MY GAZE DARTED to each student. I was caught. I should have told them my past, but I hadn't had any time. I'd just started to gain their trust.

Being an Empath, I could tangibly feel the terror, betrayal, and fear that wafted off of my students. Dammit, and things had been going so good.

Isaiah's emotional state screamed betrayal. The look on his face sent a knife through my chest.

"It's only happened once," I tried to explain, exuding as much calm emotion as I could.

"Are you fucking shitting me?" Camila had crossed her arms. It wasn't in defiance. It was a measure of self-protection. She looked utterly terrified. Her eyes were huge.

"I want everyone to calm down. Seriously, you'll all be fine," I tried to assure them. Looking for that spot in my head, searching for it frantically, I needed to reassure them they were safe.

"Fuck this shit," Chris said. He was starting to hyperventilate.

"Chris, calm down. You'll lose control," I warned him. Where was that spot?

"Like I fucking care at this point? So we're actually in a twisted concentration camp. Where are the gas chambers in here, huh? We're all going to die, and you knew it."

Find that spot...damn it...ah...there it is. Clenching my mind, I pushed a big bubble of soothing, warm, relaxing feelings.

"No one's going to die." My voice was smooth, like silk, layering the emotion I pressed outward.

"You don't know that, though, do you?" Isaiah said, with a tremble in his voice. His eyes welled up. "I told you, I don't want to die."

They weren't picking up on my emotions. "Isaiah, I don't want anyone else to die. I'm stuck here just as much as you. I'm just as trapped. But I really want you to calm down."

"Wait. What the fuck does that mean?" Camila spun and looked at Isaiah. "You knew about this?"

"No! I didn't know about the CMRD part of it," Isaiah said.

"What other fucking part is there?" Camila screeched.

"The Tonka part," Isaiah stated. He said it in such a way that just the mention of the coven leader's name sent chills down my back.

"How the hell does that affect me?" Camila said.

"It doesn't," I said. "But it does affect Annabelle, Ning, and Isaiah."

"How?" Annabelle asked. Tears were streaming down her face.

"If we don't figure out how to manage our demons, they will exorcise them from us." For the briefest moment, Ning and Annabelle appeared to have a slight glimmer of hope. "But rarely does the human survive the exorcism."

Ning's shoulders slumped forward. "I'm afraid," she whispered and then started crying.

"So I'm stuck with these things?" Annabelle sobbed.

"Look, everyone just stop," I pleaded with them. "I don't have all the answers. I don't want anyone to die, and if I could, I would take away all your demons and be done with all this shit. But that's not the reality right now. I don't know what to tell you. You have to get your shit together and get a handle on this magic."

I grabbed the first student near me, which was Camila, and pushed relaxation into her hard. She was resisting, though, and I had to fight her. There was a tug of war of emotions.

Her head jerked towards me as she glared. "Don't you dare! Don't you dare make me feel something I don't want to!"

"It's for your own good, just chill. I can get us all out of this mess." I forcibly shoved every ounce of serenity I possibly could into her.

I could tell she was fighting, her eyes fluttered, her jaw clenched, but ultimately, she lost the battle. Her mouth slackened, and then her head lolled to the side. She visibly softened. At that point, I had her. I told her, *grab Chris's hand.* She did as she was told, and I pushed even harder. Another battle began, but there's a funny thing that happens once I have one person under my control. If I push it through someone else, it amplifies, as if the other person becomes a battery and revs up my ability. It didn't take long before Chris's face relaxed.

Grab the next person's hand.

Chris leaned over and clasped hands with Annabelle. "What will happen to us if we do get it together?" Chris asked.

Another push and Annabelle's sobs slowed. She then reached for the next person, Isaiah.

"A very good question. I don't have answers for all of you, but I know the United Nations is interested in Ning for her language abilities, CSIS is interested in Camila, and the military wants you, Chris."

Isaiah relaxed and then grabbed Ning.

"What about Annabelle and me?" Isaiah asked.

"I don't know," I said, my eyelids were growing heavy.

"They're not just going to let us go—you know that. Annabelle and I are way too powerful," Isaiah said as he looked at Annabelle and tried to smile.

Push. *Warm sunshine. A forest clearing covered in wildflowers. A glorious hot beach with palm trees.* I thought of all the images I could think of that were soothing and relaxing. I had to close my eyes.

"That is most likely true," I said. A wave of exhaustion rippled through me. My knees buckled.

"Then what's the point?" Annabelle let her head hang. "I may as well just let the demons eat me."

"Eat you?" Isaiah glanced at her, horrified.

"Yeah..." Annabelle replied very quietly.

"Holy shit," Chris said.

"No one is going to be eaten by anyone or anything. Look, a good portion of this is going to be figuring it out together. I don't have all the answers. But I can tell you what we need to do, and if we can accomplish it—no one will die. Period."

"All right, Teach, what's the big plan then?" Camila scowled at me.

I looked at each of them, carefully weighing the situation, and thought, it's now or never. The plan I had conjured the other night after being in the medical bay—that needed to be shared. But I couldn't risk Miriam eavesdropping in on us and hearing it.

They'd all relaxed enough. I let go of Camila, outstretched my hands, and created a bubble, just like the one that had contained the demon head. And then I enlarged it. It became huge and was almost pressing up against each of us.

"Step inside," I said.

"Are you crazy? I'm not—" Camila started.

"Dammit, girl, listen to me and do it."

Each of them stepped into the shimmering bubble, and it made a weird *bloop* sound as we entered.

My shoulders drooped forward as a wave of exhaustion passed over me. I wasn't going to be able to handle this for very long. My brain fogged over, making it hard to concentrate.

The bubble would act as a shield, a cone of silence. We could say and do what we wanted in here, and Miriam and her cameras wouldn't know what we were doing or saying.

"Demon management, anger management, and astral projection management, in a nutshell. You guys figure that shit out; then we get everyone the hell out of here. Once that's done, I get to help my sister, if it's not too late."

"Your sister? How does she play into this?" Camila asked.

"She's been missing for a while, has addiction issues, and ..." I swallowed hard, not ready to say the next part out loud. "She's started using Blood Magic."

"Good fucking Christ," Camila snapped. "No bloody way."

"Shawna has always had problems." I loved her. She was my only sibling, but I was always cleaning up her messes.

"Like?" Isaiah asked. Out of any of them, he knew the kinds of trouble that could be found in the forgotten back alleys of the city.

"All right, family history time. I was just like you. Seven years ago, I was rounded up and brought here because my Psyche abilities were getting the best of me, and I had hospitalized several people, including my father." I had just started to gain their trust. I didn't want to lose it. Especially after Cody's stupid rant. If they were going to continue to trust me and forget about Cody and his ridiculous display, I'd have to put all the cards on the table.

"What happened?" Ning asked cautiously.

"My father found me and my sister in a local nightclub. I was drunk and stoned. I got angry, very angry. I didn't want to go home. Our parents had always pushed us to be, you know, the perfect family, overachievers, honours students, the whole works. Most of all, he wanted us to be *normal.* I tried to get away from him that night. I pushed out a force field so violent anyone who came into contact with it was tossed off their feet. My father was thrown through the club's front window. The broken glass did a number on him. He was in the hospital and rehab for months afterward."

"Oh, Mr. James, that's terrible," Ning said and then stepped up to my side and put her hand on my arm.

"No one died. I was lucky. But in the chaos, my sister fled. She disappeared on the streets that night, and since then, she's been in and out of homeless shelters, hospitals, and various forms of rehab. She's a mess. I just want to help her. But she's mad at me for not going with her. She's angry that I left her on the streets. She thinks I sided with our parents."

"And what about your parents?" Annabelle asked.

"We don't see each other anymore. The magic was okay as long as it was silly parlour tricks, but when they realized how deadly I was, they didn't want me around."

"I know the feeling," Annabelle said as she took a step towards me.

"Look, I just want you all to have as normal a life as you possibly can, with the talents you have. And then I want you the fuck out of here. Miriam and I haven't always gotten along, but this time, she's changed. She's done a few things that have made me question the aim of the CMRD. She's too quick to use the excuse of extermination if she thinks it's 'safer' for society. She's lied about Chris's past. I refuse to lose anyone else. We're going to get out of here, and once you're safely beyond her clutches, I need to focus on finding my sister."

And with that, the group settled for the moment. I was done. The room was spinning.

"So, are we all okay?" I asked.

"Not really. But I don't think we have much choice," Isaiah said while looking at the others for approval.

"That's probably the best answer I can hope for. We just need to take it all one day at a time." The room was swayed violently to one side as I lurched forward. I couldn't hold them calm and this force field any longer. I felt hot and clammy.

"Whoa, you okay, Mr. Martin?" Chris asked.

"I...um..." I hit the floor on my knees as the world turned a fuzzy kind of grey. A *pop* sounded as the force field blew apart.

Isaiah was suddenly wrapping his arms around my chest. "I got ya."

So cute, so warm.

Eighteen: Recess

I WAS COMFY, really comfy. The bedsheets were wrapped around me, and I was warm and could smell Isaiah.

Sweet Isaiah, smells so good, kind of like leather and cloves and that sweaty smell right after a good workout.

My body was reacting to his aroma as well, an excited stiffening reaction.

My head rolled on the pillow while my eyelids reluctantly peeled apart.

Sitting straight up in bed and looking around, I realized I had no idea where I was. The bed was comfortable, but a double size, not the king that was in my apartment. The room was dark, except for a lamp that illuminated one corner of the room, shining on a desk.

Isaiah sat with his back towards me, books all around him, and he was studying.

"What am I doing here?" I croaked. My throat was scratchy dry. My muscles, however, were screaming in agony—like when you *finally* return to the gym and work out way too hard after not having pushed your body for months on end.

"Oh cool. I was starting to worry you weren't ever going to wake up," Isaiah said as he spun around. He smiled at me.

"How long have I been here? Has Miriam come down?" I threw the blankets off me but then realized I was naked and exposing too much of myself in front of Isaiah. Way too much. I tried to be nonchalant about moving the sheets back over my lap and covering myself up.

"Relax. You've been out for—" He glanced at his watch. "—oh, like close to four hours. Don't worry, you're good. Like really good." Isaiah winked at me while glancing towards my crotch.

Well, so much for decorum.

But then reality set in, embarrassment about a boner or not, there was a more pressing issue. If Miriam caught me out there, there would be hell to pay.

"No, I need to get back to my apartment or else Miriam will storm down here, and that won't be a happy thing for anyone." I swung my legs out of Isaiah's bed and tried to move as fast as I possibly could—except I just wasn't budging. "Where are my clothes?" I said, panicked.

"James." Isaiah stood up and came over towards me. He put a warm hand on my bare shoulder and gently pushed me back. "Please, just sit for a minute and let me explain."

Something in his eyes—a pressing need, the adultness, I wasn't sure—but his resolve halted my motivations momentarily, and I sat down.

Isaiah settled in next to me. He was dressed in shorts and a tank top, and his bare leg rubbed up against mine. His leg hair brushed my bare skin, sending shivers of excitement through me.

"We took care of all of it. You get to have a break for a bit."

"I don't understand."

"You passed out. You overexerted yourself, and you did that trying to help us. So, the instant you collapsed, we all had the same thought."

"Free time, recess?"

"No." Isaiah laughed. It was more like a chuckle, but it was genuinely filled with light and happiness. "No, we knew that Miriam would be marching down, and then we'd all end up back in our cells and locked up for who knows how long. None of us wanted that."

"What did you do?" I squinted my eyes with suspicion as I glanced at him sideways.

He bumped my bare shoulder to his equally naked one. As I studied him, a devilish smile spread across his face.

"Well, Camila is pretty damn good with illusions. Who knew?" Isaiah quipped.

"What did you do?" I said now with alarm.

"Relax, we got this." Isaiah threw his arm around my shoulder and gave it a gentle squeeze, laughing as he spoke. "Right now—you're not gonna believe this—Chris is in your apartment living life to the fullest. Last I checked on him, he was munching on popcorn and watching movies on your Smart TV. Nice digs, by the way. You, mister, are going to have to share your cigarettes. But don't worry, Miriam will never catch on. Chris looks an awful lot like you currently."

"What?" I was momentarily confused, and then it dawned on me...glamour? "Camila knows how to cast fascinations? Smart move."

"A fascination?" Isaiah asked.

"Yeah, how do I explain it? Those Magicals with the ability can create visuals with their magic. Sometimes that's sparkling lights, swirling colours, and people can be quite fascinated or enthralled by it. Enchanted might be a better word. But if you're truly adept, you can cast far more complicated illusions. For instance, changing Chris to look like me?" I hazard a guess.

"Chris was the closest one to your height and build. Camila said it would work better with Chris. Good guess. By the way, you're pretty thick."

"Excuse me?" I was immediately reminded that I was lacking all manner of clothing—exactly what was Isaiah referencing?

"Shoulders, dude, shoulders. You've been to a gym once or twice. We debated who would be the easiest to use. But Chris and you are similar in body height and you are both physically similar in size—like linebacker size. I'm a little smaller and a lot wirier. The girls are all tiny in comparison to you, and Camila explained it's easier when the size is similar. You should've seen Chris's face when Camila started changing his facial features to match yours. It looked painful."

"I bet. But that doesn't hide me here," I said, casting a side glance towards Isaiah.

"Oh yeah, don't worry about that. Annabelle knows a couple of tricks. Despite the fact she hates her demons, she can smokescreen using demon fog. Coolest shit I've ever seen. She's got the hangar covered in a black mist thicker than pea soup. Ning frosted up her cube so nothing can see in, and she's asleep in Chris's bed in case the mist reveals the cubes momentarily. If nothing else, it will just look like Chris retired for the night."

"Wow. You guys did this all for me?"

Isaiah cocked an eyebrow as he studied me, then put his hand on my thigh. I should have pulled away, but...

"We like you," Isaiah said as he patted my leg, then left his warm hand on my leg. "You're one of us, which is better than the last few we've had in here. The Norms were kind of stupid. You've also stood up to us in front of that class A bitch, Miriam. No one likes her."

"Yes, well, don't piss her off."

"No shit." Isaiah snickered nervously. "But more than anything else, you exhausted yourself trying to make us feel safe. Oh and then there's this promise that you're gonna break us out. That would have played pretty heavy with everyone. By the way, can I ask a favour? I mean—I know you're like just waking up and all, but your blackout—that severed all the connections you had with us, and I'm starting to get a little whirly upstairs." Isaiah circled his index finger at his temple.

"Oh, that's not good. We don't want you out of control." I grabbed the hand he'd left on my thigh.

"Are you sure? Can you handle it?"

"Just you and me. Yeah, we're good." I was already revving up the old emotion engines and thinking about serenity and calm vibes.

Isaiah put up no resistance to me placing his hand in mine, and I passed the emotion on. His face immediately reflected the connection between us and the absorption of the emotion.

"Can I ask?" Isaiah continued to hang on to my hand. I wasn't pulling away either. His palm was hot, and the human contact was familiar. There hadn't been anything like that for me in a long time.

"Ask what?" I glanced up at him. His copper brown eyes were solidly focused on me.

"Is what Cody said for real?"

"What do you mean? Was he telling the truth?" I asked, and Isaiah nodded. "Yes, they euthanized him. Miriam made me watch. And I'm sure they've done it to others, but Cody was the only person I saw it happen to."

"Was he your boyfriend?" he asked sheepishly, and he dropped his head and looked at the floor of his cell.

"Yes. Yes, he was. But no one knew. Miriam doesn't like gay guys. I've heard her make more than a few disparaging remarks. If she had found out about Cody and me, I'm sure the consequences would have been worse."

"I'm not sure it could have gone any worse for Cody."

"Yeah, fair." That burned a little, because the reality was, the tough consequences would have been actions against me, not Cody. "I tried everything I knew to get him in control of his abilities. I even tried to bust him out once I found out he was scheduled for..." The memory of Cody, dressed in white, lying strapped to the execution table took over my thoughts.

"It's okay. You don't have to talk about it. I can't imagine having to sit and watch anyone die, especially someone I loved."

"I left the CMRD. I wasn't fit to be around anyone. I haven't been too much on the sober side since it happened. Miriam dragged me back in here. I am, after all, under contract. I still owe them."

Isaiah stood and walked over to his desk, picked up a book, and turned around and stared at me, "How much do you know about what's in these things?" He waved the book at me.

"A lot," I said but couldn't quite look at him when I said it.

"You think you can help us all out?"

"I want to. You guys are all good people, and holy shit for talent. In the short few days we've had, each of you have shown me incredible abilities. But unfortunately, Miriam is not wrong. If we can't get a handle on what we can do, we're deadly."

"Were you shitting us when you said you'd break us all out?"

"No. I'm done dealing with Miriam and her cause. I was like you guys. I was here and Miriam helped me get control of my abilities. But when I left this place, I got into a lot of trouble, fell in with the wrong people, did some crappy things. Miriam brought me back here—kind of forced me to sign a contract with her and this facility. It was okay at first, but things have slowly changed and now she's way more bent on making money. I'm done dealing with her. I'm done with her crazy. I can't be part of it anymore. For me, it's more important to find my sister and get her out of whatever crap she's gotten herself into this time. That is, after I'm done making sure you're going to be all right."

"Okay, one last question."

"All right."

Isaiah dropped the book on his desk and took a few steps to stand in front of me. "You really think I'm cute?"

A wave of crushing nerves consumed me. I could feel my cheeks start to burn, and I was quite certain they had turned red.

I glanced up to look at Isaiah, so handsome, so intense for his age. The warmth eating up my insides was burning hotter by the second.

Isaiah smiled a little, took the bottom of his tank top and with two hands, yanked it off, and pitched the garment into the corner of his room.

He crawled onto the bed, placed one knee on each side of my thighs and sat on my lap, his face right up to mine. We were nose to nose.

"Tell me the truth. You're not fighting this too hard."

"No, I'm not." I gulped.

"Something else is getting hard again." Isaiah cocked an eyebrow and smirked.

"Isaiah, I can't do this," I said as I looked away.

Isaiah grabbed my chin in his hand and gently redirected my attention towards him. Staring directly into my eyes, he asked, "What colour are my eyes right now?"

"Brown, with those crazy gold flecks."

"Who's talking to you? Isaiah or the demon?" he asked.

"You are."

"I won't force you into anything. I want you to know that. But I do find you distractingly attractive. If you're going to be my teacher, then I absolutely want private lessons. I trust you. I believe you, and I think you have our best interests at heart—despite what happened to you in the past. I can't imagine how horrifying that was. I will do everything I can to get control of the magic in me, but I want you to know something," he said.

"What's that?" I whispered. I was totally entranced.

"You touched me in a way that made me feel safe, complete, and whole. For the first time in years, my mind settled and I could actually see straight without the demon or crazy-ass powers getting in the way or taking over. I don't think that was just your Psyche abilities.

"I also don't believe in love at first sight, but I can tell you, because of you right now, I'm a different person. And if you've affected me this much in the space of a few days, I want to see how much we can change each other. I want to at least try that."

"Isaiah," I started, but how could I explain?

"What's holding you back? Cody?"

"Partly. Yes. I can't ever go through that again."

"I understand that. So this will take time for you. I'm okay with that."

"That's only part of it. How can I possibly be your teacher, a guide, a mentor, and have the others wonder or question if there's anything going on between us? That would make you more important to me than them. That's not fair to them."

Isaiah nodded and stroked my shoulders, then ran his hands over my chest. "My demon was right."

"About what?" His touch felt so good. I shivered. Goosepimples formed where his fingers had lightly stroked my chest. It had been so long since I'd had human contact. I suddenly found myself craving more from Isaiah. I'd told myself I wasn't allowed to think about those things.

"He said you would be a challenge, and he also said you'd have just a dusting of hair on your chest. I love that too." He ran his fingers through it. "Let me share another little tidbit with you." He continued to touch and explore my arms and chest.

"Oh god, Isaiah, please stop," I begged.

"James..." He leaned forward and whispered in my ear.

"Yeah?"

"The others already know, and they don't care."

Isaiah nibbled on my earlobe as I brought my hands up and held Isaiah closer to me. His back muscles spasmed at my touch.

Just this once. We'll get it out of our systems.

Isaiah pushed us over, and suddenly, he was lying on top of me. I was pinned beneath him and enjoying every last taboo second.

"Really? They all know?" I whispered.

"It's not hard to see your feelings plastered all over your face when you look at me." He smiled mischievously. "Can't say I'm any different when I look at you. They've all noticed."

Isaiah leaned in and kissed my lips. Hesitantly, I'm sure—gauging my reaction.

All I could feel was his bristly beard up against my face, his warm wet lips pressed to mine, and his very hairy chest rubbing up across my skin.

"Oh. Well, I..." I tried to reply, but Isaiah kissed me again. "How long can the others keep their magic going?"

"Well, they were prepared to do it all night."

"Oh" was all I could manage. Isaiah's charms and constant kisses had won.

Oh my god.

Nineteen: Show and Tell

I SNUGGLED INTO the warmth of the body I was holding, and the sensation of stroking the furry chest and tummy made me relax into the softness of the bed.

Isaiah mumbled and pushed his body closer to mine.

Oh! Shit! What the hell have I done?

I propped myself up on one elbow and looked at the sleeping man in front of me. He was peaceful and content, and a stark contrast to the first time I had seen him, levitating with IV tubes coming out of him like spaghetti.

"Isaiah, I need to go..." I said softly, gently nudging him awake.

He rolled over, flopped an arm around my midsection, and held me tight. He slowly opened his eyelids, smiling, and reached up to stroke my face. He gave me a quick kiss.

"Isaiah, I can't—" I started.

"I swear, if you say anything along the lines of 'this was a mistake,' I'll set my demon after you," he said.

He was so beautiful, handsome, and his voice was deep in its half-sleep state.

I was his teacher, and I shouldn't have given into this.

I pulled myself out of his grasp and crawled from the bed. Upon finding my clothes draped over the back of his chair, I started to get dressed.

"Okay, say something to me. Clearly, you're not happy."

"What do you want me to say? Was this a mistake? Yes. Did I want to do this? Yes. But it's wrong, Isaiah. What are the others going to say? And if Miriam finds out, then we're in for a whole different world of trouble."

"You worry too much," Isaiah said and rolled over onto his back, tangled up in bedsheets, but most of his lithe body was exposed.

"Look, if this had happened out there in the real world, I wouldn't be freaking out like I am right now. I'm not going to lie, Isaiah. I find you incredibly attractive, and I'm very turned on by you, but I just..." I didn't know what to say to him.

"How about this? We'll just take this slow. Wait. You'll see the others don't care. I get the difficulty this might pose with her royal bitchiness, but I thought we were all planning on breaking out of here? Right? Those weren't just empty promises?"

"No, they weren't. I need to get out of here as much as you guys do."

"All right then." Isaiah got out of the bed, stark naked, and my god, what a sight to behold. I stopped pulling on my sock from my seated position at his desk and took in everything about him. He walked over to me, took my face in both his hands, and kissed me. He tasted so good. "Please don't dismiss this. I need you. In more ways than one. And I like you. Can we at least try? Even if it's at a glacial pace?" He canted his head, raised an eyebrow, and smirked a little.

I sighed and closed my eyes, resting my head against his palms.

"Isaiah, I need time. I...I just..."

He sighed and let me go. "You get to have all the time you need. But I'm stubborn and usually get what I want. Just warning you."

"Yeah," I said while pulling up my pants. "Okay then. I'll see you in the class at nine. Can you bring the others?" My face was burning. I should have known better than to do this.

"Sure." He smiled, but it wasn't an eager grin. If anything, I was positive I saw regret in the look on his face.

I finished getting dressed, and as I left his cube, I turned to capture one more peek at him. He gave me a half-hearted grin. "I'll see you in a while."

Walking across the hangar to my apartment, Annabelle's demon mist was, as Isaiah had said, thick. Disorienting, actually. It took me much longer than I thought it should have to make my way across the hangar. When the mists finally parted, I could see the TV from my living room flickering away.

Another version of me was passed out on the couch. The bright fluorescent blue numbers on my digital clock said 4:21 a.m. Too early. There was no way I was going to get any sleep. Not now.

I went to the kitchen cabinet, opened the door to my stash—generously supplied by Miriam—and pulled out the cigarettes.

Not wanting to wake Chris, I threw a blanket over him, turned the TV off, and then headed for my bedroom. After closing the door, I stripped and lit a cigarette.

The nicotine assaulted my body as it coursed through the bloodstream, and I felt lightheaded. Then I sat and wallowed in my own misery, absorbed in the guilt of what I'd done.

I could still smell Isaiah on my skin.

I swear I could still feel his hands...all over me.

As glorious as it had been, I felt dirty, like I had shit on the memory of Cody and betrayed the other four students.

I snubbed out the remaining cigarette, wishing I had never lit it in the first place, then made my way to the bathroom, scrubbed the smoke from my teeth with copious amounts of toothpaste, and stepped into the shower.

No amount of soap was going to make me clean.

WHEN I HAD built up enough courage to walk out of my bedroom, I discovered Chris had left. I hadn't heard him leave, which just proved how lost in miserable thoughts I had been over the past few hours.

That and several cigarettes.

I wasn't looking forward to class today at all. And I was quite sure I couldn't look Isaiah in the eye.

"Well, here goes," I said to myself as I started the trek across the hangar.

The demon fog had dissipated slightly. It still ebbed and flowed, billowed and separated as I walked through it. If I wasn't exactly sure where I was going, I could have been wandering in circles around the giant warehouse space. The thought occurred to me that perhaps the shroud might have been imbued with confusion as a magical quality. Embedding emotions within its vapours would be a clever trick—something I'd have to sock away for later.

As I finally entered the classroom, Ning, Isaiah, Annabelle, and Chris were already seated, books splayed out before them, and looking very studious. It was only 8:30 a.m.

I stood in front of the teacher's desk with my arms crossed and watched each of them for a minute.

Finally, Ning looked up and smiled. Not just her usual friendly smile. Her entire face seemed to glow with happiness, "Good morning, Mr. James."

Chris was just outright staring at me, looking like himself—not me, which was a shame. I wished I'd had the opportunity to study the glamour Camila had used. He gave me a nod and a quick grin, then returned to his book.

Isaiah was stealing peeks at me from behind a rather old-looking tome. One of the beastie books that Tonka had left. I was sure he was dying as much as I was? I couldn't see his entire face. It was hard to tell.

Annabelle, however, gave away everything. She was pretending very hard to be reading before looking at me—a glance to see if I was watching, then covered her mouth and giggled.

The rest of them all glared at her with stunned and slightly angry faces.

"I'm sorry. I can't." And then the hand disappeared into her lap and she laughed aloud, which of course, made the rest of them follow suit—except for Isaiah. He was watching me carefully. I think it was the first time I had ever seen Annabelle laugh, and it was good to see on her.

"Okay, okay—you all know." I rolled my eyes toward the back of my head. My cheeks were surely the same colour as a tomato. My ego was about as tender as a bruised one.

"Know? Dude, we could hear you," Chris said and burst out laughing.

"Oh shit." I covered my face with my hand. Was it possible to just crawl under the bureau and die?

"Mr. James." Ning, still smiling, got up from her seat, walked over, and gave me a huge hug. She pulled back but left her hands on my shoulders. I still had my arms crossed. "We are happy for you, and for Isaiah." She glanced in Isaiah's direction, then returned her pretty, bright gaze to me. "It was very easy to see that the two of you liked each other, and in this...facility...we haven't seen or felt anything good in a long time. I was only too happy to help out with our sneaky plan."

"Seriously? You all feel the same way?"

There was general nodding.

Isaiah was right. I'm such an idiot.

"You are still going to bust us out of this joint, right?" Chris added.

I gave him a glare, as did all the others, at which point, he realized his error. There was always the potential that *they* were listening, or at least we had to assume that.

"Well, we won't speak of it again," I whispered and then nodded and gave Chris a wink, and he acknowledged it with another nod of his head and mouthed the word sorry. "So, really? You're all okay with this?" I waited for the other shoe to drop. It was all a joke. It had to be a joke, right?

"Really," Annabelle said. "Now, I need help with this." She flipped her book around and showed me a horrendously difficult sigil.

"Ah, okay. You know I'm not good with this stuff, but let's have a go." I started to walk over, then realized Camila wasn't present. "Where's Camila?"

"She said she wasn't feeling up to it this morning. She's still in bed," Ning said.

I gave Ning a side glance. "I should go check on her. Sorry, Annabelle, can it wait?"

She nodded, "Before you go—" Annabelle stopped me. "—we were wondering if you had enough energy? I mean we don't want to have a repeat of yesterday, but honestly, your empathic abilities put things right in my head for me."

I shrugged. Of all the emotions to push, stillness was probably the easiest. "I think so. Camila's not here, so that's one less—although I'm still gonna check on her."

"I think I'm okay today, Mr. James," Ning stated.

I had already made the connection with Isaiah, so it was just Chris and Annabelle. It was a quick exchange and easy to do. I gained a small amount of pleasure watching whatever demons and rage melt away all their struggles, knowing that the empathic push was keeping their mental bonds intact.

I turned to Isaiah. "Can we chat?"

"Sure," he said, a little unsure.

We walked out of the classroom and into the hangar, waist deep in swirling darkness, thanks to Annabelle.

I turned to look at him once I thought we were a reasonable distance from the others. The mist wafted and intermittently obscured the classroom.

"I had nothing to do with their reactions and I didn't say anything!" he began, but I cut him short before he could say anything else.

"So, I'm an idiot, and I'm sorry, but—" I started.

Isaiah interrupted. "Look, I get it, I do. Us"—he used his index finger and gestured at the each of our chests—"being okay with the others is one thing. There's still Miriam, and I think the bigger issue is your past. I'm not an idiot, James."

"No. No, you certainly are not. I'm a little relieved? I don't know what to think to be honest. Right now, embarrassment is pretty high on the list, but it's going to take time for me to deal with the Cody issues."

"That's okay—I told you it was."

"I don't know what to say," I stammered.

"You don't have to say anything." He leaned forward and had to stretch a little to kiss me on the cheek. He placed his hand on the back of my neck and pulled me forward until our foreheads were touching. "I told you, you get all the time you want. I need you."

I sighed deeply. There was a part of me that needed the human contact, and Isaiah's touch was electrifying, literally and figuratively.

Isaiah pulled away. "Go check on Camila. Come back to class when you're done."

I nodded as I studied him.

Dealing with my ghosts wasn't going to be easy. If a year of inebriation didn't kill my haunted past, then frankly, I wasn't sure how to deal with it.

"I'm gonna try, okay?" I said.

"I know." He patted my shoulder, then let his hand trail down my arm before he turned back towards the classroom and left me in the swirling mist.

I sighed again and rolled my eyes, feeling like the biggest dumbass ever.

Twenty: Study Session-Camila

I WALKED OVER to Camila's cube and peered through the glass wall. It was dark inside, but I could just make her out, curled up in bed. I rapped on the glass.

No answer.

"Camila, it's James. Are you okay?"

Still nothing. Was she asleep? As much as I didn't like teleporting myself into someone's private space, her safety and well-being were more important.

Tingly feet and then...

Standing in the middle of Camila's room, the first thing I noticed was the mess. Most of the other students were pretty tidy. Well, Ning was fastidious, and both the boys kept their rooms clean, but they weren't big on organization. In Annabelle's cube, it was impossible to see anything, and considering the possible denizens, I wasn't sure I wanted a view.

Camila was crumpled in her bed, blankets wrapped around her tightly. She was facing the wall.

"Camila, I'm sorry for intruding. But I need to know—are you okay?" I asked.

"I'm fine, just leave me alone." It was so quiet I could barely hear her.

"Are you feeling sick? Should I call the nurse?"

"No."

"You're not feeling sick? Or you don't want the nurse?"

"Yes."

"You're not helping." I sighed, took two steps, and then sat on the edge of her bed. I put a hand on her shoulder. She immediately retreated from my touch, edging in closer to the wall of her cube.

I pulled my hand back quickly.

"Please, just let me sleep. Or die, whichever."

"Ah, no one wants you to die. Camila, are you sure you're okay?"

"Yes. Please, just...no. I just want to be left alone."

Camila was an adult. It wasn't like I could force her to go to class or see the nurse. If for whatever reason she needed a day off, to herself, who was I to take that away from her?

"Alright, I'll leave, but if you need me, I'll be in the classroom or my apartment."

"How would I get out of here?"

Oh, shit, there was that. Either Isaiah or I had been popping the others in and out of the cubes, which in the end, was ridiculous. These kids needed to feel like they could come and go as they needed. No one was getting beyond the hangar anyway, but still.

The black plastic remote that Miriam had taken out from the wall panel—I had forgotten all about it. I could fix this one issue.

"I think I might have a solution. For now, I'll let you be, but I'll come back and check on you later."

"Fine." She squirmed farther into the corner and enveloped herself more in the blankets.

Frowning out of concern, I stood up from her bed and then concentrated on being on the outside of her room.

Woosh

Peering into the dense demon fog before me, I made my way across to my apartment. Once there, it didn't take me long to locate the black remote Miriam had left for me. It was on the kitchen counter.

I picked it up and examined it. There were a sundry of buttons, a series of which said Open Cell One, Open Cell Two, etc.

Well, why not?

I pressed each of the open buttons. Nothing happened, no huge explosion, no screams. This was as easy as it should have been.

Still...you would have expected—

An ear-piercing screech echoed throughout the student hangar.

Shit.

I stuffed the remote into my back pocket and then made my way back to the classroom, only to find the kids all standing outside, gaping at their cubes.

"What?" I asked.

"What did you do?" Isaiah asked.

"I pressed these buttons." I said, taking the black plastic thing out of my back pocket, and then I remembered Miriam's warning, "*Under no circumstances are you to push the red set.*"

For fuck's sake.

"What happened?" I swivelled to see what they were gaping at. Miriam. Miriam was walking through the fog. "Shit, back to the classroom with you."

They escaped to the safety of the classroom, not wanting to be anywhere near where an argument or unpleasantness was about to erupt.

Miriam stopped dead in front of me, then gestured through the fog.

"Honestly, do you know what you've done, James?" she snapped, snarky as ever.

"Good morning, Miriam. How are you?" I smiled at her, knowing that would irritate her beyond what words could express.

She walked over and snatched the remote out of my hands. "They *were* locked away for protection," she snarled.

"Miriam, look." I pointed in the direction of the classroom. Thankfully, the demon mist was relatively thin on this side of the hangar. All four were there, behaving like students, immersed in books, and taking notes. Miriam glared at me. I wiggled my eyebrows at her, as if to say, *So there!*

"Fantastic, where's the fifth one?"

"You mean, where's Camila? She's having a sick day. That's allowed."

"This is going to cost money we don't have to fix," Miriam said.

"What are you talking about?"

"Look, you idiot. Open Cell One is this button, the one you pushed, the one that just cost me thousands of dollars. It does not mean Cell One Door, that button is right here."

I looked at the remote to where she was pointing. Sure enough, there were the buttons that would have opened the actual doors on the kids' cells, not lift up the entire glass front of each cube.

"Oh. Oops?" I smiled at her with a stupid little grin to indicate I was sorry.

"Did I not leave you instructions about the series of red buttons? Something to the effect of do not press them?" Miriam was going red herself, never mind her buttons, which I had pushed.

I glanced over Miriam's padded shoulders, to see the damage I had created.

Even through the foggy mist that was *still* swirling about in the warehouse, I could see the front of each of the cells had lifted up, exposing the cubes.

Way off in the distance, Camila stood, still dressed in what appeared to be pyjamas, gripping her bedspread in one hand while it draped and puddled onto the floor around her feet. She held out her hand where the glass front to her cube had once been.

I waved at her, smiling, which was supposed to tell her *See, problem fixed. Come get me if you need anything.* Camila didn't wave back. Instead, she turned and withdrew back into her room.

"I will have to get maintenance to come in here and fix this," she said.

"Why? Fix what? At least they can come and go as they please."

"There are doors for that, James!" Miriam was almost purple, redder than her rouge for sure.

"Well, you should have told me that. Isn't there a Close Cell One button?" I asked ignorantly. It would just stand to reason.

"No, James, there isn't. This button was to be used in case of an emergency. The individual walls were never meant to be reattached once assembled, only disassembled once the project was over."

"Wait. The project?"

"We will discuss this in my office," she sniped through gritted teeth. Her jaws were slammed tight. I was in for a treat.

Twenty-One: Called to the Principal's Office

IT TOOK US almost twenty minutes with an armed escort to arrive at Miriam's inner sanctum office. The room was just as I had remembered it. Lavish with comfort, leather upholstery, intricately carved bookshelves, and a large desk in the center of the room. Also not surprising; there was no computer anywhere. After seeing how well Miriam took to technology, I was sure the IT department was glad for that fact. There also wasn't a window anywhere. Weird.

"Sit down," Miriam barked at me.

"You know, it wouldn't kill you to be nice." I pushed the corners of my mouth up with both index fingers, turning my lips into a smile. I sat in the visitor chair across from her desk.

"We are not running a kindergarten. These are not grade-schoolers. How many times do I have to tell you how dangerous they are?" Miriam used her index finger to jab the surface of her very solid desk to make the point clear.

"They are also still people, Miriam. Human. Beings. People who deserve far better treatment than what you've been giving them. Honestly, when was the last time they saw sunshine? What is wrong with you?"

"This isn't up for debate."

"You're right, it isn't. Have your men fix the cubes if you want, but if you don't give those kids the ability to come and go out of their rooms at their own will, I'll have them blast the entire fucking thing apart. Don't think they can't do it."

"Actually, they can't. Each one of those cubes is designed to house them as individuals. Ning's cube has cold detectors in it that will start a heating process to ensure she doesn't freeze herself or the plexiglass. Chris's cube is the opposite. Isaiah and Annabelle and Ning also have the most up-to-date and complicated wards and protection sigils created in ultraviolet paint that protect and keep their demons in their cubes, and those same wards are then duplicated on the outside of the hangar. Don't you think it was odd that Isaiah's demon didn't actually stampede its way across the arena to get to you?"

"Oh." What else was I supposed to say?

"Do you know how much money those sensors cost? And those wards and sigils aren't created by just anyone. That expertise has to be called in. Not to even mention the mechanical damage you've caused." Miriam shook her head. "We also keep them separated at a distance so they can't conspire with each other. There's danger in letting them out. I know that's a risk I have to take when you're there, but I was hoping for adult supervision on your part. You've disappointed me again, James."

"Okay, but you know, while we're on the topic of discussing everyone, let's talk about Chris. He told me that he was basically kidnapped and woke up in his cell. He has complete control over his abilities."

"Oh really. Is that what he said to you? Have you seen him get angry?" Miriam cocked an eyebrow at me.

"Yes, I have, but then, given his treatment here, I'd be just as angry if not worse. Honestly, what were you expecting to happen?" My hands were becoming more animated the angrier I got.

"You were given instructions, James. Get them to control their abilities, and I distinctly remember telling you to work on anger management with Chris. He can't be passing out from anger and exhaustion when he's conscripted into the military!"

"And I'm telling you that giving me false or half information doesn't help me or them in any way." I glared at her, leaned forward, and this time, I pushed a finger onto the top of her desk in front of her to make *my* point.

Miriam sat back and crossed her arms. I could tell from her reddened cheeks that she was still livid. "You were given instructions. I expect you to comply with them. But since you've arrived here...you're different, James. I'm afraid what happened in your last class has affected you too much, distorted your ability to see what's a priority."

"Oh my god, are you serious? Of course it affected me. You're heartless. I watched Cody die. Doesn't that bother you? How do you sleep at night?"

She spun her chair around and scooted over half a foot to a filing cabinet, where she pulled out the bottom drawer, riffled through her files, pulled out a thick one, and then from that, a single sheet of paper.

Miriam placed it on her desk and slid it to me.

"I sleep just fine. Due to unforeseen circumstances, their dates have been advanced." Her voice was dead and monotone. This was Miriam as angry as I'd ever seen.

"What are you talking about?" A chill touched my spine. If this was... I looked at the words that ran across the top of the page:

Termination Date for Project CMRD58/5/JMAR-Vault 21b:
~~180~~ 90 days from inception.

Underneath the date were the full names of each of my students. My stomach knotted and fell out. The room spun slightly. They couldn't be serious.

Oh my god, I'm gonna lose Isaiah...

"Is this what I think it is?" I asked, knowing exactly what it was but not wanting confirmation. Cold sweat formed a slick across my back.

"It is." Miriam stared at me, her face as still as a statue. The anger blowing off of her was as palpable as a heat wave.

"Why? Why would you do this? We were supposed to have until March! You've cut my time in half." The faces of each of them flashed in my head. Ning and her smile, Camila and her mischievous ways. Isaiah...oh my god, Isaiah. Memories of Cody resurfaced.

"There was a benefactor meeting yesterday. At one point, James, I had sponsors for each of them. I'd even found parties that were interested in Annabelle and Isaiah. But after reviewing footage of your teaching efforts, your side trips to the medical ward, and where each of them have progressed to, I've lost interested parties. So, let's just call this funding cuts. Which now more than ever is an even bigger issue with the damage you've caused to those cubes." Miriam was flipping through papers from the file she had pulled out, "After watching what little progress you've had, the council doesn't see you being able to pull this off."

"Are you fucking kidding me? I just got them to trust me. Oh my god, you're such a—"

"Careful. Not another word or I'll chop off another month. I have no funds to keep you housed and fed. Right now, you're riding on my generosity. I'm hoping I can find other interested groups. Besides, we received notice from Tonka. Her people will be here next week to conduct their tests. I expect by the end of next week, you'll only have Camila and Chris left anyway, as I just don't see the others being ready enough for Tonka's tests. And honestly, you're not going to succeed with someone who has bipolar disease. So, all you have to do is focus on Chris."

It's bipolar disorder, you witch. Wait...what?

"Camila has a mental illness? Did you not think that might have been a key thing to tell me at the onset?" I couldn't contain my rage. This had gone to hell. Three of my kids might have demons, but this bitch beat all of those unearthly beings hands down when it came to evilness. "Does she have medication? Are we getting her therapy?"

"James, it doesn't matter. Did you not hear me? Tonka is coming next week. You'll never get the Arcanes ready, and I don't see Camila getting better." Miriam squinted and made her mouth scrunch over to one side. "Just babysit them and do your best with the Elemental shapeshifter. Despite your failures, the military is still interested in him and willing to pay dearly as well."

"When the hell did Tonka send notice?" I was livid and absolutely terrified.

"Two days ago."

"Why are you just telling me now?" I was coming close to screaming.

"James. Really. This facility is huge. Yours is not the only class we are currently hosting. And I'm afraid, in this economic environment, we're not finding enough potential investors. Every single class is being scaled back. Even though you have a few of the more powerful students, you do not, by any means, have the most important ones. There are others here with more marketable talents. I'm sorry. This is nothing personal. It boils down to dollars."

"You're un-fucking-believable. Is that all you're concerned about? Money?"

"I might add that out of the benefactors we do have left, *some* are of the mind that Arcane abilities should not be allowed to perpetuate in the human genome."

"So, now you're talking about genocide." I bounced out of my chair during my rant and paced in front of her desk while she remained seated, and completely still, despite the rage she displayed for my insubordinate behaviour. If I had thoughts before that I needed to bust these kids out, now I was absolutely certain.

"No, James, the definition of genocide is the extermination of a particular ethnic group. I don't care who you are or where you come from. If you can't control them, then extermination is our only option. And I have to repeat this to you. Without patrons for each student, I can't continue to run the facility. I don't understand why you can't accept this." She threw her hands up dismissively.

And that was the end of that. Miriam's lips were pursed so tight, you couldn't even see the red lipstick.

"And what about Shawna? What happened to that promise?"

"James, you saw the video. I just don't know what to tell you. If she's involved in what we think we saw...well, I can't risk the reputation of the CMRD and get involved in Sanguimancy. I mean we'll try, for whatever good it might do. I did promise you, but I think you have to come to terms that she might be a lost cause." Miriam grimaced in disgust and shook her head.

That's it. Fuck this, fuck her. We are all out of here.

Twenty-Two: Group Work

I WAS POLITELY escorted back to my apartment, which now seemed even more like a prison or concentration camp. And really, politely was being generous. Rodney, the guard, had his weapon drawn.

But it was a good thing I had been removed from Miriam's presence, because I was beyond enraged. I'd never been so angry, and it was obvious. I was losing control of my own magic. If I hadn't had one of Miriam's henchmen at my side reminding me I was still "under contract," there would have been far more damage to the halls of the CMRD.

As it was, little spheres of force field formed around me and flew off at alarming speeds in random directions, only to dissipate a short distance away. They weren't powerful enough to hurt anyone, but being hit would most likely feel like getting chunked by a speeding baseball. The dents in the walls proved it. Rodney didn't look like he was having a good time.

While I was making a subconscious obstacle course for my escort, I was also devising a quick plan of action. I needed to gather all the kids together.

I was deposited back at my place, with a definite look of relief washing over Rodney's face as we arrived. I immediately ran out into the hangar to fetch each of the students.

They were busy with their textbooks, studying, except for Camila, who was still curled up in her bed. Sheets and comforter were wrapped around her as she sat upright and rocked back and forth. I finally noticed the damage from the fronts of the cubes being opened, with bits of metal and gears hanging limp from several arms that held up the broken and splintered plexiglass. I saw no workmen, though. It was easy to gather each of the kids as I passed their open cells.

My chest ached as I walked past Camila's cube, seeing her lying in her bed. I felt bad for her and couldn't begin to imagine what was going through her head. I needed to get her the necessary help, but that meant breaking her out of here.

She declined my invitation to come with me.

"Please, I...I just can't. Not now. Maybe later. I have to stay here." She white-knuckled her bedspread. I wasn't going to argue with her.

"Okay. Would it be alright if I dropped in and visited tonight then?"

"Yeah, I guess."

The others followed me, asking questions as we returned to my apartment.

"What's the hell's going on?" Chris asked. "You look furious."

"Are you okay?" Ning, who usually had a smile, was now frowning.

Isaiah put his hand on my shoulder and made me stop. "James, what is going on?"

"We can't. Not out here. Just come with me."

Once everyone had settled into my tiny living room, I took several deep breaths. I had to calm down, had to find that center where life was good and everything was going to be fine. I lit a cigarette and inhaled deeply, took several drags, and then chucked the pack at Isaiah, who promptly lit his own.

The kids looked at each other with side glances.

I needed to tell them. But before I could, we needed privacy. A cone of silence.

I had to look hard. That elusive spot in my head retreated whenever I was highly emotional, and it took me several attempts to find it, but once I did...

The silver shimmering blob of a force field grew in the center of us and expanded to fill the entire room, swallowing everyone up in the process. Once I was sure we were all within the radius of the private sphere, I tried to find the words they needed to hear.

"What is going on? You look ready to kill." Chris acknowledged my rage.

"I am. Isaiah, can you do whatever it is you do to make the cameras go a little more wonky than normal?"

"I think so." He scrunched up his face a little and the air inside the bubble suddenly turned. It felt like those hot summer nights when the atmosphere is heavily charged and an electrical storm is coming. "I don't know how to tell you the information I was told. I just had a meeting with Miriam. It didn't go well."

"Why?" Annabelle asked. "And why isn't Camila here? She should be here, no?"

"She should. But she needs time to herself right now. I'll tell her later. Okay. Um…apparently, Tonka will be here next week to test you three," I blurted out.

"What?" Annabelle's eyelids stretched open. "Oh my god, we're nowhere near ready for her and her tests!"

"I'm afraid that's not all."

"How could it possibly be any worse, Mr. James?" Ning had snuggled up to Annabelle and wrapped an arm around her. She was by far the kindest person I'd ever met.

"Remember what Cody said?"

Suddenly, there were four pairs of eyes glued to my every word and action.

"They've scheduled an actual date. Miriam has no interest in saving anyone except for Chris, and that's only because the military is willing to pay large sums of money for you." I focused in on him. "It just means you are the only one making money, which in turn, results in the continuance of the CMRD. Our efforts have been evaluated, and to date, they weren't enough. Miriam has lost the other sponsors she had for Camila and Ning. Isaiah and Annabelle only briefly had interested parties, but they've back out as well."

"Are you fucking kidding me?" Isaiah, who had been cross-legged on my floor, leapt up, clenched his fists, and started pacing, getting dangerously close to my psychic barrier.

"Oh my god." Annabelle's bottom lip quivered and her eyes filled up with tears. "She's going to kill us."

"They can't fucking do that." As Chris said the words, flames erupted from his palms.

I grabbed his shoulder, thrusting a more calm state of mental well-being into him, which was difficult considering my own emotional upheaval. But having him decimate my apartment in flames or, worse, having the wolf take over wouldn't do any of us any good, and it would cost Miriam more money.

Ning was crying.

"Okay, just, everyone stop. Please." I gestured with my hands to get everyone to sit back down. "There's no way I'm letting this happen."

"What the hell are you going to do about it? You're locked in here like the rest of us," Isaiah said.

"We've only been together, what, a week? That was time we spent getting to know one another. We're going to spend the next few days getting the three of you ready. And Chris and Camila are going to work equally as hard to find the cues and triggers that send them off. If we can prove to Miriam that you're making progress, we might be able to get that date changed until you're all ready for the tests. Hopefully even attract a patron or two. If not, then we're going to get out of here, guns a-blazing."

"Why don't we just fucking do that now?" Chris said, sparks of fire ignited in his eyes and under his skin.

"Chris, calm down, please," I said, then added, "The CMRD is not a simple, backwoods operation that will be easy to just bust out of. Those cubes you've been living in? Each one of them had measures put in place to make it difficult or impossible to break out."

"Such as?" Isaiah asked.

"Well, around you three, there are wards. An Arcane's demon is controlled through use of sigils and wards. And they may not be visibly apparent to you, but I guarantee you there's a healthy amount of magical script around each of your cubes. There will be more around the circumference of this area as well. For Elementals, the plexiglass has sensors in them to detect heat and cold and to counteract as necessary. Plus Miriam will have made sure other anti-measures are put in place to contain the Psyches."

"What do you mean?" Isaiah asked.

"We're a little harder to contain." I stated. "Some view Psyches as the weakest of the three classes. Yet, often the opposite is true. We can be the most powerful. Miriam will ensure that armed guards are ready to take us out. I saw them while I was being dragged around. That's new. But she'll use them."

"Shit. Fuckers..." Chris said. His fists still hadn't unclenched.

"Chris, I'm not going to tell you again. Calm the fuck down."

"How the hell am I supposed to do that? You're telling me that they're going to murder each of us because we don't measure up—but they're not giving us the time to get up to their stupid standards. And you think we actually have a chance in hell of getting out of here? Lightning boy there can't control shit, and Camila's sitting in her bed, wrapped in blankets. She can't handle it." His voice was raised.

"Whoa, dude, uncalled for." Isaiah grimaced and looked a little hurt.

Ning used the back of her hand to wipe away tears. "Chris, stop. We have to work together. We won't make it out of here unless we're all in this together."

Annabelle was glaring at Chris when she abruptly said, "I'll possess you if I have to."

"Okay, enough. We're all going to work together. Right, Chris?" I turned to him, trying to elicit a granule of cooperation.

"Yeah, I guess," he retorted.

"Look, I get it. You haven't spent a lot of time together as a group. I get that there might be some hesitation. But like I said, we're going to play their game for a bit, and then...then we're going to bust our way out of here. But it won't be easy, and all six of us are going to have to work together in order for that to happen."

"Please, can't we just do that now?" Annabelle looked scary, frowning and her brows furrowed. Her stare was intense and black demon mist was pouring out of her.

"Whether or not you want to believe it, you're not ready. You guys haven't had basic instruction, and although you've all managed to figure out a few things on your own, you have the potential to do so much more, and once those talents of yours can be funnelled and directed, then we'll be able to get out. We can do this, but you're all going to have to work bloody hard."

"All right," Isaiah said, "I don't see any other choice. If this had happened a year ago, I would've said 'stick the needle in.' Not now. I've got enough reasons to live. Let's do this. And I want to see that bitch's face when we walk out of here." Isaiah's gaze drifted over to me as he spoke.

"Well, that's one of you. What about the rest?"

"We'll do it," Ning said, wiping away more tears from her cheeks.

Annabelle nodded.

Chris just growled, but it seemed like I had consensus. Now, if I could just figure out what was going on inside Camila's head and then get her to a place where we could work together.

"All right then. Tomorrow morning we start fresh, and early, and we study and work like we've got nothing to lose? Agreed?" I lit another cigarette and sucked on it mercilessly.

"Except we've got everything to lose," Chris said.

"Well, you don't," Isaiah commented, with a demonic touch to his voice. "But it's good to see you're as pissed off as the rest of us." Isaiah glanced back up at me from his seated position. "Agreed. Fuck them."

The girls said in unison, "Agreed." But no one was fooling anyone. They were all terrified, and I was too.

I had a very small chance to get these kids out of there alive.

THEY DIDN'T STICK around much after that and, as a group, left for their cells. I sat there, my thoughts still going a mile a minute.

How the hell are we going to get out of this one?

I grabbed the pack of smokes on the coffee table. I was sucking them back one after another as if I had an endless supply of them.

I pulled a cancer stick out of the smooth plastic package, held it up to my lips, and inhaled the rich sweet smell of the tobacco as I flicked the lighter and brought the flame up to the tip. That crackle when it lights, I loved that sound.

I inhaled deeply and closed my eyes.

"You gonna share, or can I have another one for myself?"

I damn near jumped out of my skin.

"Jesus, mother loving…" I clutched my chest as the wave of fight-or-flight endorphins pulsated through me. "Isaiah, we talked about this, boundaries!"

"Sorry." He hung his head. "I just don't want to be alone."

"Well, you could go talk with the others," I offered.

"Chris has shifted into wolf form, Camila is…well, being Camila, and Ning and Annabelle are coping by having a girls' night. Try as I might, I don't look good with purple sparkle nail polish."

"You've tried this colour in the past?" I asked, just being an ass and, in part, getting back at him for scaring the hell out of me.

"Maybe." He cocked an eyebrow, testing me.

"I'm not judging."

"Better not be."

"Yes, help yourself to one." I pointed at the pack.

"Well, we could just share?"

"Isaiah—" I started.

He stopped me. "Look, full disclosure. I need to be around someone. I've just been told that my life expectancy has been considerably decreased. I am *not* okay with that. I also know that you're not keen on us…" Isaiah pointed back and forth between our chests.

"I never said that. In fact, if I remember correctly, I said that if this had happened outside of this arena, I'd have been all over this." I pointed at him and then myself, mimicking him. "There are ramifications, Isaiah."

"What could possibly be worse than it is right now? We have a death date, Miriam's or potentially Tonka's. I need you to fucking hold me before I completely lose my mind."

My heart ached. It felt as though my entire body burned with the sensation of helplessness. I could only do so much for them, and they were all good people, none of whom deserved any of this shit.

"At this point, I don't care what that queen bitch Miriam has to say about anything. And if I make it through Tonka's witching ceremony, believe me, I'm not gonna let Miriam send me off into the great unknown. I need you, right now, James. I don't want to beg, but please." His chest hitched as he inhaled a breath.

Good god. If you are at least half human, buck up, mister. It's time to own this or let it go.

I shook my head. "I don't want you feeling like this, and I'm not sure there's anything I can do to help you get around what's coming. But I'll teach you as much as I can beforehand." I patted the couch next to me.

Isaiah sat down. I put my arm around his shoulder and gave him my cigarette.

He inhaled and blew out a steady stream of smoke.

"Oh man, instant dizzy when you don't get them on a regular basis." He chortled. "I keep forgetting that, but it feels good. You feel good too."

We sat there for a few minutes, passing the cigarette between the two of us.

Isaiah snuggled in beside me, then suddenly stood up and said, "Okay, early start tomorrow, right?"

"If we're gonna do this, yes." I got up, expecting Isaiah to go.

"It's bedtime then." Isaiah turned and walked toward my bedroom. As he did, he pulled off his tank top.

I was gonna argue with him, but his voice rang out from the bedroom. "And no funny business either, mister. I need my damn sleep. This metaphysics teacher of mine is one tough son of a bitch."

So then cuddling it is. Fuck you, Miriam.

Regardless of the warmth and company, I didn't sleep that well.

Twenty-Three: Biology Lesson

"CAN ANYONE TELL me why talents and abilities don't usually show up until you reach your early- to mid-twenties?" I asked. I had been firing rapid questions at them for the past twenty minutes. Most of the answers I had to pump out of them. Perhaps we had started too early in the morning. They all looked sleep deprived.

Everyone had gathered and were seated in the classroom by eight in the morning. Except for Camila. I had not checked back in with her the previous night. Instead, Isaiah had monopolized all my time. So a visit with Camila first thing before class had been required.

HANGING JUST OUTSIDE Camila's cube, I noticed her bedroom looked as if a bomb had gone off. Stuff was scattered all over the place. I was fairly convinced that her Astrals had wreaked havoc on her small bedroom.

"Can I come in?"

"If you want." She was still in bed.

"Look, I want you to know, there were events that happened yesterday. Not good things either, but I don't want to upset you any further. We are going to study hard this week. And as a group, we're going to help get Ning, Annabelle, and Isaiah ready for Tonka's tests. She'll be here next week. We'd like it if you'd come join us, but that's up to you."

"I'll see." She grabbed a fistful of blanket and pulled it up closer around her.

I didn't know what else to do. I patted her leg through her layers of blankets and left with "Whenever you're ready."

As I walked away from her bed, three Astrals appeared in various spots around the room, and although they looked like Camila, the snarls and menacing stares suggested I had entered territory that I had not been granted permission to.

I backed away slowly. They didn't advance but darted around the room, grabbing items and throwing them at me. I had to duck a few times. Their aim was pretty good.

Well, at least Camila hadn't flinched away from my touch like she had the night before. Who knew? I hoped she would come around sooner rather than later.

BACK IN CLASS, Ning raised her hand to answer my question. She was always willing to answer when no one else would.

"Yes, Ning," I said.

"Because the frontal lobe in the brain doesn't finish maturation until the early to mid-twenties in humans."

"Correct. And what is the frontal lobe responsible for?"

"Expression of emotion, language, judgment, and *sexual* behaviour." Isaiah emphasized the suggestive word while waggling his eyebrows and winking at me.

There was a collective *ooooh* from the class.

"That's enough. God, you guys are like a bunch of teenagers sometimes."

"Our frontal lobes aren't mature yet," Annabelle quipped, which at first left everyone shell-shocked. And then collectively we laughed, including myself. Another first for her. She'd never attempted a joke before. She was slowly coming into her own.

"So then, what do you think that has to do with your magical talents?" I asked.

Crickets.

"Come on. Think about it. It makes complete sense."

"Because our brains found a different way to express emotion. We have a new language, so to speak, and the additional abilities give us new ways of solving complex problems." Ning let her head hang to one side, her bangs partially obscuring her deep brown eyes.

"I think you're entirely right. And if we focus in on Ning, what's her greatest gift?"

"Her smile," Camila said from the edge of the classroom.

Everyone turned to see her standing there, a little shy and very self-conscious.

I smiled and waved her in. "Come, come, have a seat, Camila. And I love your answer, because you're absolutely right."

Ning blushed.

"Ning has an extraordinary ability to learn languages," Annabelle said.

"Exactly," I said. "Although her smile is pretty damn awesome too."

Camila took a seat, and Ning reached over and grabbed her hand. They smiled at each other. It was good to see this group starting to come together.

"Okay, now let's put that to use!"

"What do you mean?" Chris asked.

"Exactly. You guys have never had this kind of training. Let's all go out into the hangar and do magic."

"Cool." Isaiah jumped up and was the first one out of the classroom.

Annabelle's demon fog, which had hid Isaiah and me, had gradually dissipated, and now there was only the odd wispy trail left swirling around our feet.

They all lined up together.

"Spread out a little. Give yourself room. Here's the exercise. I want you to just stand there, close your eyes, and listen to the sounds around you. The hum of machinery from the complex, the breathing of the people next to you, anything, but just get lost in that. When you think you're centered in on that, put your hand out in front of you, like you were telling me to stop."

I stood there and waited.

And waited.

After a while, all five stood with their hands outstretched, hands flat and palms facing me.

I moved off to the side.

"Okay, good. Now I want you to think of yourself walking down a forest path. It's bright and warm, but the sunlight is only breaking through the forest in shafts of light. You see moss growing on an old tree stump, and in the distance, you can hear the gurgling of a little creek as it ebbs and flows through the wild lands.

"There are birds flying, chirping, and you can smell the humidity in the air, it hangs heavy, but it's comfortable, not oppressive. More like you're wrapped up in the security of a big thick blanket.

"As you walk through the forest, you can't help but think of happy things, pleasant things. You feel secure and proud and, most of all, magical.

"Now, take a moment to feel that sensation—of being happy and proud—and then push that feeling out of you with your magic and create."

It was almost comical watching the five of them. The looks of concentration on each of their faces meant they were thinking too much and not feeling enough. I knew exactly how to change that.

I came in close behind Isaiah, wrapped my arms around him, and placed one hand on his tummy. I leaned into his ear and whispered, "Feel happy. Don't think happy."

"Oh, I feel happy now," he said, then snickered, but that's all it took.

As I removed my hand, Isaiah's feet lifted off the floor. He smiled and I actually felt the bubbly emotions of happy, warm, proud, and most importantly, magical. Considering the shit storm that each of them was facing, it was good to sense a lighter and buoyant attitude prevailing from each.

"Okay, now open your eyes," I said to them, and as they listened to my instruction, their faces morphed from deep concentration and worry, to surprise and joy. They were nothing but smiles.

"Whoa!" Chris exclaimed. He too was rising upward, and before I knew it, all six of us were floating. Isaiah had once again achieved the impossible. Levitating more than just himself. He was doing it to everyone.

Camila looked ecstatic as she rolled over backwards, enjoying the free-flowing weightlessness when suddenly prisms of dancing light and sparks like fireflies illuminated the air around us.

Annabelle sucked in a breath of surprise. "It's so beautiful!"

"Isaiah, this is a fascination spell," I said, reminding him of our prior conversation.

"I don't care what it's called. It's amazing!" he said as he waved his hand through a rainbow-colored beam of light.

"Well done, Camila," I said. "Okay, three more. What are you gonna add to this?"

"What about you, Mr. James?" Ning giggled.

"How about this?" I closed my eyes and called forth a myriad of tiny mirrored bubbles, little force fields that bounced and ricocheted off of Camila's light show, refracting and enhancing the display.

Ning burst out laughing as she flicked a few of the spheres at others, while spinning in what felt like zero-gravity. Her hair floated outward.

Ning closed her eyes and spread her hands out, and the air around us chilled but only slightly. Big heavy snowflakes fell from the air around us.

"Oh wow, Ning, that's so cool!" Chris said.

It was truly magical, ethereal, and beautiful to be surrounded by the gentleness of our abilities combining together, working in tandem to create an experience none of them had ever seen before.

"Okay, hold up. I got this..." Chris interrupted my thought process. "I'm not sure if I can, but—"

A moment passed by and then—

"I can smell it. I can smell it!" Ning said.

Spicy perfume floated through the area. An earth smell. It was the first time I had seen Chris use any of his Earth Elemental abilities. He was usually so bent on fire and anger.

"I've done it before, but it's hard not to be so angry all the time, and if I'm angry, I can't do the Earth stuff."

"This is brilliant, you guys. Well done!" I complimented them all.

"What about you, Annabelle? Can you add something?" Ning asked.

"All my magic comes from my demons. I'm not sure dark creatures would be at home in such wonder." Her voice was airy, she was happy, but I could feel the stab of disappointment from her, knowing that her beasts didn't relish such light-hearted emotions.

"Annabelle, I wonder," I started. "Can any of your horde call upon lesser creatures?"

"I'm afraid to ask."

"Try it. We're not going to learn and grow if we're afraid to branch out and try new things."

Annabelle grew still and sat, floating in the air, cross-legged. She curled in on herself as a gentle breeze blew that took all of us, the snowflakes and floating globes, the warm sunshine and jasmine-scented air, and slowly churned us all in an easy-flowing counter clockwise motion.

A bright light erupted as a small nix appeared in the form of a serpentine dragon. Its face was flat with teeth that hung crooked and sideways. But despite the fierce dentures, its aqua-blue eyes contrasted sharply against the albino scales that covered its body.

Undulating through the vortex, it played chase to Camila's pretty lights and bounced around my little mirrored force fields.

The kids all laughed.

"And there we have magic built from the thoughts of being happy. It can be done, from each of you, regardless of your talent. Nicely done, folks!"

Nothing had gone wrong, everyone was in a good mood, and the moment etched itself into my mind.

I caught Isaiah studying me, his gaze was filled with wonder and the slight smile on his face let me know that for the first in a very long time, he was truly happy.

Well, shit. Maybe we can actually pull together as a team.

Twenty-Four: Learning Cursive

THE NEXT FEW days flew by, and by the end of each, I was exhausted. I'd learned my lesson in that I wasn't able to force all five of them into a state of calm and keep that up all day, but I alternated between Ning, Camila, and Annabelle. They had better control over their emotional states and didn't need me as much as the guys.

Chris and Isaiah needed the constant empathic connection, and often, Chris needed additional doses. But beyond the transferring of emotion through touch, the vast slew of lessons required to get these kids up to speed meant we started early in the morning and worked until late at night.

And then there were the practical sessions.

Magical theory is all well and good, but being book smart was only half the battle. They needed to *do* as much as possible. Teaching Camila and Isaiah about force fields, teleporting, auras, empathic resonance, and other Psyche talents came as second nature to me, and thankfully, they were quick and adept students.

At one point, Ning had turned the entire floor of the student hangar into a skating rink with a thin sheet of frost. Chris then spent the good part of two hours using flames to thaw the damn place out. So, not everything was going smoothly. All of them were still lacking that reliability of constant control.

But anything I threw at Isaiah was learned quickly, especially if it was Elemental based. Although, we rapidly discovered that his go-to element of choice was Electricity.

"Yeah. If I hear "that's shocking" one more time…I swear," Isaiah said, threatening me with a pointed finger that released a few zaps.

We even had rudimentary sigil lessons, which oddly, Chris and Camila got into. They didn't need to learn a single hieroglyphic mark, but they showed solidarity with their Arcane classmates and took instruction on everything from protection wards and circles to Entrapment Stars and Angel Script. Ning, Annabelle, and Isaiah had also created a Binding Box— basically a little tool kit that was specific for their type of demon. The kit held all the tools required for summoning their creatures or keeping the things at bay.

But I was starting to exhaust my level of understanding with the ancient symbols. In truth, the demons scared the bejesus out of me. Given the choice, I'd never teach another Arcane student ever again, but then, after this class—if we survived—I had no intentions of ever doing anything else with the CMRD. I was hoping that this would be the last time I'd ever have to be there.

The one thing we hadn't attempted yet, and needed to ensure, was how to cast a perfect Contract Circle.

The Contract Circle was a one-time spell. It was a combination of Entrapment Stars within a Security Circle, but with one direct channel for physical contact. It was a strange contradiction, as theoretical studies made it very clear; an actual physical connection between a demon and their host was horrifyingly dangerous and not to be attempted unless absolutely necessary.

Of course, once you knew you had become "chosen," a Contract Circle was an essential beginning step to life with a demon. Basically, the summoner stood within the Security Circle with their Binding Box, and then the demon was raised within the Entrapment Star. The Connection Channel that existed between the two diagrams allowed for the physical touch with the demon. It was during that linking that the human discovered why they were chosen and what their demon demanded of them in return for the use of their supernatural powers.

It was a ritual that normally took several weeks to perfect.

"Annabelle, are you sure that's right?" I pointed to one of the symbols. It just looked off.

"It has to be like that," she said, as she stood and brushed the white chalk from her hands against her black leggings. "In the original text by Slagenoffen, if you use a single hex scratch, then you open up one Connection Channel, right?" She opened the largest of the texts that were scattered about the floor to show me and pointed at the open page. "But I don't have a single demon. If I change that mark to a Sumerian infinity symbol, then the number of connection points will blossom from the Entrapment Star in correlation with the number of demons within my horde."

"Oh, I see." I half understood what she said. I was more impressed that she had absorbed as much knowledge as she had.

Ning giggled. Her etchings not only looked perfect, they were better organized and clearer than the examples in the textbooks.

Isaiah was struggling. "I can't draw this stuff for shit!" He threw his chalk in frustration.

Annabelle walked over and spun around slowly, inspecting the entire circle. "I don't know. Looks okay to me..." She continued to peruse Isaiah's work. "Oh, except that there." She pointed towards one end. "One of your protection sigils has a tail going outside of the outer ring. You can't ever do that. The outer ring is always intact, and nothing can ever break it, otherwise—"

"Yeah, I know." Isaiah looked frustrated. "It'll eat me."

"If you're lucky." Annabelle cocked an eyebrow and frowned at Isaiah as she spoke. "Mine keep telling me that's the last thing they're going to do. You don't want to know what else they'd like to do if I gave them the opportunity. Play with me has very different connotations where they're concerned."

A wave of cold air crept down between my shoulder blades at hearing that. The hair on my arms rose too.

Damn demons.

"Okay, well that's enough of that. Shall we erase these and start again tomorrow? It's already past dinner," I said.

"No, I think it's a good time to put these to use." A cold familiar voice said from all around us.

The large doors on the far side of the hangar swung open, and in walked Tonka with her crew, the swirling black mist heavy behind them. They were a gruesome sight. Miriam trailed behind them with her constant cohort of bodyguards.

"Fuck," I whispered. "Fuck, shit, fuck, shit."

"Careful, Mr. Martin. We've discussed your language before," Tonka warned.

Miriam frowned as well.

"I'd like another day with them, *please.*" There was a tight knot forming in the center of my stomach. It was too early. Isaiah needed more time.

"Nonsense. If Annabelle can already figure out substitutions, it sounds like they're ready." Tonka nodded her head towards the girl. "And we must return home soon. Our business elsewhere involved capturing a rogue entity, which we have contained, but containment only lasts so long."

"Thank you for leaving the texts, Mistress Tonka," Annabelle said and gave a short curtsy.

"You're welcome. I see you put them to good use. And I see you wear the medallion I gave you. I'm pleased. Now, let's start. Bogdan, I want you behind Ning. Dieter, you'll be in charge of Isaiah, and Siren and I will supervise Annabelle. Places everyone. Let's start."

Isaiah glanced at me with dread and terror. Dieter was leering at Isaiah, and it took everything in me not to walk over and punch him in the head.

"Just give me a minute," I said shortly to Tonka, then waved the kids over to me and whispered, "Okay, we knew this was coming, right? I know we've only just started these, but everyone has to do this spell. If everyone has to do it, it can't be that hard, right? You guys can do this."

"I wish I had one more time." Isaiah grimaced. I squeezed his taut shoulder in an attempt to give him a little comfort.

"I do too. But I'm going to be right here, and if anyone has any issues, I'll throw up as much of a barrier as I can to protect you from *them*." My hand was still on Isaiah's shoulder and I gave him a couple of pats—more assurance. What I wanted was to hug him tight and tell him everything would be okay. But I wasn't sure of that, and Miriam was glaring at us. Last thing I wanted her to know was that anything had happened between Isaiah and me.

But Miriam couldn't do anything about a group hug, so I brought them all in towards me, and for the briefest of moments, I hoped they felt better. "Let's do this."

Ning, Isaiah, and Annabelle walked over to each of their Contract Circles and stood in the middle of them. Isaiah looked like he was going to throw up.

"Deep breaths, buddy. You can do this," I said, trying to encourage him.

He gave me a curt nod and stepped into his Security Circle. He was about to settle himself when he remembered what Annabelle had told him. He bolted out, found the one spot where the outer ring had been breached and wiped that away. He inspected his circle one more time, double-checking everything. Finally, he returned to the center.

"All right now. Begin," Tonka commanded.

Ning bent over and opened her Binding Box, pulling out several items required for the summoning. Her hand shook a little, but she continued.

Annabelle stood very still with her eyes closed, while Isaiah stared at me with saucer eyes.

I nodded at him and mouthed "You can do this" to encourage him.

He got to work.

There were only three things needed for this particular spell. A piece of chalk, a needle, and an herb mixture of shaved rowan wood, Acacia pods, and dried St. John's wort. When sprinkled at the summoner's feet, the three are supposed to protect the spellcaster and anchor the soul to the body.

The chalk was for the final inner circle and pentagram; once those were drawn, the last step was the needle.

A pinprick for a single drop of blood. Just the mere mention of blood made me think of Shawna. I needed this to go okay, so we could get the hell out of here to find her.

It also made me wonder...blood in an Arcane ritual, regardless of the amount, wasn't much of a departure from Sanguimancy.

Ning jabbed herself and squeezed out a single droplet. The second it hit the ground, the etchings illuminated until they glowed a bright blue-white.

Isaiah fumbled with the pinprick but eventually got it.

I tensed up.

This was it.

A darting line shot out towards the Entrapment Star, glowing and building in brightness.

Once the outer edges of the Entrapment Star glyphs had sprung to life, a writhing mist formed in the center and grew vertically. From within the undulating smoke, solid forms were appearing.

Except for Annabelle's cast—things there were going a little different. The one Entrapment Star split and became two, and then each of those split again, becoming four, and then once again, until there were eight stars surrounding her circle.

All of Tonka's crew stood at the ready behind their charges.

Behind Annabelle, Siren took watch over one side, Tonka supervised the other. Based on the look in their eyes, I wasn't entirely convinced they had the capacity to handle four demons each. And then it dawned on me— Annabelle had eight creatures living within her, taunting her with visuals, whispering unseen pieces of knowledge to her, and begging to be let out. I shook my head.

From within Ning's trap, the Yuki-onna emerged. The swirling grey smoke had turned crystal white, revealing the snow woman in all her glory. She was beautiful, with long flowing frosted silks billowing out from her body and snow-white hair. Her skin was dappled white and grey, but her eyes and lips were blood red. The snow demon lunged forward, extending her hand towards the Connection Channel, and Ning mimicked the action from within her Security Circle.

Ning pushed her foot forward, erasing a small section of the circle, opening the channel. The minute that seal was broken, a burst of wind encircled her, whipping her hair around as snow began to fall, but only within the column of her sphere. You could see a thin white line, a string of connection between the snow demon and Ning.

Ning's head whipped back, and she screamed as she rose off her feet. Her chest heaved with heavy breaths. Her outstretched arm became bio-illuminated. I would have sworn I could see her skeleton.

Ning arched her back, and just as suddenly, the glowing light was gone, as was her demon. She crumpled to the floor, sobbing uncontrollably.

Isaiah looked terrified as the Asmodeus demon was almost done forming, and it was huge. A low growl permeated the room, shaking everything.

"Oh shit," Isaiah said, his eyes expanding.

From beside me, I caught a flash of white. *Cody swirled into being.* He was laughing his ass off.

I didn't have time to deal with him or his nonsense.

Isaiah howled in pain as he was lifted off his feet and bent backwards, his arm outstretched towards the massive horned fiend. The flesh on his arm split open and blood poured from the open wound.

The demon revealed its face and licked its lips with a black forked tongue. Its heavy brow and flat nose was reminiscent of a bull. Ice blue eyes locked onto Isaiah, and then it scoped the room and found me. The tongue flickered out again, tasting the air like a snake, before it threw its head back and bayed. The noise made me wince, and Isaiah screamed again in pain.

Gazing at the face of the demon made my skin crawl, like it was covered in inchworms. Every muscle in my body clenched and tightened. I wanted to protect Isaiah. I took two steps towards him, but Dieter put his arm out and stopped me.

And just like that, it was over and Isaiah was passed out inside his chalked-out circle.

The sight unfolding before Tonka and Siren was more than all the horror movies I've ever seen combined.

Columns of smoke rose from the centers of each of the Entrapment Stars and formed writhing and seething whirlwinds within the eight symbols.

Annabelle looked very small standing in the center. Tears streamed down her face, and her chest was heaving with sobs as her tiny foot inched forward slowly to erase the chalk line that would open the Connection Channel.

The first form to show itself was a half-rotted corpse, more skeleton than anything, with long flowing black robes. One demon was tentacles and goo, while another star held a towering stretched humanoid that was hidden by a thin shroud.

The chalk line was gone, and a swirl of air rotated counterclockwise within the security of Annabelle's inner circle. Dark threads from each of her demons wound their way towards the one opening, the demons' first touch at the tiny girl.

Cold sweat slicked my back and the heavy stench of rot and decay filled the air around us. Annabelle was bent violently backward until her head almost touched the floor, and then she slowly lifted off the ground. The winds took her and she spun slowly. The threads from eight demons had made their way through the Connection Channel and were whipping like thin nematode worms, little parasites looking for purchase.

They elongated and stretched, stretching towards Annabelle, until one of them came into contact with her arm. Within the inhale of a single breath, the filaments wrapped around any part of Annabelle they touched first.

The light in the hangar, which was dim at best, blinked out.

I could hear whispers. The dead were sneaking up from the shadows while their decayed tongues told secrets, scratchy little voices with malicious ideas and twisted thoughts. A wail sounded within the hangar. The screech of a trapped soul, a banshee announcing its presence to the living. That was usually an omen; the oncoming death of a condemned soul.

I heard the skittering of sharp claws pass me. The glyph marks were the only source of light. Their glow throbbed, revealing Annabelle dangling twenty feet in the air, floating, arms outstretched, with the demon threads of connection wrapped around her like a cocoon. She was mouthing words, but no sound was coming from her, and her eyes had gone milky again. And then, the skin on her face shrunk and desiccated. Long black veins ran across the surface of her skin as her eyes sank into her skull.

I glanced at Tonka. She looked concerned.

Annabelle was rotting.

Her skin was flaking, and her ear dropped off.

"This should not be happening, mistress," Siren said loud enough for me to hear.

I took another few steps towards my students. Ning and Isaiah had survived, being tended to by Tonka's coven mates, but my Annabelle was in trouble. I headed towards her.

Tonka's head whipped around at me and she hissed, "Stay back!"

Annabelle screamed.

It was the highest-pitched and longest scream I had ever heard.

She dropped the twenty feet and crumpled to the floor.

The hangar descended into blackness again.

A pounding was coming from the other end of the hangar, and as soon as the dim light returned, the hangar doors burst open and Miriam's henchmen flooded into the arena.

I ran out to collect the kids, but Tonka and Siren were already attending to Annabelle, trying to force water down her throat. Isaiah was closest to me, and as soon as I got within his proximity, he grabbed me and clutched tight. He was drenched in sweat and shaking uncontrollably. Dieter had wrapped his arm with bandages.

"Are you okay? What do you need me to do?" I asked.

"Just don't move. Oh my god, don't ever make me do that again."

"We have to get Ning. Can you come with me?" We shuffled closer to Ning's circle where she lay still on the ground, but the minute I got close enough, I could tell something wasn't right. Bogdan was standing over her, but he looked confused.

Ning was shaking and shivering, and she was covered in a layer of frost. I bent over to pick her up, but as soon as my hand touched her, my skin darkened with frostbite. The ground beneath us had formed a layer of ice. Ning swung her head towards me.

One lock of her jet hair had turned snow white, just like her Yuki-onna, but it was her face that shocked me the most.

Half of it was covered in crystals and resembled more of the snow woman than Ning. Her one eye was crystal white but rimmed red with blood.

"Chris!" I yelled. He came running from the sidelines, Camila not far behind.

"What?"

"Can you help Ning?" I pointed.

"I can try." Chris closed his eyes and banged his fists together, and as he did, sparks flew. He continued until the embers within his skin became apparent, little burning fires erupted beneath the surface of his skin.

He reached out and grabbed Ning, holding her close as she fought him. A tornado of fire erupted and swirled around the two of them, and then within seconds, it was gone, and Chris was holding onto Ning, the frost gone. But she was like Isaiah, completely soaked and shivering. The lock of hair still ice white, although her face was back to the Ning we'd all grown to know. Her radiant smile, however, was gone.

She staggered over to Isaiah and me with Chris's help.

"Are you okay?"

She nodded.

Miriam stormed over, glaring at me and Tonka. "You should have briefed me on what was going to happen. Did you see those things? Oh my heavens." She was shaking. "I should have been placed behind protective walls, and so should have my staff. God only knows what could have happened if one of those things had broken free! You endangered our lives!"

"This was necessary, Miriam. You were never in any danger. Only the caster. Each Arcane has gone through the same ritual, and it is a stepping stone in developing a relationship with one's demon. I forced his hand because I needed to see that these students could handle the beasts within." Tonka turned towards me. "You've done well with these young ones. No one died. Although it was close." Tonka reached behind her to grab Annabelle's shoulder and brought her forward.

Annabelle was shell-shocked.

"Tell them," Tonka demanded.

"Tell us what?" Miriam spat out from gritted teeth.

"Each of them know what their entities require. Tell them."

Ning started, "She wants blood. Regular feedings or she'll rip me apart and take my own. She also wants me to find her body. She's somewhere in the Kamikochi mountains."

"Blood?" I said.

"Yes." Ning looked disgusted.

"That is not all that unusual, my dear. Be thankful. One girl I know who had a Yuki-onna was made to eat the flesh of her victims," Tonka said.

We all shuddered.

"Tell them, child." Tonka ushered Annabelle forward.

She whispered so quietly I couldn't hear a word.

"Louder. Own this, Annabelle. Own it and be strong, or they *will* consume you."

"They want more," she said, slightly louder, her bottom lip quivering as her eyes filled up with tears.

"What do you mean, more?" Miriam said indignantly.

"Her horde wants exactly that. To become more," Tonka explained. "They wish to grow in size. Annabelle will have to feed willing souls to her horde and grow the Legion within her."

"I can't deal with more."

"Holy shit," Camila said.

"All right, this can't get any worse. Isaiah? What happened? We need to get your arm stitched up as well," I said.

"You're not gonna like this," he said while shivering and clattering his teeth.

"I already don't like any of this, damn demons." I gripped his shoulder and gave Tonka a dirty look, like this was all her fault. After realizing what I'd said, I turned my frown away from her. The glare she had thrown my way told me she wasn't impressed. "It's okay." I hugged Isaiah to me. "Tell us. What happened?"

"You happened."

"What do you mean?" I asked.

"It wants you," Isaiah said. The fear in his eyes was unmistakable.

"I don't understand," I said.

"It *wants* you," Isaiah said and gave me a look that told me exactly what his demon wanted.

If I wanted Isaiah to be able to keep his demon happy, I was going to have to let his demon play with me. I had to submit to it.

No fucking way I'm being some demon's chew toy.

Twenty-Five: Detention, Again

"MY OFFICE, NOW!" Miriam shouted, then spun and strode off, her high heels *clicking* their way through the hangar.

I looked at Isaiah, my eyes wide. "What do you mean, it wants me?"

"He wants you," Isaiah said, and his face burned a rather unhealthy shade of red. "Just go. I'll explain it later."

"Oh for fuck's sake." I rolled my eyes.

Tonka looked at me with a lifted eyebrow, judging.

"What?" I asked shortly.

She said nothing but turned and glided off in Miriam's direction.

"Alright then. Listen," I said, pulling the kids together, beckoning them to come closer with a wave of my hand. "Chris and Camila, I want you to watch over these three. Clean clothes, warm blankets, and happy thoughts. No one is to be separated tonight. Got it? I'll be back as soon as this is over."

They all nodded and agreed. Ning and Annabelle were visibly upset. Isaiah wouldn't look me in the eye. I was pretty sure I had a damn good idea what his demon wanted, and the thought of it made my skin crawl. But then, I also knew my choices in the matter would be limited. Isaiah was going to have to fulfil his contract with the beast, and that sounded like it was going to include me. If I wanted Isaiah...

I left the hangar and the students to themselves, following the wispy trails of black demon mist that wafted off of Tonka. The lithe woman was quick on her feet, and by the time I caught up to her and Miriam, I was almost out of breath.

"Is this necessary?" I huffed out once I finally caught up. "The kids had to go through this. Right, Tonka?" I gaped at her, my eyebrows raised as far as they could go, pleading to her with a help-me-out-here kind of look.

Miriam didn't say anything as she continued the long march towards her office. The deafening silence and the extended walk were meant to foster feelings of distress and shame. Damn her. It had worked. By the time we arrived at her luxuriously decorated domain where she toiled all day creating evil plots and schemes, the knot in my stomach was tight enough to make me want to hurl.

"Sit down," Miriam barked and pointed.

I grabbed the chair and sat, then realized Tonka was standing behind me. I chanced a glance to find her with arms folded across her chest, defying the command. Her focus was on Miriam, and the energy from that glower was nothing short of frightening. She reminded me of Morticia Adams, but Tonka had the death glare mastered well beyond what the TV character had ever managed. Even Miriam squirmed a little waiting for the woman to have a seat.

She finally gave up. "Fine, stand." Miriam then rustled a stack of papers on her desk, pulled out a single sheet, and flipped it towards me.

"What new hell is this?" I asked as I perused the paper filled with a bunch of lines, dates, and numbers.

"It's the project timeline and budget. Concepts that may be beyond your comprehension. You'll notice the large negative numbers in red. Those are the investors that have pulled out. I have not been able to secure any other financiers. I may be forced to terminate this even earlier than I had last discussed with you. I can't afford it, James. Even Major Harris is now wavering on their investment in Chris."

"What?" My voice cracked as I said it.

"What are you referring to?" Tonka questioned, her thick accent seemed harsher than normal.

Shifting in my seat so I could see the Bulgarian coven leader, I explained to her, "The CMRD will euthanize the kids if they can't get everything under control before their final tests. Or, in our case, if they can't make money off of us."

Tonka snatched the piece of paper out of my hands and perused the ledger, then refocused her stare on Miriam. "This is how you treat the rarest gifts in your country? This is barbaric. Let me make one thing very clear to you. You called us for help. We don't travel halfway across the hemisphere to offer assistance only to have you kill one of our own."

"We'll do as we please with them. These are our people, and they are not safe to be left in the general population." Miriam's usual rant fell from her pursed lips. The red lipstick she wore stained the little wrinkles and creases that furrowed the area around her mouth. The colour made her appear angrier and madder than normal.

Tonka floated closer to Miriam's desk. I swear, she didn't move her feet, she simply slithered forward as her dark presence expanded and filled the room. "No, let me make this very clear to you, madam. If you harm

Annabelle in any way, you will answer to me. I will come for her when I am ready. She requires tutelage, but there are preparations and rituals that need to be completed in order to accommodate her horde. When I return, she will be here, she will be of sound mind and body, and she will wear a smile on her face. Is that understood?" Tonka pressed a single finger onto the giant wooden desk's lacquered surface.

Veins of black rot ran across the surface of the desk and a loud *crack* sounded throughout the room.

The desktop split down the middle.

"You don't scare me, woman." Miriam's fists came down onto her desk. "And how *dare* you threaten me." Miriam stood as she spoke.

"You are mistaken, madam. I am not threatening you." Tonka's darkness intensified. They were squaring off. "I am simply telling you an unalterable truth. Annabelle will be left for me to claim when I am ready for her. Failure to ensure this will be your demise." Pallid demon arms unfolded from behind Tonka's back. The skin covering them hung loosely, as if the flesh would fall from the bone at a moment's notice. Clawed hands tipped with black talons made ominous gestures towards Miriam. The darkness behind Tonka deepened and the shadows in the office ran across the floor and up the wall.

Tiny whispers from hundreds of voices sounded from within the depths of her gloom. Shivers ran down my spine.

"Get out," Miriam yelled and pointed towards her office door.

"Don't test me, woman. You will not win," Tonka said. She flung out an arm, dragging her cloak upward and hiding her face. As before, the material folded into itself, and within a flutter of fabric, like a flag waving on a windy day, she was gone.

Miriam sat back down in her chair and grabbed her tablet.

She pushed the device towards me. "Turn it on. Damn things confound me." I search for the power button on the side of the tablet and pressed it. Miriam froze in her seat. She never moved, but her gaze burned hellfire holes through my face. A video clip played. But the image was full of static and blurred. Didn't matter, though, I knew exactly what it was. It was my bedroom.

It was Isaiah and me in bed together, naked. He was straddling me and we were both laughing.

My face flushed as a wave of heat started at the base of my neck and rushed towards the top of my head. I wasn't sure if I was embarrassed or angrier than Chris's fire wolf.

"What the fuck is this? You're filming me? You have footage of me taking a shit too?" I was gripping the tablet so tight, my fingers were white.

"I told you, the CMRD will not tolerate this behaviour!" Miriam lashed out.

"What behaviour is that?" I questioned her, my voice raw with anger.

"Let's start with you sleeping with one of your students. You don't see anything inappropriate about that?"

"They are all adults, Miriam. They get to make choices about their lives as much as I do."

"Not while you're in my employ. I told you last time we spoke, our benefactors are watching everything. What do you think happened when they saw this? I had to keep everything open and available to them.

"James, we have investors who will not tolerate these kinds of actions. Personally, I don't care who you sleep with *on your own time,* but you are not on your own time right now. Don't think I didn't know, James. About Cody? Don't think I haven't had an idea about *who* you were. But I put that aside. You were so talented. You had so much promise!

"You could have done great things with these...these..." She couldn't find the word to describe the kids. What was she trying to say? Monsters?

I interrupted her before she said anything else. "You *knew?*" I was vibrating. "You knew about Cody, and yet you still made me watch as you killed him?"

"He wasn't safe—" She started in on the rhetoric, but I cut her short.

"My choice of who I sleep with is none of your damn business. Who I have sex with or, in this case, share a bed with is none of your goddamn business. You fucking bigot." I got up to leave.

"It's not me, James. Our investors—"

"Bullshit!" I spun around to face her, spit flying from my mouth as I yelled. "Veiled homophobia. *'I don't care, but what about what the others might think.'*" I did my best Miriam impersonation, complete with pursed lips.

Miriam's lips tightened even further. She was shaking she was so mad.

"My facility. My students. My goddamn rules. And you will not dictate anything around here. As of right now, you are costing me money." She grabbed the ledger and scribbled words on it, then flung the paper towards me.

Final Testing Date: December 15

The shortened three-month date had been obliterated with Miriam's vicious pen strokes. Miriam had just reduced our time to fourteen days.

Two fucking weeks.

"You hateful bitch. You will get what you deserve, Miriam, because not only will I have these kids ready, but I'm gonna make sure that I hunt you down after the whole thing is over. I will pull you down along with every brick of this institution."

"You and your kind. You're all sick, just like my ex-husband. You're all just filthy bastards!" she yelled.

I stopped for a second. What the hell had Miriam just exposed?

"So, which is it, Miriam? Your ex was gifted? Or did you walked in on him having a tryst with some handsome young guy? Is that why you're always so bitchy? Why you hate us so much? Because you're such a cold bag you didn't stand a chance in satisfying your spouse? Did he have to turn to men to get his rocks off?"

"Get out!" she screamed, picked up the stapler from her desk, and flung it at me.

Stupid woman should have known better.

I held up my hand, and instantly, a telekinetic barrier formed causing the stapler to bounce off my shield and fly backwards. There was a dull *thud* as it smacked her in the forehead.

She fell back into her chair, grasping her head in her hands. Blood trickled from in between her fingers where she clasped the wound.

"Get out," she whispered through laboured breaths.

"Gladly. Bitch." I turned and left the office, slamming the door on the way out.

The amount of damage I caused on the way back to my own apartment was significant. No escort could come anywhere close to me as anger fed spherical force fields flung out randomly, thrashing the hallways of the CMRD.

The walls looked like a car after a hailstorm. But nothing collapsed, and no breaches were made.

It's going to be damn near impossible to get out of here.

Twenty-Six: Fire Drill

ONCE I FOUND my apartment within the CMRD, I passed straight through it and strutted out to the hangar to fetch everyone. My mind was whirring, and all my plans for teaching the kids with a slow and steady pace flew right out the window.

We didn't have time, and there was no way I was going to be able to teach them what they needed to know to pass Miriam's tests. And, at this point, I was pretty sure Miriam would expect them to pass skill levels that even I couldn't attain. We had two weeks. In that short period, we were going to have to concentrate on how to break out, and learn any spell we needed to get out of this hell hole of a prison.

The group had collected inside Ning's cube, which made sense as hers was the cleanest and nicest, and complete with a TV—although it wasn't turned on. Annabelle was studying, Ning was practicing creating little snowballs, while Chris was attempting to sublimate them. Isaiah was scribbling things into his Book of Ways, and Camila was staring off into thin air.

I worry about you, girl.

"Okay, how are we all doing?" I asked them while leaning up against the outside frame of the cube, trying desperately to mask the inner rage that was still making my blood boil, even after having walked around the CMRD for so long.

Camila looked right at me. "Better than you. What's going on?"

"That obvious, huh?" I snorted in response to her. Clearly my mask wasn't that effective.

Isaiah put his pencil down, stood up, took the couple of steps over to me, and took my hand. "What happened?"

All of them were staring at me with questioning gazes. They knew Miriam was a monster, but they had no idea how much of one.

Cody's white smoke filled the corner of the room as he slowly formed his putrefied corpse. Tattered white clothes and flesh hung from his frame. He was decaying more and more. Then he pointed at all of us and started laughing.

"I swear if I could kill him again, I would," I whispered under my breath and sneered at him.

"You know, we could get rid of him." Annabelle batted her long black eyelashes at me with a slight of a grin.

"What do you mean?" I said.

"He's a ghost, right? We all see him, and frankly, he's angry and annoying. We could exorcise him and then you'd be free of him. We would all be free of him." Annabelle replicated my sneer as she glared at the apparition. She had no love for Cody either.

"We can do that?" I asked.

"We can. Well, I can." She lifted one eyebrow and glared at me, which reminded me of Tonka, as she held up a book and pointed to it. "There's a ceremony in here we could follow."

"You know, there was a time when Cody was just like all of you," I said. Suddenly, I wasn't sure how I felt about exorcising him.

Cody's hand gripped my shoulder, sending a trickle of ice down my spine, as his cold breath blew on my neck. "You need me. You can't get rid of me. You said you loved me! How could you ever lose me? Remember what you said? You promised to protect me."

I shuddered as I closed my eyes, remembering back to when Cody and his fellow classmates occupied a similar space within the CMRD. Annabelle's tiny hand pressed itself against my chest in an attempt to comfort me. Isaiah gripped my hand tighter—he hadn't let go.

"Mr. Martin, it's okay. We all hear the lies and confusion he murmurs to you. It's not really Cody, you know." She removed her hand from my chest as she continued. "Once they get stuck in the spirit realm, they get a little twisted. Especially if they're holding on to anger, and clearly, Cody is doing exactly that. He's rotting, and he's getting worse every time we see him. Spirits don't rot, Mr. Martin. The anger is eating Cody up. If we exorcise him, hopefully he'll move on. He'll go to the next place where the anger won't continue to destroy him, or us." Annabelle tried to calm me. That was a switch.

I had to think about that for a minute. It sounded like a good idea.

"Okay, tell you what. I'll think on the Cody thing. He's the least of our problems right now." I spun around and looked at the decomposing ghost. "Leave. You're not welcome."

Cody snarled at me but slowly dissipated. A faint *hiss* sounded as the white smoke evaporated with little trails of vapour that ascended into nothingness.

"Okay, tell us what happened with the old bitch." Chris piped up after the last vestiges of Cody had left the room. I had to snicker at what he called her. Old bitch was so appropriate.

"She was angry, very angry. I don't think she's particularly happy that Ning, Isaiah, and Annabelle sealed the contracts with their demons. Which, by the way, I'm all super proud of you for getting to that step. I knew you all could do it."

"James, what did she say?" Isaiah prompted me.

I turned to look at him. My stomach flipped a little. If at one point I had been unsure about what I wanted to do about Isaiah, Miriam solidified my gut instinct. Spending more time with him was what I wanted to do, and because of her bigotry and hatred, I wasn't a hundred percent sure that was going to happen. I wanted there to be an "us," and evidently that extended to his demon as well? Not sure what that meant, but every time I looked at his light brown eyes that had just a touch of sadness to them, I wanted to hold him. I wanted to tell him everything would be okay. "Miriam is an angry person. She showed me a video," I started while looking at Isaiah and then glanced back at the other four, my cheeks flushed as I continued, my gaze drawn back to my bearded magician. "It was the two of us when you slept in my bed the other night. *They* were watching." I pointed my finger up towards the ceiling.

Isaiah studied me, and a smile spread across his face. He looked over at his fellow classmates, and then suddenly, he laughed. "And? So what?"

"So what? Well, let me tell you, Miriam was purple she was so angry."

"Angry about what?"

"That I would be so inappropriate with one of my students," I said, a little sheepishly. After all, she wasn't completely wrong. Bedding down with Isaiah, given that I was supposed to be mentoring him, wasn't exactly the most professional move.

"I'm not sixteen. And we're so close in age that if we'd met outside of these circumstances—you can bet your sweet ass I would have been all after you. My god, what's her fucking problem? I'm an adult. I'm possessed by an Asmodeus demon for Christ's sake. Do you know what they are famous for?"

I shook my head, I had no idea.

"They're ancient Babylonian demons who would create chaos and amass power and wealth by controlling the relationships between people. Sexual relations. They are like the highest form of succubus or incubus.

They thrive on changing or altering possible outcomes in people's lives by influencing probabilities. They create connections, building new ones or inserting untold strife and unrest within existing relationships. They control lust. Some can even hypnotize people and make them do whatever they want. The more powerful ones have been known to sway entire armies.

"I have that creature residing inside of me, and *she* has the nerve to tell me who I can and cannot sleep with? Fuck her." Isaiah's cheeks were redder than normal, and a shadow of black cast over his eyes. Little sparks of blue flickered in his irises. The demon within him was lurking.

"Listen, calm down. She clearly has her own personal history with gay guys, and seeing the two of us didn't sit well with her. She compared me to her 'bastard' of an ex-husband. That tells me we're stirring up bad things for her."

"How does that relate to us? Oh, right it doesn't." Isaiah was mad. I wanted to comfort him, allay his anger. I wanted to run my fingers through his beard and the hair on his chest, to either soothe away his disgust or stoke those powerful energies into more productive emotions.

"It doesn't matter what's right or what should be. Right now, Miriam is pissed and she's taking it out on us." I stopped. All five of them were once again glued to my every word. It felt so weird to be back in this role as teacher. It wasn't a position I wanted. I didn't want them relying on me. Honestly, I wasn't sure I could save them. I wasn't convinced that we would be able to break out of this fortress. Miriam had resources. She had weapons. What did we have? Five very young adults who didn't have a handle on themselves. Our chances of success were slight. But I damn well was gonna try.

"Well, fuck her," Isaiah said. His defiance made me proud. I pulled him in and gave him a hug. I couldn't help myself.

"She's changed the date," I said while gripping him, as if holding him close would ensure his rage wouldn't bubble over. Truth was, I should have had a hold on Chris.

"What the hell do you mean?" Chris said. The wave of heat that surged through Ning's room was tangible.

"Easy, Chris."

"No. What the hell, man?" Another wave.

I was attempting to untangle myself from Isaiah and get myself over to Chris, when one of the stuffed animals on Ning's bed started to smoulder.

"Isaiah, let go. Ning, freeze that thing!" I pointed to her teddy bear.

"Oh my god!" She ran over and threw her arms out, but all that succeeded in doing was throwing a layer of ice over everything.

Chris was still stewing. Under his skin, his veins glowed bright like little streams of lava.

"What did she do?" Chris said between gritted teeth.

I reached out to grab Chris's shoulder and started pushing relaxing thoughts into his body, but it wasn't taking.

"She upped it again, didn't she?" Camila said. "She just wants to kill us."

"Yes, she did. We only have two weeks," I responded.

Despite my touch, Chris exploded, literally, into a stream of black smoke. It was the weirdest sensation to touch the tense shoulder muscles, heat radiating from them, and then in a blink of an eye, steam and billowing vapours waft through my fingers.

The column of black smoke erupted with embers and flames, and then as fast as the explosion occurred, the entire column solidified, but instead of Chris, it was the black wolf. His dark eyes were lined with orange. The interior of his nose huffed out soot and sparks. His jaw opened and a long tongue licked its muzzle. The saliva that dripped out steamed as it hit the ground.

"Oh shit," Annabelle said.

"Everyone huddle in close," I said.

They all cautiously crowded in around me as I pushed out one of my silver shimmering force fields, until I realized that Camila was still standing on her own.

"Camila, come on. Slowly walk over here."

She dismissed me with an indifferent wave of her hand. "Phttb. I got this."

Oh dear god. Camila walked towards the wolf. It was snarling and smoke was rising from it. Little embers had dropped from its fur and fires would be erupting soon.

"Camila, please, come over here," I whispered to her, then turned around to see Ning standing behind me with her hand pressed over her eyes. "Ning, you're going to have to control the fires."

"I can't watch!" she said.

"I can try," Isaiah said.

I looked at him, momentarily confused, but then, Isaiah was everything. "Can you control water if we need you to?"

"Like I said, I'll try. That's not an element I've played much with."

"Oh man." We were screwed. Meanwhile, Camila was still advancing on the wolf as it crouched, getting itself into attack posture as she advanced.

"Camila! You're a Psyche. You should have some empathic abilities. Calm him down. Don't piss him off any more!"

"He's not going to calm down. He needs to be knocked the hell out," she said, and within a blink of an eye, there were six Camilas. Each one facing the wolf, encircling him and trapping the beast. Which didn't go unnoticed by the animal. Saliva foamed around its mouth. It snarled and snapped at the astral projections.

In a coordinated attack, the Camilas pounced, striking the wolf with round after round of telekinetic bursts.

She never ceased to amaze. I had seen Camila's Astrals grab physical objects and use them as weapons, which was rare enough, but now I was watching as each of her Astrals displayed magical abilities. I was flabbergasted. But, at the same time, six Astrals unleashing energy grenades onto one entity, a wolf that was otherwise known as her classmate, wasn't going to turn out well.

"Camila, what the hell? You're going to kill him!" I yelled over the snarling and yelping.

Little fires were erupting from the increasingly annoyed and trapped wolf, and in between Camila's attacks, it was launching fire bombs of its own. Of course, the Astrals took no notice of the physical flames. They weren't physical themselves, but Camila on the other hand was in danger.

A ring of flames had ignited, and it encircled Camila and her projections, but she was so glued to her task, she hadn't taken notice.

I turned to Isaiah. "Dude, now!"

"Okay." He scrunched his eyes tight, held his hands out, and within seconds, it was pouring rain, but only inside the protective shield I had wrapped around us, trying to create a barrier between us and the wolf.

"Isaiah, how about you do that outside the force field?"

"Ha! Oops." The ring of fire around Camila was now obscuring the fight. I couldn't see much and the crackle of the flames was getting louder. I heard more snapping and yelping and barking, but I was also hearing sounds of pain from Camila too.

This wasn't going well.

"Isaiah, any time now would be good."

"I'm trying."

The pouring rain inside the force field had been a bit of a deluge, but spread out in the space of the hangar, it was more of a light sprinkle. Still, things were getting wet, and the flames were now hissing with evaporating water, but it just wasn't enough.

Camila screamed.

"No!" Ning was visibly upset. She held her hands out towards the ongoing battle. Isaiah, Annabelle, and I watched as a rapidly forming ice sheet covered everything in front of Ning. Within seconds, a crystalline veneer had formed, freezing everything in its path. The fire was out as sparkling ice encased the floor, the wolf, Camila, and her Astrals.

That lasted a short breath before the Astrals disappeared and their ice cover disintegrated, collapsing into itself, sending a cascade of *tinkling* shards to the floor.

Except one.

One astral burst free of the frozen hold, and it looked pissed. It launched itself towards the ice enshrouded wolf and started pummelling it. Chunks of ice broke off and fell away. Within a few punches, the wolf was almost free of Ning's ice imprisonment.

Camila was still covered. If we didn't break her free from it quickly, she would suffocate.

"Oh shit," Isaiah said, as he took a step back.

"Oh no! I'm so sorry. I'm so sorry!" Ning sobbed.

Annabelle took a step forward. "Let me try."

She closed her eyes and stood deathly still.

From within her shadows, a hand emerged, dark skinned and clawed. It stretched forward, piercing the floor with its talon, and pulled the rest of the body forward. The misshapen form was human but twisted and bent in odd angles. It lifted its head from a neck that was too long. The only facial feature was a huge mouth. As it opened and exhaled, it blew out an ever-expanding cloud that looked like black sand.

Little swirls and whirlwinds twisted and spun as it inched towards Camila, the wolf, and the rogue Astral. A snakelike tendril wound up the wolf's leg, around its shoulder and neck growing until it wrapped over the snout and disappeared into the nostril.

The wolf's eyes closed as it collapsed. In a violent eruption, it exploded into a burst of smoke and then as quickly as the wolf disappeared, Chris was suddenly lying where the smoke collapsed into itself.

Chris was sound asleep. "We have to get Camila out of that ice!" I yelled towards the others, while letting my force field drop. With the wolf gone, there was no need for it any longer.

"This I can do," Isaiah replied.

Little arcs of electricity crackled in between his fingers, illuminating his hands. The sparks increased in ferocity with flashes of current running wild from his hands to his shoulders and then in arcs across his body and into the floor in front of him.

I did not have a good feeling about this.

Bolts, like lightning, shot out and hit the encased Camila, and that was all that was needed. The thin sheet of ice disintegrated.

Camila sucked in an audible lungful of air.

Annabelle's sleep demon angled itself in a rather inhuman way and blew out another stream of demon grit, which inched and writhed its way across the floor to Camila. Upon finding her leg, it swirled and climbed her body until the stream disappeared into her nose.

Camila's eyes rolled into the back of her head, and she collapsed onto the floor, completely unconscious.

Annabelle's demon disintegrated like water poured on a sandcastle and melted back into the shadows where it had come from.

Camila's remaining Astral was still hovering over the scene, taking it all in. And then it turned to glare at me. A sneer crawled across its face before it disappeared.

"Well that can't ever happen again. Deal?" I said, exhausted.

A crackle of electricity danced over Camila's face, jumping in erratic arcs across the floor, and disappeared inches away from my foot.

We're never going to pass these tests.

Twenty-Seven: Curriculum Planning

THE NEXT DAY turned out to be a complete waste. Chris was still asleep, exhausted from his rage-filled shapeshifting and subsequent Astral attack. Ning was emotionally distraught at having encased her classmates in ice, and Camila had once again sunk into a depressive state.

I sat at my kitchen table, papers scattered in front of me, and held my rather thought-heavy head in my hands.

I was sure I had discerned a pattern with Camila. A few days of normalcy, then a gradual ascent into braggadocios behaviour, followed by insane acts of magic that inevitably turned helter skelter, followed by a period when her gloomy and bleak emotions made it impossible to get out of bed.

I couldn't imagine how draining it would be to ride that constant roller coaster. I stretched out, popping a few vertebrae in my neck.

And then there was Chris, who wasn't much different. Little things would trigger his anger, and without a constant empathic connection to me, his rage would eventually spiral out of control, followed by a wolf-induced rampage, ultimately leading to a collapse into exhaustion.

Was that a pattern of behaviour for us? Were we all on our own versions of out-of-control roller coasters? Was Miriam actually protecting us from ourselves?

I sat there for several minutes contemplating my newly formed theory. My brain couldn't accept a possibility that Miriam was attempting to help us.

Chris needed therapy and ways to combat his rage—and I still didn't know why he incubated such energy. Camila needed to be on meds that would balance out the extremes and level them onto an even playing field. Neither of them was going to find that stuck in the CMRD. If anything, Miriam would continue to allow the high and low swings until Camila required institutionalization or euthanasia, and Chris...well, the military would have either fixed him or killed him, but it seemed that was no longer an option for him. Major Harris had revoked his interest.

I had had my doubts about his future forced enlistment. In my opinion, Chris required a wide berth with a happy life. An environment that allowed him to temper his hotheadedness, not a structured regime where others made decisions for him. I didn't see that going down well. The fact that all the benefactors had pulled away, maybe this was a cue. The universe was telling us...get out.

It was time to plan our exit from this hell.

I let the kids do whatever they needed as a day to recoup while I planned and plotted. Thankfully, Camila and Chris being out of commission meant they'd be down for the count for several hours. Isaiah, Ning, and Annabelle were working together, studying from Tonka's reference materials.

I tapped my pencil a couple of times on the paper in front of me, trying to sketch out notes on things I remembered about the facility. Trying to pinpoint any holes in security I could remember or glaring weaknesses. I wasn't having much luck.

There was a knock on the wall behind me.

I swivelled in my chair to see Isaiah standing there, with a lopsided grin on his face, dressed in his usual tank top and loose-fitting jeans with a pair of old worn sneakers. His baseball cap was on backwards and dammit if he didn't look like the cutest thing I'd seen, ever.

"Hey. Want company?" he asked.

I sighed, trying to disengage from my thoughts, which wasn't hard while looking at him. "Sure. Come on in."

Isaiah sauntered over to where I sat and wrapped his furry muscled arms around me, hugging me while I sat in the chair. His rough beard nuzzled my neck as he slid his nose through the hair on the back of my head. Once he reached my earlobe, he gave it a little nibble and then squeezed me tight.

"Hmmm." I settled into his hug, melting slightly. "You know there are cameras in here and they're probably watching everything."

"Yup, probably. What's she gonna do? Burst through the door and haul me away? I doubt it. She knows I'd zap her ass into next week the moment I had the chance."

"Yeah, but then you'd obliterate everything around us, too, including me."

"Possibly." His index finger and thumb found one of my nipples and gave it a pinch. "Could be stimulating." He giggled.

I chuckled a little. His affection and closeness was getting me aroused. "I don't think electrocution would be considered fun."

"Well, how do you know if you've never tried?"

I shook my head. "Come on, sit down. Let's try something."

Isaiah slid his hand under my shirt and ran it over my chest. "Hmm, 'kay, let's start with trying this."

"You are a bad boy. Come on. We can play later. If the others are all occupied, let's get you practiced at toning down your overenthusiastic abilities."

"That's not nearly as much fun," he whispered into my ear.

With his arms still wrapped around me, I squirmed my way out from the chair and swivelled around to stand chest-to-chest with him.

He was a lot shorter than me. So our current position meant Isaiah was on tippy-toes and I was hunching down.

Still.

Sigh.

His light brown eyes were partially concealed by relaxed eyelids, but I could see random flecks of ice blue appearing and disappearing within his irises. His demon was in there and stirring around, probably instigating this behaviour. But damn, that gaze of his, looking at me with a come-hither look. How could I possibly rebut this flirting?

I gave him a kiss, my mouth soft but intent on tasting his lips, which were pliable and receiving. I held his furry face in both hands and gave him another quick peck.

"Come on. I promise, play time later—" I winked at him. "—*if* we can figure out how to obscure the cameras, but right now, let's at least get a little practice in? Please? I need assurance each of you can attempt to handle yourselves without being deadly."

"I don't know. As scary as yesterday was, we managed to work ourselves out of it. We're kinda good as a team. Except for that thing Annabelle conjured. Good god, that was hideous."

"Please?"

Isaiah cupped my crotch in his hands and gently squeezed. "Promise? Later?"

"You are incorrigible. Yes, later," I said, then swatted his hand away. "And you still need to tell me what your demon really wants."

He sighed but then grinned. "Okay." He took up residence in the chair on the opposite side of the table. "The demon wants you. I told you that."

"What does that even mean, though?" I had a good idea, but I wanted confirmation.

"Don't be dense. He *wants* you. As in naked, spread-eagle on the floor."

"Oh god, *seriously*?"

"Just one fuck. That's all he wants. He—or it? I'm still not sure yet." Isaiah screwed his face up while pondering the nature of the beast inside him.

"Are you freaking kidding me?"

"Nope. What's the problem?"

"Ah, well, let's see. I don't roll over for anyone? And I certainly don't let other species use me for their pleasure!"

"Oh, come on. How do you think it's going to happen? It'll just be me, except it won't really be me. Remember, it lives inside me. It can manifest itself for short periods of time outside of me, but only in its true form. Anything extended where it wants the sensory experience has to happen while in my body."

"Oh. Well, that's not so bad then. But why? What's the big deal about me?"

"Yeah, okay, that's the part you're not going to like. That kind of interaction creates a bond, a connection. One where you and I are sort of tethered together."

I thought about that for a moment. That wouldn't be so bad if Isaiah and I were on a path to a long-term commitment, but we hadn't even started a relationship yet, never mind discussing unyielding love between the two of us.

"Ah, okay. Well, that's something we can talk about *after* we get out of here."

Isaiah rolled his eyes to the side.

"What?"

"I don't know if he'll wait that long."

"You can tell him if he's going *there,* I have all the say. I'll determine when it gets to happen. Not the other way around."

"Okay. Sure." Isaiah nodded curtly, then skirted that particular topic. "What's the lesson?"

I didn't believe the agreement from him. I had a bad feeling his demon would be taking what it wanted, whenever it wanted.

"I need to figure out how to get us out of the hangar. Then we have to get past the outside walls of the CMRD. Once we're free and clear from that,

I'm hoping that you can teleport yourself and Ning, I can take Chris, and Camila can take Annabelle. This is assuming that Camila can master the ability. The last round with her didn't go so well." Everyone's abilities were a little different and manifested in subtly altered ways. For instance, my teleportation was more of a fast movement that could happen through solid material. Isaiah disappeared and then reappeared wherever he chose. Camila ended up stretching her Psyche abilities to make portals, but the few things we sent through the portals didn't always come out on the other side in one piece. Plus, she always created two portals, one several feet away, and the other directly in front of her, almost like a tunnel. I wasn't sure if sending people through that passageway was a good idea, yet.

"I might be able to take more than one person," Isaiah offered. "But why not just teleport directly out of here?"

"We have to get beyond the confines of the facility and be outside of any sigils or wards that would keep your demons in line and contained. I have a suspicion that those magical hex marks are going to keep you all within your designated areas. We need to find a way past them first. But then we also need to stand guard and keep away from any weapons that could take us down."

"She'd shoot to kill?"

"She'd stick a needle in your arm to kill you, so yes, she most certainly would. The quieter we can make our exit, the easier it will be."

"I think I'm better making a big bang," Isaiah said while waggling his eyebrows at me.

I glared at him, shook my head slightly, then continued. "I wonder if I'm thinking about this the wrong way then. I think what we need is a quiet escape."

"What do you mean?" Isaiah asked.

"We have been planning a blowout of an escape route, counting on resistance and a show of force, right?"

Isaiah arched his eyebrows in question.

"But if we sneak our way through the facility..." I stopped, thinking of the possibilities.

"How so?"

"Camila," I said.

Isaiah kept one eyebrow raised well into the hair that fell from underneath his backward baseball cap. "I'm not following."

"Camila's teleportation ability, not strong. But her ability to create illusions and fascinations are stellar! I've never tried to push her with those, but guaranteed, she can do them. What if she created one that looked like us? Maybe I'm teaching a class or we're all in our rooms sleeping, or…I don't know, pick a scenario. Then we can sneak out. It might take them a long time to figure out that we're not the illusion."

"Oh wow. Yeah, that's good." Isaiah looked impressed along with cute, furry, and sitting so close to me. "But we still have to get past the blast doors open at the end of the hangar, and without any noise. And there will be guards on the other side, right?" he stated. "Oh I know! How about Annabelle's sleep demon? I bet she could put the guards to bed."

"Nice. I like it. Now, we need to get you to open the doors," I said.

"Me?"

I nodded. "All the doors here will be electronically controlled and locked. So, a quick jolt, and…" I raised an eyebrow at him.

"Ah, gotcha. Except—"

I interrupted. "Except I need you to electrify the door, not fry the entire facility or us in the process. A focused effort, not a mass effect. Think you can do that?"

"No." Isaiah scrunched up his face with disappointment in his inability.

I laughed. "And that's why we need to practice. It took me years to get a hold of what I can do today. But there were a few talents that came quicker than others. You're apt with the lightning stuff. You should be able to control it pretty quick."

"You're just saying that to make me feel better."

'Yes and no. There's some truth to it. When you have to force yourself to use your abilities or control an ability you're not comfortable or familiar with, then it becomes harder to master. But you create sparks like nobody's business." I meant that in all the ways it could be taken, but I'd let him figure out the double entendre.

"You think so?" he said with a smile.

"I do. Now, let's see." I grabbed the pencil I'd used to jot down notes and placed it in the center of the white kitchen table. "Let's see you zap that. Move it."

"Should you put on a rubber suit or something?"

"Pretty sure that's not in my closet, and no. You got this. You can do it."

"Okay, can't say I didn't warn you."

Isaiah sat in the chair opposite me, with his stare locked on to the pencil and his right hand on top of the table, his index finger pointed towards it. His lips pressed together in a thin line of concentration.

A *zzzt* sparked from his pointed digit and arced over to a knuckle.

He shook his head, inhaled a deep breath, and tried again.

"Does that hurt?" I asked.

"Nope. Don't even feel it. Well, that's not entirely true. There's a little tingle, like when your foot goes to sleep, but that's about it, and it lasts for just a second. Now, shush...this is hard."

His tongue stuck out, just a little, and his forehead wrinkled as he concentrated. This time, an electric-blue lightning bolt zipped across the surface of the table and just missed the pencil. I jumped to the side to avoid getting hit.

"Hey! Not bad," I said. "Keep trying."

"This is impossible." He threw his hands up in the air.

"Drama much?" I snickered.

He gave me a dirty look.

"I never said it would be easy. Look, don't try so hard. You kinda look like you're constipated," I said jokingly.

"Ha-ha." His fake laugh was an attempt to insult me. It didn't work. He was still cute.

He closed his eyes and, instead of pointing his one finger, raised his hand just slightly above the table top and stretched all five fingers towards the pen.

"Just let it flow naturally. What did it feel like when it happened before? Were you excited? Did you feel angry? There's usually an emotional trigger, but not always. Sometimes, people think about a single thing and that's their on switch. You just have to find yours," I said, trying to encourage him.

He took a deep breath.

And exhaled.

Nothing.

We waited.

Nothing.

"See I can't just do this," he said in frustration, and then...

Five massive arcs of white-hot lightning shot across the table and through the pencil, melting it to the table's surface. Stray bolts arched around the kitchen, bouncing from the ceiling to floor. I threw my hands up in an attempt to protect myself, and if I had been smart and was thinking, I would have thrown up a shield. But it all happened so fast. One errant fork of screaming electricity scorched the air in front of me, bounded directly towards me, and as I could smell the odour of ozone—

All I remember was seeing bright white light. No shapes, no depth, just pure white. It was blinding, and then excruciating pain made every muscle in my body clench and spasm at the exact same moment. Violent, convulsive seizing shook me like a rag doll as hot fire ripped through my body, and it felt like everything it touched erupted in flames.

Then I gave in to the blackness.

Twenty-Eight: Pep Rally

"JAMES! JAMES, WAKE up. Oh shit, oh shit, oh shit!" I could hear Isaiah. It sounded like he was coming from the inside of a tin can, but even the dulled noise hurt my head. "I'm so sorry! Oh my god."

I groaned as hands grabbed me and hoisted me into a weird position. The tug and jostle on my body made muscles scream out in agony. I peeled an eye open to find Isaiah had cradled me in his lap, trying to help, but his attempt at a rescue was filled with panic.

Isaiah placed a hand on my shoulder and I screamed. Hot searing fire licked its way up my shoulder through the neck and buried itself deep into my brain.

"I'm sorry," he said again, retracting his hand. "I barely touched you."

"It's okay." I tried to comfort him. "I think that's where I got hit." I reached across my body and tugged at the sleeve of my shirt. The charred fabric smelled sweet, but chemical. I pushed it up, revealing the injury.

"No way!"

"What?"

"Look at your arm!" Isaiah pointed, his gaze unwavering and eyes wide.

I glanced down to my wounded arm only to see a strange mark, like a tattoo, but it was bright red and looked like a fern? Branches of a tree? I wasn't sure.

"Oh, that's a Lichtenberg figure!" Ning said from behind Isaiah.

"A who?" Isaiah asked as Annabelle seemed to float up beside him. Black mist wafted off behind her. She was going darker and more shadowy since the contract-sealing ceremony.

"A Lichtenberg figure. They're very rare. It happens when someone is struck by lightning, and considering the bright flash of light we saw, we know what happened. Explains the smell too." Ning wrinkled up her nose.

I still wasn't used to her shocking white lock of hair. It stood out amongst her jet hair and was quite striking, almost as much as my new tattoo.

"It won't last long. Hours or a few days. Eventually you'll heal," Ning said.

Isaiah grimaced.

"It's okay," I said to him, then held my other hand out, asking for help to get my knocked-over ass off the floor.

He slid both hands behind my back and gently pushed me up.

My shirtsleeve, electrified and shredded, fell off, revealing the full extent of the tree-branch mark.

"Oh my god." Isaiah hung his head.

"Okay, enough." I needed to go change my clothes. "Stop berating yourself, but this is exactly why you all need to practice. Huge blowouts are useful and have their place, but only when you're in control of them. The most effective magic are often the things you can make happen in the palm of your hand."

Isaiah's shoulders dropped and he shrunk into himself as I turned and walked towards my bedroom.

Ning and Annabelle discussed my new wound as I attempted to remove my shirt, as gingerly as possible, and pitched it into the garbage can in the corner of the room. Upon opening the closet, I found another shirt and started to put it on, but the rubbing material made me cringe in pain.

"Ai yai yai..." Well, that wasn't going to work. Then a thought occurred to me. I didn't like it, but I also didn't have much of a choice.

Dammit.

"Isaiah? Can you come here?" I called out.

He popped his head around the corner. I was standing in front of my mirror, shirtless, examining my new wound. "Um, I hate to ask this, but..."

"What? You can ask anything!" His face was still pulled into a knot of concern, and I would have bet he was willing to do anything to make up for nearly killing me. However, standing in front of Isaiah half naked was changing his expression to something verging on a leer.

"Stop that," I said, half smiling. "Can I borrow a tank top? Everything I have has sleeves and hurts."

"Ha!" Isaiah bellowed his boisterous laugh. "Of course you can, but they're gonna be a bit tight on you, Mr. Muscles."

"I'm not that big."

"You're bigger than I am. Just stay put. I'll go get you one."

He disappeared, and while he was gone, I inspected the mark further. It was actually quite beautiful. It made me think. Forked, branched, multiple end points.

I wonder.

It didn't take him long, and he returned with a bright-red tank, one I had seen him wear before. As he tossed me the flimsy shirt, I could smell him on it.

This is not going to make life any easier. That delicious intoxicating smell of Isaiah—leather and sweat.

When I pulled on Isaiah's shirt, I discovered he had quite correctly surmised how his clothes would fit on me. Although the tank was long enough, it wasn't nearly wide enough, and the material pulled across my chest. It did actually make me look like I'd lived in a gym, which couldn't have been further from the truth. Perhaps at one time, but certainly not now. I had to chuckle a little, because the reality was, Isaiah saw me as Mr. Muscles, as he put it, but I only saw how out of shape I'd become.

But for now, I didn't have much of a choice.

"You probably like this, don't you?" I asked, motioning to my torso like a game show model.

He just cocked an eyebrow and smiled mischievously. "Really? Of course I do."

"All right, out!" I shooed him from my bedroom and followed after him. The girls were still in my kitchen, inspecting the melted pencil.

I poked at the now-useless writing instrument. "Miriam will have a fit. She'll call it wanton destruction of facility property." I shook my head. "I'm sure she'd spank me if she could."

Annabelle giggled and Ning looked away, her cheeks reddening slightly.

Annabelle, who was always thinking, spoke up. "We've been talking about what you said about the small stuff being just as powerful." Annabelle wove her hand through the air just above her head. A trail of black demon mist formed behind her motion, but as she dropped her arm, the vapour hung for a moment and then began to swirl, wrapping itself around the four of us. It grew quickly until we were concealed and blanketed. "That should conceal us from any cameras and microphones picking up our conversations. For the last few days, Ning and I have been thinking. Each of us have different abilities that can help us get out of here."

I studied the writhing mist, almost hypnotized by it and completely amazed that Annabelle had successfully cast yet another dark spell. "Oh? And your proposal would be?"

"We think, as a group, we can get past just about any security guard, which will allow us to walk out of the CMRD and leave it behind."

My eyebrows rose.

"Well, I've been scheming about exactly that. I think it's time we put our heads together and come up with an escape route. There's just one catch," I said. "We can't kill. I wouldn't be able to live with myself if I knew that we caused a massacre on the way out of here, and furthermore, it would prove Miriam's point about you all being lethal and unfit to be part of the world."

Ning's one eye iced over as half of her face grew frost crystals. I had not seen this side of Ning before, but it was rather evident that her Yuki-onna was just beneath the surface. She pointed one finger and touched the top of my shoulder where the Lichtenberg mark started. As she grazed my skin, frost crystals formed, changing the mark from bright red to a dazzling electric blue.

It didn't hurt at all. In fact, it felt soothing as the coolness eased the constant burn from the electrical current that had writhed its way through my body.

"Small, controlled, but powerful," Ning said in a voice that wasn't completely her own. "And not necessarily deadly." Her one eye's pupil glowed an eerie red.

"We can do this. We just need to get a little practice in," Annabelle said with a slight tilt of her head and a half smile.

I nodded as the little shimmering crystals of ice on my arm melted away. Trickles of water ran down my arm.

I shivered. Partly because the water was cool, but mostly because I'd just witnessed Annabelle and Ning's control, and both were staring at me with a steady, icy glare. One was an Elemental cold, the other was deathly Arcane abilities. Didn't matter, they both meant business.

Now we had to get the others into that same state.

TWO DAYS LATER, in the classroom, everyone was present as we put together our plan. This time, it was Camila, back in action, creating an illusion to shield us from the CMRD and hide our true intentions. If Miriam or any of her watchdogs were checking up on us, as I'm sure they were, all they would have seen was us in the classroom reading books, sketching notes and glyphs, and chatting about magical theory.

In reality, we were in complete mutiny mode.

"So, as soon as Isaiah blows the doors open, you want me to release Mora and put anyone out who's guarding the hallway?" Annabelle asked.

"Mora?"

"The sleep demon."

Everyone else in the room grimaced. Mora wasn't particularly pleasant to look at.

"Okay, well, assuming we get the doors open and manage to get the hallway guards asleep, then what?" Chris asked, skeptical.

"We make our way out," I said.

"That's not much of a plan. Do we know which way is out? I don't think I've ever seen the front door to this place," Chris added.

"Yeah, I can't remember either. The CMRD is built to be a maze for a reason," I said.

"Damn." Isaiah shook his head. "This is not the best plan in the world. I'm not inspired. In fact, I'm thinking we're never going to get out of here."

"Oh hold up, Tesla boy," Camila said, rolling her eyes. "You guys underestimate the power of multiple Astrals going all over the place. I've been wandering these halls for a good portion of the past year."

Every head turned to look at Camila. I damn near slapped my hand to my forehead.

Of course. Why didn't I think of this?

"You think you can help us navigate out of here?" I asked.

"Ah, yeah. I know these halls backwards and forwards. I also know the guards and when they switch shifts. There are a couple who are total assholes. We want to avoid them, but there's a couple others who are dumber than sticks and totally afraid of me," Camila said, confident and way too sure of herself for my liking.

"Um, well then, problem solved?" I said hesitantly.

"I got it. We're good. So, this has been a great pep talk and all, but the real question is when?" Camila asked.

"Yeah, when are we doing this?" Isaiah seconded the question.

"I don't know. It's gotta be soon for obvious reasons, but at the same time, I don't want to push you into a situation you're not ready for." This very question weighed heavily on my mind. Just thinking about it made my stomach lurch. "And I'm going to reemphasize, a peaceful exit—no bloodshed."

"Unless they start it first," Camila said, with a raised eyebrow. This girl was scary. "And then I don't hold back."

"Yeah, what she said." Chris nodded his head in Camila's direction. Ning, Isaiah, and Annabelle didn't look convinced.

Neither was I.

Dear lord, this was going to be ugly.

Twenty-Nine: Exorcise Class

THE GANG AND I spent the next few days practicing everything we could. Small spells and big ones. If anyone had looked in, it would have appeared that we were running through drills, getting them ready for their CMRD finals, not beefing up their abilities in order to escape. But each day that passed had me questioning at what point we should be leaving. Time was ticking away. Their death date was drawing near.

I was seeing improvement, and we had successes. They really were getting better. Ning was able to coat surfaces in varying thicknesses of ice with three dimensional properties like stalagmites and stalactites. Isaiah was able to hypnotize his classmates using his demon, Camila was researching the hallways and creating a map on which way would lead us to freedom, while Chris learned how to set up fire traps.

That development was rather interesting. Annabelle had found a rune that would activate upon touch, and Chris had learned how to imbue that symbol with fire. The result was an exploding magical symbol. Rather clever, I thought.

Annabelle's demons were still giving her grief, and she struggled to deal with their constant barrage of horrifying images. But slowly, she was learning to take the energy that was driving her fear and redirect it into her studies.

"Mr. Martin." She approached me in class on the third day after our decision had been made to bust out. "We need to do something about Cody."

"You know, at this point, you could call me James if you wanted," I offered. "And yes, you mentioned an exorcism before." I was putting a stack of books on the shelf behind the desk I was sitting at.

"Yes, it's time," she said, then added, "James." It was awkward.

I glanced at her, uncertain how she had discerned such a thing. "What makes you say that?"

"Them," she whispered, then gently nodded her head over her shoulder, indicating the horde that was always lurking behind her in the shadows and mist that perpetually hung around all Arcanes.

"Oh. I see. Care to share more?"

She fidgeted a little while, standing in front of me, obviously uncomfortable with the entire situation. "I suppose it's only fair that you'd want to know how I came to that conclusion, but I'm not sure I can share anything other than, *because they told me.*"

"So, the demons inside you said that Cody was going to be a problem?"

"No, they said Cody would do everything in his power to make sure *you* didn't leave the CMRD. So, I think it's time we got rid of Cody."

"Ah, well, I don't know, Annabelle. I mean, what happens to him?"

"He goes away."

"No, I mean, does he get destroyed? Does he move on? If so, where does he go? Cody's spirit, what happens to that?" I asked. After all, at one point, I had *cared* about Cody.

"Oh. Ah, well, I guess that sort of depends on Cody. If he fights it, it could destroy him, but if he sees reason, then he'll most likely move on to wherever it is he needs to go. Regardless of either of those scenarios, if we don't do something about him before we...you know—escape"—she whispered the last word, while shifting her gaze around the room— "then the demons said Cody will thwart our efforts and be successful." Annabelle's tone implied urgency. "But if we do nothing for him, he'll continue to rot. Eventually, he'll turn into a worse entity than just an angry spirit of your dead ex."

"What do you mean?"

"Don't you know?"

"Honestly? Arcane magic makes me super uncomfortable and I don't understand it well. Lately, I've had a hard enough time dealing with Miriam and the CMRD, and even though I'm supposed to be helping all of you, I've made it perfectly clear to them that I don't have an expertise in your domain. I'm afraid I didn't even know a spirit could rot. I thought that only happened to dead bodies," I said.

"Well, you're not wrong on that; what Cody is going through is certainly unusual. Sometimes a spirit is so angry, it tears the soul apart. I think that's what's happening." She lifted her hand and clasped between her fingers was a thick yellowed tome. "It says so in here." She flipped open to the page she had bookmarked, then plopped the book down on the desk in front of us. I could smell the mouldy pages even from where I sat. She pointed at a line drawing of a hideous creature. "It's called a Shtriga."

"Oh, that's not pretty." A grimace formed as I studied the drawing in the book.

"No, not pretty at all, and they're quite distorted. It's kind of sad, really. Cody is going to end up being a soul-sucking killer. If he devolves into this form, he'll attack whatever he can to absorb the life energy from it. Every kill will damn his soul that much more. I know you don't want that for him, regardless of his current bad behaviour."

"You're right. I don't. What happened to him was not his fault. What do we need to do?"

"I'll get it set up. But everyone should be present and within a protected space, otherwise, Cody might lash out and hurt someone."

"Great." Suddenly, I wasn't as convinced about this being a good idea.

Annabelle smiled hesitantly at me and then placed her small hand gently on my arm.

"I am sorry, James."

"Thanks, Annabelle. You know, though, I'm super proud of you. Look how far you've come. From hiding in the mist in your cell, to suggesting we exorcise a ghost because it might become something worse. You've grown an incredible amount in a short time."

Her cheeks flushed and her small smile brightened and spread. "Thanks, James. I'm not sure I could have done it without you and the others. Despite the hellish chaos inside of me, I see there's good I can do too."

I nodded at her, put my arm around her shoulders, and gave her a supportive squeeze.

"I'll set things up and let you all know when I need you." She floated off with her book, intent on her purpose.

Look at that, she's evolving, and you're helping her get there. We can do this.

We can get the hell out of here.

I HAD TO say I was impressed with all five of them. Even Camila, who could be extremely cocky, was attempting to harness her often-wayward Astrals. Other than the theoretical knowledge we had access to in numerous texts, the vast majority of getting a grip on their talents was from practice.

Practice, after all, makes perfect.

Well, sort of.

Annabelle had spent all afternoon and part of the evening in the center of the hangar, creating an elaborate glyph marking on the floor of the warehouse. Various concentric circles, overlapping pentagrams, and other magical scribbling, which meant nothing to me but everything to the spirit realm, were drawn with precision in white chalk.

As I passed by Annabelle, she looked up, her hair mussed and hanging forward, covering part of her face. Her nose was covered in chalk dust. Still, she smiled.

"How's it going?" I stopped and crouched near her, inspecting the intricacy of the working area.

"Not too bad. I'm almost done."

"Do I want to know what all of this does?" I asked.

"Well, it's complicated, but each of these circles"—she pointed around the perimeter—"are for us, except you." She then pointed to the center. "That big one in the middle is yours. Once you step inside, you'll need to call Cody and attract him here. You'll be caught with him, and then I have to recite this verse here." She grabbed a book from a pile she had collected, leafed through several pages, and then pointed at an incantation. "That should do it."

"I thought there was more holy water and waving of crosses involved."

She looked at me and smirked. "You watch too many horror movies."

"Well, other than the hours you've spent out here, it just all seems too simple, no?" I asked.

"That remains to be seen. I have a few backup plans in case Cody decides that moving on isn't what he wants. If I have to force him out, then there are three other possible scripts I can read. I have them bookmarked. But I hope it will be as easy as you think." She looked at me, a little exasperated.

"So, tomorrow then?"

"Oh no, we're doing this tonight. It's better done during darkness, not that you can tell day from night in the middle of here—" She waved her hand above her head, indicating our current environment. "—but the energies are better at night."

"But you look exhausted."

"I'll be okay. Besides, I've got all of you to lean on afterward." She smiled.

"ARE YOU SURE about this?" Isaiah asked as we walked out into the hangar. Everyone had had dinner together except for Annabelle who was still in the hangar getting ready for Cody's ceremony.

"Annabelle is convinced we need to do this," I said, "And so, I trust her, and I don't want anything to happen that would jeopardize our plans to make sure you guys 'pass your finals'."

We were all careful not to use any statements that might lead Miriam into believing I was doing anything other than exactly what she wanted from me: Babysit them until the Bulgarian Coven gets Annabelle. To hell with the others.

"Pass your finals" had become our code words for "get the hell out of here."

As we approached the magical circle where Cody was about to transition from this world into the next, Annabelle appeared from the shadows. Swirls of demon mist parted as she walked out from her own darkness.

"You're just on time. We need to start now; the moon is in the right position in the sky."

"Sure," I said as a tickle of uncertainty fluttered across my stomach and settled lower into my guts. "What do you need us to do?"

"Well, you're the main attraction so carefully step into that circle. No! Don't step on the writing, you'll have to manoeuvre around the lines. Remember the tail that Isaiah had outside his protective circle? Same principle. Don't wreck the sigils." She waved a finger at me, just like my mother used to when I was doing something wrong.

"Okay, good, just stand there," she said once I had positioned myself. "Isaiah and Chris, you stand there and there." She pointed at two spots opposite each other. "And then Camila and Ning, here and here." Annabelle walked over to a small pile of books and picked up a few volumes, then headed over to the last blank circle in the massive hex mark.

"This is kind of scary," Ning said.

The others nodded.

"Okay, are we all ready?" Annabelle asked.

There were tentative nods all around, however I wasn't seeing or feeling optimistic enthusiasm from anyone.

"James, when I point at you, I want you to call out to Cody, but you have to say it with importance and force. Got it?"

"Yup. Got it."

"Here goes nothing," she said as she tossed one of the books out in front of her. It abruptly stopped, floating briefly and then hung in one spot suspended in mid-air. Annabelle waved her hand over the tome. The cover flipped open and several pages rustled as she made her way to the correct incantation. It stopped on the desired page. Annabelle started reading.

"Here in the night,
Where spirits roam without light,
We call upon the ghost, and the one it calls a host.
Tethered and linked, cast together, indistinct,
Come to us, reveal your intentions,
Not just a shadow, no apprehension,
Just you, and us, an ascension."

Annabelle's voice lilted with the rhyme. She sounded otherworldly, and for the briefest of moments, I could have pictured her as a benign forest nymph, not the dark girl possessed by a demon horde. And then, she pointed at me.

Random old memories of Cody swarmed my head as my hands turned dead cold and clammy. In that moment, I regretted giving Annabelle the permission to do this. But it was too late now.

"James, now," Annabelle whispered, but despite the breathy words, the urgency came through.

"Cody," I yelled, as fear and betrayal clawed at me with sharp talons.

We waited as the air around us became heavy and still, but that didn't last long. Annabelle's dark mist wafted on the air currents, expanding gradually. Snaky white vapours writhed their way across the floor, winding into the middle of the circle where I stood. The space within the charmed circle filled up, leaving us knee deep in ashen-tinted fog. Cody's corporeal body gradually formed, but this time, he was missing a good chunk of the skin from his face. Fingers had fallen off and one ear hung from a black sinew of flesh. It turned my stomach looking at him. He floated closer and put his lips a breath away from my earlobe.

I shivered uncontrollably.

"This is different. You called me? Do you want me? Have you ditched the other one, the one you cannot save? Look at me, touch me...like you used to."

"No, Cody. It's time. You don't belong here," I said. The hairs on the backs of my arms were standing straight up as Cody brushed up against my back.

"I belong with you."

Annabelle recited the next verse in her spell book.

"Through the doorway,
Pass from this realm,
A new place awaits,
With Golden Oaks and White Elms,
The pasture of the goddess,
A place of peace, of love, of solace."

The sigils in the center of the circle glowed an eerie yellow as the air took on a similar tinted haze, and the smell of sulphur became weighty and thick when Annabelle recited the Arcane invocation.

Cody's face morphed from sexy tempter into a scowl of rage. "What are you doing?"

"What we should have done a long time ago," Annabelle said. She slammed the text shut with a wave of her hand. The sound of the closing book made everyone jerk their heads to look at it. Black demon mist swirled in towards the book. Skeletal fingers formed from the fog and grasped it.

"What are you doing?" Annabelle said with a scowl. I had to assume she was talking to the bodiless hands that gripped the book.

Annabelle stepped forward and grabbed the book and tugged it, hard.

"Let go! This is not yours," Annabelle hissed.

Without warning, another disembodied hand formed out of the dense black vapour and scratched the back of Annabelle's hand. It left huge red welts and one long scratch that wept blood.

"Ow!" Annabelle pulled her hand back and cradled it, but as she let go, the demon claw released the book and let it drop. The book spun slightly and moved into the circle, obliterating one of the hex marks.

"No!" Annabelle screamed.

The rest of us standing in our circles were terrified. Isaiah made moves to leave the hangar.

"You can't leave. Don't! Stay where you are," Annabelle commanded.

Demon voices screamed out from the mist behind Annabelle, and Cody hissed.

Everyone whipped to look at the book as its movement smeared more of the carefully written magical symbols.

Cody laughed. "You won't be doing anything now."

Cody began to dissolve back into smoke, as tails of his vapour edged its way out of the ritual space. The broken circle was his way out.

"There will be no escape for you," Annabelle said, except it wasn't her voice. "You are now ours." The speech was layered, several tones spoke at once. Her horde had addressed Cody as one entity. Annabelle blinked, and her eyes morphed into black orbs as dark as the pits that contained her demons.

She curled her lips back and bared teeth.

Undecipherable words in a language I'd never heard flew from her quick moving lips. Annabelle was gone. The voices came from all over, her words echoing.

Cody's white wisps lashed out at the encroaching demon mist. He shrieked as demon hands emerged from behind Annabelle and took hold of Cody's vapour.

"Oh my god," Camila said as she covered her ears.

I stood in the center of it all, feeling the temperature drop suddenly. I glanced over at Ning, only to see her Yuki-onna in full form, standing in her place. It was crouched, ready to strike, with blood-red eyes. Frost crystals crept out from her circle, forming intricate geometric patterns.

I could see my breath, my chest heaving as the fear that had started only moments ago erupted into a bubble of terror that was quickly erasing any sensible thought in my head.

Run!

I had never lost control of my power in this way. Fear translated into a wayward sphere of emotion, tinted and shadowed in varying shades of black. If the bubble of emotion touched anyone, absolute chaos would erupt.

Chris was on fire.

Isaiah stood still, shell-shocked, and then he pointed past me towards Annabelle.

From within her dark fog, an impossibly tall thin demon materialized and took a few steps towards Cody, who was still screaming. *His ethereal gasses churned and twisted, attempting to break free of Annabelle's grasp.*

"I see you..." Annabelle's raspy voice squeaked out.

Cody's rotting corpse reformed from the swirling white vapour. He glanced at me, and scowled, then returned his glare to Annabelle.

"No, you can't touch me. James, you said you would protect me. You promised. I'm dying again. Don't do this!"

The thin fiend stretched out a clawed hand and pushed it into Cody's chest.

All of us lurched forward as we felt the stabbing pain of the demon's hand puncturing into Cody's rotted torso.

Annabelle continued to mumble out incantations, indiscernible, her eyes still pitch black, her hands splayed out to her sides, but now, she was levitating. Her toes gently brushed the concrete floor as the ancient words tumbled out of her mouth.

Writhing black mist swarmed us, encircling between our legs. The pain in my chest was tight and I thought my heart had stopped beating. It was impossible to get any breath into my lungs.

"Annabelle! Stop, you're killing us!" Camila screamed.

The thin demon stretched himself forward, towering over Cody, and gripped his head in an impossibly large hand. And then he pulled up.

The shriek was ear-splitting as Cody's head was removed from his body, and the embedded demon hand ripped open his putrid trunk.

I knew none of it was physically there, but it was hard to tell, it all seemed so...real.

Cody began to dissolve into tiny tails of white fog, swirling and undulating. Points of light erupted from where Cody's heart should have been and burst forth like a little firework eruption.

Annabelle opened her mouth wide and inhaled. Her breath was raspy and wet. The tiny fairy lights swirled in the air and then, just as swiftly as they appeared, were sucked up by Annabelle's distended maw.

She paled to a deathly white, the same colour Cody had been. Her eyes shifted from dead black to snow white.

The demon, the black fog, the remains of Cody's body, and his white vapour all swirled and imploded into Annabelle, as she remained floating, centimetres above the floor, her toes grazing and scraping against the cold floor.

Annabelle fell limp. Her hands dropped to her sides and her head hung awkwardly to one side, her mouth open, tongue hanging out.

I rushed over, grabbed her shoulders, and shook her. I could feel the others tentatively approaching behind me, concerned for their classmate but unsure of their safety.

I peered into Annabelle's open eyes. No iris or pupil existed, just white orbs, with tiny threadlike red spider veins skittering across them.

New veins began to appear.

Help me.

The words formed in red within the orbs as if someone had scratched them into white paint with blood. I continued to shake Annabelle, yelling at her. "Annabelle, wake up, wake up!"

Thirty: Health Class-Basic Arcane First Aid

ANNABELLE COLLAPSED ON the floor.

Everyone came rushing over. Camila pushed me out of the way and knelt down to Annabelle, then scooped her up into her arms and cradled her.

What the hell?

"They've known each other far longer than any of us," Isaiah whispered from very close behind me. He put a hand on my back as he peered at them from over my shoulder. I knew he was standing on his tippy-toes. He was shorter than I was, so I stepped to the side, allowing him to be closer to his classmates.

Annabelle started seizing.

"What do we do?" Camila cried, looking at me.

"Let's place her down on the floor and roll her to her side." I move forward to help Camila. Annabelle's eyes fluttered as her limbs spasmed and her back arched.

"She's stiff as a board, oh my god," Camila said, tears rolling down her cheeks.

"Just calm down. She'll be okay. Ning, get your phone out, time her. Make sure this doesn't last any longer than three minutes."

"What happens at three minutes?" Ning asked.

"We'll have to get her help. Help we can't provide."

The seizure didn't last very long, another thirty seconds or so after we had her rolled sideways.

She relaxed visibly, and shortly after the muscle spasm stopped, Annabelle's eyes peeled open.

I leaned in close to her and put a hand on her shoulder. "You okay? You had a seizure."

"A w...w-what?" she stuttered.

"You had a seizure, after your demon, the demon fog, and Cody imploded and you sucked it all in. Are you okay?" Isaiah said from behind me.

"I think so. Really? I had a seizure?" She pushed herself up into a sitting position with one hand and wobbled a little. "I haven't had one of those in years, like since I was a kid."

"Hmph. Wow. Well, that's not in your file," I said.

"No, I only had a couple and Mom and Dad never took me to a doctor. They happened at home. They kept it secret because they didn't want the congregation to find out I was having them. They were afraid we'd be treated differently."

"The congregation?" I asked. "It says in your file that you grew up in a very religious household, and in all honesty, a lot of Arcanes come from a strict religious upbringing."

"Yes, the congregation. My parents were devout believers of a Christian sect. It was very old-school, hellfire and brimstone. Sort of backwards. No music, no TV, a strict moral code. That sort of thing."

My eyebrows raised at the description, and Annabelle caught me with the expression on my face.

"Please don't judge my parents. They are good people, and truthfully, I miss them. The congregation was kind of nice. We had a community. There were always people to call upon for help. But certain medical conditions were viewed as intrusion of evil spirits or demons. If the elders had known, they would have put my family through terrible times." Annabelle slumped forward, "I guess they were right. Look where I am now."

"Can you stand up?" I asked, "We should get you back to your cell so you can lie down."

"I think so," she said. She attempted with Bambi legs, but almost fell over.

From out of nowhere, Chris was beside her, holding her up. "I'll take you."

They were about to turn away when Isaiah asked, "But where'd Cody go?"

Annabelle's head dropped, and she closed her eyes. Embarrassment rolled off of her in palpable waves. Thunderous rolling breakers that I'm sure any psychic in the vicinity would have felt.

Annabelle pointed to her chest.

Then she started to cry.

"I can feel him. He's so angry."

"You mean you absorbed him into your horde?" Camila asked.

I was dumbstruck.

"Yes," she sobbed, "I'm sorry—I didn't mean to." Annabelle cried, looking at me through weepy eyes.

I didn't know what to say. What was I supposed to say? I wanted Cody to move on. He should have been in Heaven, or wherever. The next plane of existence or lounging in meadows being fed peeled grapes. He should have been safe. Not embedded in the hell that possessed Annabelle, and yet, how could I blame her? Had she had any control over any of it? After all, that's exactly what her demons wanted. More.

"Is he safe, Annabelle?" I asked. "Please tell me he's safe. That he won't turn into that thing you showed me."

"The Shtriga? I...I don't think so. I don't know." She sobbed, "I'm so sorry."

I was numb. Cody had been gone for a long time, even if his ghost had hung around. I had always thought it was just my subconscious. At first, he had tormented me with his visits, making his death fresh each time he showed up. Now, so many months later, learning that he had chosen to haunt me, my feelings for him had changed. Love had turned to guilt, which morphed into frustration and then annoyance. Still...

I wasn't sure what I was supposed to feel.

"I am so sorry," Annabelle said, her bottom lip quivering.

Chris turned her around and the two headed off towards the student cells.

I stood there as they walked away. Camila ran after them not long after. Ning followed.

"Are you okay?" Isaiah put his hand on the small of my back.

"I'm not sure," I said. I turned to look at him. His chestnut eyes conveyed a sense of worry as he glanced at me and then away. "It's okay. At least Cody won't be bothering us anymore. I hope."

"Do you want company?" he asked, sliding his hand into mine.

I squeezed it. He was so sweet and good to me and always far too flirtatious.

"No, I think I need time to think." And with that, I turned, walked in the opposite direction from the student cells, and left Isaiah standing all alone in the middle of the vast hangar.

I GRABBED THE pack of smokes that I had left on the kitchen counter, slid one out, stuck it between my lips, and lit it. The smoke was thick as I inhaled, as that soothing rush of nicotine flooded my lungs. It calmed me briefly, allowing me to replay everything that had happened in the past hour.

Cody was gone.

Except he wasn't. He was trapped in a demonic horde.

It took the entire length of the cigarette for me to realize that the emotion I was feeling was, after all, guilt. Even with his taunting and inappropriate comments, I *had* promised him that I would look after him. And I hadn't done that. And that translated into my current predicament. I couldn't look after the kids I had now.

"Stop that," Isaiah said from the doorway. "What happened wasn't your fault. Can I come in?"

I stubbed the spent smoke out onto a plate I was using as an ashtray. Another reason for housekeeping to hate me.

"*You* stop that." I pointed my finger at Isaiah as heat flamed the back of my neck. "We've had multiple conversations about boundaries. And I said I needed some time." I was angry, and guilty, and not worthy of looking after anything, including myself.

"That right there. You need to stop that kind of thinking," Isaiah said, leaning up against the doorjamb. "And fuck you and your boundaries. Most of the time I have no control over the thoughts that barrel over me. Ever thought that as an Empath, you're pushing your emotions outward and not even realizing it?"

"Not now, Isaiah, please."

"I'm serious, James, I could hear you and your pity wallowing all the way across the hangar. I get it. You made promises to Cody you couldn't keep. We've all been in similar situations, letting others down with broken promises."

"If this is your way of trying to make me feel better, you suck at it," I said, while taking a seat at the kitchen table. It allowed me the opportunity to put my elbows on the table so I could put my head in my hands.

Isaiah came up behind me and rubbed my shoulders. He found tight knots and gently rubbed them with his fingers. My initial anger melted away with every knead of my muscles.

I sat up and rested my head against Isaiah's chest. "I'm still not comfortable with us."

"I know. It's interesting. Your mind is one thought fighting against another. You have to give yourself more credit. We're going to get out of this."

"You're so sure of yourself. You have no idea how devious the CMRD and Miriam can be."

"I can see those things from your past experiences. I know. But they've also never dealt with the five of us. We've gotten better, in a tremendously short period of time. Not good enough to be able to control much of anything, but we're better. More importantly, we have each other. Each of us have developed bonds, and I know, as a team, we're going to get out of here. Now, show me these maps that Camila's been working on."

"When the hell did you get to be so mature?" I asked.

"There's lots you don't know about me yet."

"There's lots you don't know about yourself yet," I pointed out.

"True, but for right now, let's concentrate on making a plan. Ning and Chris are practicing fire and ice games, and Camila is looking after Annabelle."

I pulled the papers I had around the table, trying to find the notes and maps Camila had made. When I uncovered them, I pushed them towards Isaiah.

He picked them up and studied them for a moment, then bent the paper in half so he could look at me with an arched eyebrow, and asked, "How's your arm?"

I rubbed the spot where the lightning bolt had marked me. "Still tingles every now and then, but it's almost gone." I'd been able to wear my own shirts again too.

"Let's see," Isaiah said.

I rolled up my sleeve far enough to show the lingering traces of the red branching brand he had inadvertently placed there.

"Damn, I was hoping you'd just take off your shirt." Isaiah smiled and winked. "But it looks much better."

I shook my head. "You are terrible."

"Hmhmm," he hummed. "So, what do I do to actually make you take off your shirt?"

"Isaiah—" I started to say more when Chris burst in through the door, flames erupting randomly all over his skin, and his chest heaving from sucking air.

"What the hell is going on?" I asked.

"Come quick. Now," Chris huffed out as sparks burst from his hands, landing little embers on the floor of my apartment. I stood up and stepped on them several times to make sure they were out.

"Chris, calm down, or you're going to set the entire place on fire," I said. "Do you need me to calm you down?"

"No, I need you to come now!"

"Has something happened to Annabelle?"

"Yes. Well, no, but...yes!" he stammered.

"Chris, what the hell is going on?"

"Miriam's guards, they've come to get Annabelle. They are trying to drag her out of her room, but Camila is fighting them off."

"Oh shit," Isaiah said.

We were off running towards the students' cells.

Thirty-One: Hall Pass

CHRIS, ISAIAH, AND I arrived in front of Annabelle's cube, panting and sucking in air from the run just in time to see Jason and Rodney, Miriam's guards, attempting to haul Annabelle out by her legs, as if they were going to drag her to a secret cell within the depths of the CMRD.

Camila was having none of it. She had projected several Astrals who were throwing little energy spheres towards the two men. They were busier trying to smack away the orbs and protect their faces than actually escorting Annabelle anywhere.

"What the fuck is going on?" I yelled.

Camila looked in my direction and, upon seeing me, relaxed slightly. Her Astrals began to fade. But Annabelle was crying. She scurried away and climbed up into her bed where she curled into a ball, huddled against the wall.

Ning and Camila put their arms around her in an attempt to comfort and protect her.

The rest of us made a line across the front Annabelle's cube, forcing the guards back and away.

"I asked you once. I will not ask you again. What is going on?"

Jason sneered at me. "Miriam wants her separated. We all saw what happened. What is she going to do next, start sucking in people? She's going to be put into quarantine until that European woman comes for her."

"Like hell that's gonna happen," Chris said, sparks flying off his hands.

Rodney was watching Chris very carefully. His eyes were getting wider, and Chris noticed his frightened reaction, so he played it up a little and punched one fist into his other hand. Embers skittered in all directions, hissing as they flew.

"If you want her, you'll have to go through us," Isaiah said. Little arcs of lightning danced from his fingers, occasionally falling to the floor and scampering across the concrete. A few jumped and fell just short of Jason and Rodney's shoes.

Rodney took a step back. From the look on his face, I could tell he was questioning his career decisions. Jason, on the other hand, stood his ground, reached behind his back, and pulled a gun out of a hidden holster. He cocked it and pointed it towards Isaiah.

"That's enough, freak." Jason's lip curled back in disgust as he took aim at Isaiah. "You people are idiots if you think Miriam's ever gonna let you back into normal society. You don't belong there."

"You're right. That is enough. Put your damn weapon away, bigot." I pushed out a sphere of emotion, a bubble filled with the thought; *compliance.*

But just as the slight shimmer began to appear in front of me, Jason swung the gun in my direction.

"None of your hocus-pocus bullshit, or I will shoot you dead." Jason was too confident. The girls huddled behind us, watching everything play out, had been forgotten by these two men.

One of Camila's Astrals appeared behind Jason and cuffed him on the back of the head with a little energy grenade. A single bomb wasn't enough to do anyone any harm, but it made Jason spin around to see what was behind him.

Isaiah took matters into his own hands. With arms outstretched towards Jason, sparks of energy flickered between his fingers, rapidly growing into bolts of energy.

"Isaiah! No!" I attempted to thwart his next action, but I was too late.

Isaiah flicked his hands towards Jason as a massive jolt of pure electric energy passed between them.

Jason's body seized into rigidity and his eyes bugged out of his head. He lost control of his body, dropping the gun, then fell to his knees convulsing and shaking. The energy coursed through his body as his clothes smoked. Isaiah was relentless. He continued to push the current through our attacker's body. Jason's eyes rolled up into his head, but then collapsed in front of us, his limp body splayed out on the floor.

Jason's clothes smouldered with little wisp tails making curlicues in the air above him. The smell of burnt polyester and flesh was revolting. Rodney, not questioning his job choice any longer, bolted from the hangar, towards the blast doors on the other end, which had been left open.

"Holy shit! Nicely done, dude," Camila said to Isaiah, giving him a high five.

"Isaiah, no killing!" I glared at him.

"Fucker had it coming," he said, pumping himself full of confidence.

"Yeah, except now that's going to bring the wrath of Miriam down on all of our heads." I gave Isaiah a stern glance.

"Not if we don't get caught," Chris said slyly, glancing towards the open doors.

Everyone looked at each other.

"Guys, I don't think that's a good idea," I said.

What the hell. This is exactly what you've been waiting for. Now's your chance.

There was the briefest amount of silence between us, and then as a group, we all gathered together and walked towards the end of the hangar and the open doors.

Ning took a peek down the corridor.

"There's no one there," she said as she glanced back to us.

"Are you kidding me? They wouldn't come in here like that and leave the doors wide open without any backup? That's too easy. Miriam must be planning something devious. I assure you, this kind of a mistake would never happen," I said, and it was true. Miriam would never have allowed this to happen.

"This is our chance. We need to go. Like, now!" Camila said. She walked forward into the attached corridor and stood in the middle of a T intersection. She looked both ways, turned back to us, and shrugged, then waved us all forward.

"Now hold up—" I started to say, but the kids pushed past me, out into the hallway. "Seriously, guys, just wait!" I hissed at them.

Reluctantly, they all turned to look at me.

"Why?" Isaiah asked.

"Because, like I said, this is just way too easy. Something is not right."

"You're way overprotective," Camila said, rolling her eyes. "This is our chance. We need to take it and get the hell out of here."

"Do you think Miriam would let this happen?" I glared at her.

"Look at the size of this place! This hallway goes so far in both directions I can't even see the end. She can't possibly have eyes on everything all the time," Chris said. His fire had died down, but flecks of bright orange sparked in his eyes. He was burning hot.

"You'd be surprised what money and resources can accomplish," I said. But none of them were paying any heed to my retort, and they were ready to bust out.

"Good god, James, really? I know these halls. Besides, we don't want to go all the way to the end," she said, pointing the direction that Chris was looking. "That leads us deeper into the complex. That first hallway up on your right, that's where we need to go." Camila instructed us, and really, she was the one who had sent her Astrals wandering as far as she could. She had the knowledge of where we needed to go.

A spectral version of Camila appeared beside me and cast me a shady sideways glance but then quietly slinked down the hallway to the first intersection where we needed to go. It poked its head around the corner and then promptly disappeared.

Camila, standing behind all of us, startled me as she spoke up. "Holy shit, James. You were right. There's like twenty of them with guns hiding around the corner. The first two were bait." She whispered the last sentence and then blanched as she realized the gravity of the current situation.

"I told you," I turned and whispered to them. "Go back, now!" I shuffled them back down the short corridor that led to the blast doors and the hangar, except the moment we turned into the hallway, the hangar doors were closed.

"Oh shit," Chris said.

I closed my eyes. So then, this *was* a snare.

An audible *click* sounded from above as a speaker thrummed to life above us.

"Well, now, what do we have here? A handful of criminals who have just electrocuted one of my guards and are attempting to break out of the CMRD?" Miriam's voice ricocheted off the walls and ceiling, making it seem to come from every direction.

"Miriam, you set us up," I shouted.

"You're done, James. You were given instructions and told what to do. You chose to ignore that. I'm not wasting any more of my time or money housing a bunch of reprobates. I tried to contain Annabelle so that the Bulgarian Coven wouldn't be angry with me. I could use her in the future, but it seems she isn't being compliant, and so I'm afraid terrible magical accidents happen to students who have poor teachers. And so, all my paper documentation states how zero progress was made in having you help them develop their abilities. In fact, we have one report here that says one student killed another in a classroom exercise gone wrong. Looks like you failed, James."

"That's a damn lie, you bitch," I yelled at the ceiling.

The kids huddled around me, inching closer.

"Who is going to question me, James? Who?"

There was another *click* as the speaker shut off, and the corridor we had just left suddenly filled with the footsteps and shuffling of many guards.

Ning, with her hands balled into fists, whispered so quietly I almost didn't hear her, "What a cunt." Her face contorted into an emotion I had never seen on her—rage—as ice crystals erupted on the surface of her skin, enshrouding one side of her face. She stomped forward into the area where all the guards had amassed.

"Fuck you," she yelled and flung her hands out.

"Well, I never thought I'd hear that coming from her," Camila said, and Annabelle looked away in embarrassment.

"Don't mess with the girls," Chris said, a huge smile plastered on his face.

But as that quick conversation took place, the air around us grew cold, our breaths hanging in small clouds of fog as we exhaled. Ning blasted an icy wind down the corridor, freezing everything in its path.

"I'll go get her," Chris said and walked towards Ning.

Ning's arms were still outstretched, snow and ice crystals falling all around her, as Chris approached and gently put his hands on both her shoulders. He leaned in and whispered in her ear.

Ning relaxed and let her hands fall. Chris waved us forward again. "Brace yourselves, but you've got to see this." His eyes were wide as he glanced back towards the frozen corridor.

The rest of us shuffled carefully up to where they stood.

The scene was terrifying.

Huge pointed icicles hung from the ceiling. Several inches of ice covered the floor and walls, but worse were the frozen faces of several guards, their hands still holding on to their weapons and their faces locked in surprise.

I turned away, my stomach churning. The guards terrified expressions locked into my brain forever. There was no turning back at this point.

It was escape or die.

"Do you think we might be able to get out of here without killing anyone else?" I said, a little louder than it should have been. I braced myself against the nearest wall to steady myself, certain I was about to lose my lunch.

Ning looked at me. Shame trickled out of her and pooled at her feet. "I'm sorry…" she whimpered.

Annabelle was clinging to Isaiah.

I sighed heavily. "No, Ning, I'm sorry. I'm sorry you all have been put in this predicament. I'm sorry for the wretched treatment you've had to endure. I'm sorry Miriam is such a bitch. But most of all, I'm sorry I didn't get the time I was supposed to have with you, and I feel responsible for not getting you to the point where your talents are controllable." I opened my arms. She rushed in and hugged me. "I know you were only trying to protect us, but seriously, guys, let's get the hell out of here without killing anyone else. Please."

"Heads up. We got incoming!" Isaiah said, nodding in the direction of Ning's ice field.

A guard with his gun cocked and ready, pointed at us, took one step onto the frozen area and slipped, tumbling backwards. The gun shot off. Its *bang* reverberated down the hallway.

"Run," Annabelle screamed.

The six of us turned and ran in the opposite direction from the frozen hell that Ning had created. The wrong direction.

Hopefully, Camila could find us an alternate way out.

Fuck, here we go.

Thirty-Two: Field Trip

"WHERE THE HELL are we going?" I yelled at Camila, who was in front, having led us down several corridors. We'd turned so many times I was completely spun around. We had also narrowly escaped several armed guards.

We came to the end of a hallway that had a door, but of course, it was locked.

"I...I'm-I'm not sure." She bent over, hands on her knees, huffing.

"Oh, that's just great," Chris said, rolling his eyes.

"You think you can do better, then lead the way, asshole." Camila gave Chris a dirty scowl, as an Astral formed next to him.

Throwing up his hands and backing up a few steps, Chris retracted his statement. "No, no, sorry. Just, you know, a direction soon would be good. Where do we go from here?"

Looking around us, there was only one option—retreat a bit and go down the last cutaway we'd passed.

But just as I finished that thought, several guards came into view.

"Shit," Isaiah said.

I threw my hand out creating a force field across the passageway. We could see them and they could see us, distorted and blurry, but we weren't going anywhere, and they couldn't touch us.

Problem, though. I wasn't going to be able to hold this up forever, and we had nowhere to go.

"Can you get us through the door?" Annabelle asked Isaiah.

"Like how?" Isaiah scrunched up his eyebrows and curled his lip up in a sarcastic reply.

"Okay, quit picking on each other and figure out a way to get us out of here. I can hold them off for a bit, but not much longer." My arm was already getting tired, and my head was starting to feel fuzzy from the mental drain.

"You can't electrocute the door open?" Camila suggested.

"Oh, um…well, I suppose…" Isaiah let the sparks fly in between his fingers, and within seconds, the smell of burning ozone permeated the air in our close quarters. I could hear the buzzing and zapping coming from behind me. I cast a quick glance over my shoulder to see what Isaiah was doing.

My force field wobbled a little.

Okay, no distractions.

"This isn't going to work. The door is too thick," Isaiah said.

"Ugh!" Camila snorted out in frustration.

"I have an idea," Annabelle said. "But I'll need everyone."

The five huddled in the corner. I could hear quick short noises, but they were being secretive, which made me suspicious.

"Okay, what kind of plan are you five hatching?"

"Nothing you're going to like, but it's going to get us out of here," Chris said.

I closed my eyes and shook my head. "Look, whatever you *think* you need to do, let's talk about it first—" I stopped. A very large beetle scurried towards the force field and the hallway I was blocking.

"What the hell?" I said.

"Yup. Quite literally, out of hell," Camila said, then giggled.

"Drop the force field and then duck and get behind us," Isaiah said.

I turned towards them to argue but, again, stopped short, taking in the vision of my five students. They no longer appeared untrained or incapable.

Not in the slightest.

Isaiah's eyes were radiant blue, arcs of lightning jumping from shoulder to knee, and fingertip to chest. Ning had crystalized and was a human embodiment of ice, with her Yuki-onna's blood-red eyes. Chris's dark skin was laced with hot running veins of fire, embers dripping off his hand, and then he exploded in a puff of black smoke, only to coalesce into his large fire wolf, panting, teeth bared, fur smoking.

Camila wore the most mischievous smile I had ever seen on her, and she was amassing multiple Astrals behind her.

But Annabelle, dear god, Annabelle. Her eyes had gone to pitch with her mouth slack and gaping. She was hovering several inches off the floor. Long tendrils of black demon mist lashed out like vine whips. Bugs of every description were crawling out from underneath her clothes and dropping to the floor. Their hard, little bodies *click-clacking* as they hit. A large spider crawled out from her mouth, scampered down the front of her shirt, and then descended via silk thread to the floor.

A shiver ran down my back and the hair all over my body rose.

From behind Annabelle, a rotting black corpse crept from the blackness, pulling itself out of the void with grasping clawed hands.

"Drop the shield," Isaiah said. His voice was not entirely his own. A shadow superimposed itself over him, and for the briefest of moments, Isaiah had monster horns curled atop his head.

In that very moment, seeing them all seething with immense power, it dawned on me.

I've done this all wrong.

I should never have expected them to focus and minimalize their powers.

They needed to explode, to burst forth and give the world everything they had.

I felt bad for the guards on the other side of my wall, when I reconciled quite quickly that the five "kids" behind me were armed with much bigger guns than I would ever have. My powers were nothing in the face of everything they could summon. And they were far from being kids.

I let my arm fall, and consequently, the shield evaporated.

The *click* of many guns being hoisted, aimed, and cocked, ready to fire, echoed off the walls of our tiny area. I derived a small amount of pleasure as I studied the faces of the guards when they took in the full detail of my little army.

"Go get 'em," I said to the kids, then added, "Don't kill anyone!"

Demonic laughter rang out from Annabelle as her corpse companion nuzzled up and embraced her.

"Oh shit," one of the guards said, dropped his gun, and ran away.

Another started shaking uncontrollably and pissed himself, the dark stain of urine wetting the front of his uniform.

A swarm of pests scurried out to the first guard, and before he could surrender, he was covered in a crawling mass of legs and wings. All you could hear was the *tick-tick-tick-tick* of their tiny exoskeletons bumping into each other. Well, that and the guard's screams.

A *woosh* came from behind me, followed by a gust of hot air as the fire wolf bolted and launched itself towards another guard. He didn't stand a chance against the open maw of razor-sharp teeth clamping down around his neck. Little burning coals dripped and sizzled their way through his clothes. Blood spurted out, marking the hallway wall with spatter.

The bugs retreated and moved onto their next victim. All that remained of the first victim was a skeleton.

Ning glided past my other side, and my arm chilled from the nearness of her cold body. As silently as a ghost, she made her way over to yet another guard. And then, just like a specter, she bolted so fast towards him that she almost disappeared. With the fangs of the Yuki-onna protruding, she lunged at the man's throat, ripping it open.

"I said don't kill anyone!" I shook my head. As much as I had wanted to bust out of here with a bang, I didn't want to escape leaving a rampage of bloody carnage in our wake. The kids, however, had other ideas. Not that I could blame them after being mistreated and kept hostage for so long. Not after being lied to, told they were going to "get better" only to discover that the people they thought were going to help them, were going to kill them.

Still. These guards were only doing what they were paid to do. It was a job for them.

Lightning bolts zipped past my head and arced their way towards the last of the remaining guardsmen, hitting one right in the chest, adding a new smell to the carnage—burnt flesh. He shook violently for a moment before dropping to the floor.

Two more men released their weapons, which made a horrid clatter on the concrete, and bolted away from us as fast as they could muster.

Smart. A little late, but smart.

Astrals of Camila were everywhere I looked. She was tossing energy bombs all over the place, distracting the remaining few guards. The bloodshed in this one little hallway was shocking, but within a short few minutes, we stood amongst the corpses, walls splattered with bodily fluids and painted red. We were breathing heavy from physical and mental exhaustion as the endorphin rush of a high-stress battle situation coursed through each of us.

The corridor grew silent and still. All I could hear was our breathing.

There's something eerie about fresh dead bodies, almost as if the souls of the recently departed permeate the area with their presence and make the surrounding area dense, thick and uncomfortable.

The wolf exploded and then coalesced back into Chris. He was still glowing with fire in his veins as he looked at Camila and asked, "Okay, which direction?"

An Astral ran down the hall, peeked around the corner, then looked back at us and waved us forward.

"That way! Follow me," Camila said while pointing at the ghostly image in front of us.

We veered around the corridor and made several turns, only to find ourselves once again at a dead end.

We were in a hallway that had a door, but of course, it was locked.

"Where the hell are we going?" I yelled at Camila.

"I…I'm-I'm not sure." She bent over, hands on her knees huffing.

"Oh, that's just great," Chris said, rolling his eyes.

"You think you can do better, then lead the way, asshole." Camila gave Chris a dirty scowl, as an Astral formed next to him.

Throwing up his hands and backing up a few steps, Chris retracted his statement. "No, no, sorry. Just, you know, a direction soon would be good. Where do we go from here?"

Wait a minute. Didn't we just do this?

Camila pushed her way past Chris and the others, then cranked her head to the side as she stood next to me.

"We just did this."

"Yeah, I know, what the—" I was cut off as several guards came into view.

"Shit," Isaiah said.

I threw my hand out, creating a force field across the passageway as armed guards rounded the corner, pointing loaded weapons at us. We could see them, they could see us, distorted and blurry, but we weren't going anywhere, and they couldn't touch us.

Camila canted her head to the other side as she furrowed her eyebrows. "No, seriously, we just did this." She turned and looked at me. "We just did this. What the hell is going on?"

"We're in a time loop, or replaced, or rewound…" I said, and there was only one person I knew who could do that.

A tall man was standing behind the guards this time. He was almost inhumanly thin, but then my force field distorted our view. He put his hands on his hips, watching us.

I knew exactly who it was.

"Drew," I said.

"Who?" Isaiah asked, with an arched eyebrow and the look of jealousy on his face.

"One of my classmates from when I spent time here at the CMRD. He could rewind or reset time. But back then, he could only do a few seconds worth. Looks like he's gotten a whole bunch more powerful." Shit, we were going to have to figure out how to neutralize him, or else he'd keep us in this loop until we fell over from exhaustion, repeating our actions over and over.

Expending this much power took a toll, and we wouldn't last very long if we had to repeat ourselves.

My force field wobbled again as I turned to face the kids. "Okay, listen. That tall guy in the back, we *need* to neutralize him. Otherwise, we'll continue this little loop of disarming guards and running down hallways only to come across the same group of guards until we are completely expended. And then the CMRD will have won. You know what's next as soon as they capture us."

"I got this." Camila strutted past me right up to the force field. She put her hand ever so gently up against the barrier.

As soon as she made that contact, I could feel her; her emotions, her thoughts, and her pain. There was a swirling mess of overconfidence laced with courage that writhed within her. I could almost touch the amorphous jelly that lay behind those emotions. It was a blob of depression. Right then, she was everything and could do no wrong, but the sadness and the worthlessness was creeping up. It would eventually take over.

I knew that as soon as this high-octane situation was over, the swallowing mess of hopelessness would consume her.

Astrals had formed on the other side of the barrier.

"Isaiah, come here," she yelled as she reached out her hand. "Take my hand and start turning out the sparks."

"Are you sure about that? I'll electrocute the crap out of you." Isaiah took two steps forward and hesitantly extended his hand.

"I'm absolutely sure. Now give me your hand."

Isaiah did as he was told, generating the sparks as *zapping* sounded off from his hands. "Are you sure?" he reiterated.

"Yes, dammit, give me your hand. Now!" Camila ordered, then closed her eyes as she took a firm grip of Isaiah's electrified digits.

Camila tensed. Her entire body became rigid as she clung to him. At that point, I didn't think she would have been able to let go, but then the coolest thing happened.

Arcs of lightning sparked and flew from Camila's Astrals. She was harnessing Isaiah's power and throwing it through her projections.

As the electrical bolts skittered across the narrow hallway, bouncing off of the ceiling and floor, it didn't take long until they had also managed to burn holes through each of the guards. As the last guard fell, I dropped my shield and stared directly at Drew's big green eyes.

"So, you turned against your own kind?" I asked as the kids crowded in behind me.

"Money was too good, and besides, I never liked most of you anyway."

"You always were an asshole, even back then. Can't say as I'm surprised. Guys, take him out," I said.

Camila nodded.

Her Astrals formed a circle around Drew and then she glanced at Isaiah again. Without saying a word, Isaiah waggled his eyebrows and then said, "Hang on."

The electrical arcs started up again, until they passed from Astral to Astral in one continuous circle all the way around Drew.

Isaiah turned his head to me. "All right, James, it's time to put those muscles to use. Go out there and put him down."

With my force field no longer required, I let the tingle in my feet take me to the inside circle created by Camila and Isaiah. In a heartbeat, I found myself standing right next to Drew.

I've never been one for fistfights, but then it had been a long time since I was this angry.

"Nobody fucks with my kids," I said, then wound up and planted a solid uppercut on Drew's jaw.

He dropped to the ground, eyes fluttering in his head, and then Drew's body shifted and distorted in fragments, appearing as if he was digital. "Shit."

"What the hell just happened?" Chris asked.

"He sent himself back in time," Camila said.

"Cool," Isaiah mumbled.

"Not really, dammit. Just means he's still around. Okay, let's go, but be cautious, and if anything seems repetitive, say something. Camila, keep your Elanchu thing on."

"On it, boss." She looked at me and gave me a wink.

My chest tightened, thinking of all the things I had felt within her as she touched my force field.

We made our way down a few corridors, Camila leading the way. A couple of times, we narrowly avoided more guards, but then it dawned on me. There was no alarm going off. The entire facility should have been on lockdown.

Things were not right—again.

As we rounded the next corner, which according to Camila was only a few meters away from our final exit, we found ourselves in the middle of a four-way intersection. Ahead of us was Miriam with swarms of guards behind her.

We stopped, each of the kids getting ready to fight.

"For heaven's sake, stop it. All of you. You're outgunned, outmanned, and you're out of time. James, this is over. I've managed to use Drew to eliminate the casualties. So far, you haven't killed anyone, but I can't keep using him. The man is positively exhausted. Don't do anything stupid. If you end up killing any of my people, none of you will make it out into the world without criminal records. Think about that very carefully. Wherever you go, the police will be tailing you constantly. I know none of you want a life on the run."

"Shut up, you crazy-ass bitch. At least it would be a life of freedom, not caged up in a cell." Camila pushed forward.

"Crazy-ass bitch? Well, my dear, that's rich, coming from you."

Camila took several steps forward, with rage plastered all over her face and Astrals forming behind her.

A handful of men with guns pushed past Miriam and aimed their weapons at Camila.

"Camila, don't. Come back here," I said.

"I'm tired of this shit. I've been stuck in here for so long. I want out. And she holds my life in her hands. It's not fair!" Camila screamed the last few words, tears running down her cheeks. Waves of anger and frustration rolled off of her. You wouldn't have to be an empath to see the utter anguish on her face.

"Camila, sweetie, come here. I'll help you," Annabelle started, but it was too late.

Camila's Astrals rushed the gunmen, little energy grenades and bombs dispersed amongst Miriam's henchmen. A few guards grabbed Miriam and pulled her to safety.

"It didn't have to be like this, James!" she yelled over her shoulder as she was taken away.

"No, no way. She doesn't get off. She doesn't get to be safe!" The amassing wave of Astrals stormed the gunmen. In one coordinated motion, each guard raised their gun, aimed it towards Camila, and fired. The whole scene proceeded in slow motion. As the recoil from the guns pushed the guards' shoulders back, and the loud *bang* reverberated all around us, a wide spray of ammunition hurtled our way.

"No!" I screamed. Camila was so rage-blind I wasn't sure if she actually saw what was coming her way or not. I started to throw my hand out to place a force field between Camila and the oncoming disaster, but just as my wall was creating itself, generating that ripple that looked like heat coming off a car in the summer sun, Camila clawed her hands into the air in front of her. She ripped open a portal just where the bullets were heading.

She was using her teleportation skills to send the bullets elsewhere, except I knew where the exit to that teleportation spell would be.

A sparkle of light burst right in front of Camila's chest as the secondary portal opened.

It was the one spell she never got right when we were practicing in the hangar.

A second passed as all the kids figured out what was going on and the collective looks of shock and horror registered on their faces.

"No!" Ning cried out.

The bullets emerged from the portal, but they were hard to see, they flew so fast. As Camila's body curled inwards, the blood pouring out from the impact wounds on her chest, we all knew they had found their destination.

Camila had saved the rest of us, by placing herself in the way and funnelling all the shots into her.

More guards were coming up the other hallways. We were quickly being surrounded. Ning turned at the oncoming pack and screamed in grief. The hallway froze over. Guards slipped and fell on the ice, but she didn't stop. Layers continued to build until she had a wall of ice blocking at least one direction.

The air near us grew cold.

Annabelle ran over to Camila, hoisting her up into her tiny lap. "Camila, why?"

Her eyes fluttered as she tried to focus on who was holding her.

She reached up and touched Annabelle's cheek. "Because, clairvoyance. I knew this would happen. It was the only way the rest of you got out of here. Take me, Annabelle. It's what your horde wants, add me. It's the only way I'm going to see beyond these walls. Please, do it. Take away the loneliness and sadness. I don't want to feel that anymore," Camila whispered.

"What?" Isaiah said. His voice hitched with anger, sadness choking him.

Another hallway was filling with guards.

"My turn," Chris said with his lip turned up into a snarl, flames erupting from his eyes. Instead of turning into the wolf, he used his pyrotechnical talents and let loose an eruption of flames. It was as if his two arms had turned into flamethrowers. Bright balls of orange and red heat barrelled through the corridor, scorching everything in its path. Whatever men were starting to converge on us turned instead and beat a hasty retreat.

Chris kept thrusting the fire down the hallway as the light in the intersection where we were trapped suddenly dimmed.

I was still trying to keep up my force field, which was becoming harder and harder to do with all the distractions, but then the lights flickered and failed plunging us into darkness. There was only one explanation.

Annabelle.

Above all the noise of erupting flames, gunshots, and the crackling of ice as it started to melt from the heat Chris was creating, the multi-layered voices of Annabelle's demons tickled the back of my neck and made my hackles stand on end.

Shadows moved, and there were other things present with us.

A cold hand brushed past my shoulder, and suddenly, I could feel and hear Cody behind me, his lips brushing my ear as he spoke, *"We've got her. Maybe you saved us after all."* And then he laughed maniacally.

A light bloomed from the two figures near the floor. It was Annabelle holding Camila.

We all watched as Camila's soul left her body, and from behind Annabelle, the tall thin demon with rakish hands glided forward.

"No!" Isaiah screamed. He flicked his hands towards the demon, sending arcs of lightning towards it, but they travelled through the beast, having no effect on it whatsoever.

An apparition that looked exactly like one of Camila's Astrals walked towards the thin man. He welcomed her with open arms. They embraced.

And then the entire scene dissolved into mist and fog. Cody gradually dissolved into the rising wind and was whisked away in his signature white smoke.

The demon fog swirled violently, spinning counter clockwise all around us. Annabelle stood in the center. She raised her arms outward and sucked up the thin man demon, Cody, and Camila.

With a deafening *boom*, an explosion of energy emanated out from Annabelle, sweeping all the CMRD guards off their feet and plowing them into the walls. Chris, Ning, Isaiah, and I stood on the perimeter of the blast, and felt nothing more than a strong wind.

Score one more for the demons.

Thirty-Three: Final Exam

THERE WAS NO seizure, no convulsing, just Annabelle floating several inches off the floor with her toes grazing the concrete. Her eyes had morphed into white orbs that focused on nothing, and her hands were splayed and slightly raised out to each side as she floated down the hallway. The black demon mist flowed out behind, disappearing into little wisps and tiny curlicues. The dress she wore billowed out, gently undulating. She would have looked like a ghostly apparition if it wasn't for the fact that everything she wore was completely black.

But to my surprise, just down the corridor, deep in the long shadows and partially hidden, was one of Camila's Astrals leading the way. Isaiah and I exchanged a quiet glance between us, acknowledging the awkwardness of still having Camila with us, but not really.

What was it like within Annabelle's horde? Was Camila's mind still a swirling mess of emotions now that she resided with the demons? Or had she found peace? I hope she got what she needed.

The remaining CMRD guards that originally surrounded us, who had been blown off their feet by the demonic detonation were either staggering away from the scene or lay unconscious on the floor. Miraculously none of us had been touched.

So then, this was it. Spectral Camila was just down the hallway pointing our way out.

Overcome with relief, I grabbed Isaiah and waved to the others. "Let's go."

I could sense Isaiah's grief, which dripped off of him like tears, each droplet a memory of Camila. Despite the sadness, he glanced at me, then gave me a quick wink.

"Let's get going. Looks like Annabelle is leading this charge with a little help. I don't want to give the CMRD any additional moments to regroup."

"Yes, that's..." Ning voice caught in her throat. "That's sad. I'm not sure how I feel about leaving her." She pointed towards Camila's body.

"I hope she has some peace." I gave Ning a half smile.

Gathering ourselves up, we fell in behind Annabelle. I cast a quick glance down the corridor. One of those scenes where the memory of it will surely haunt a person for the rest of their days.

Black sear marks, blood spatter, dents in the walls, and bodies were strewn all over the place.

My focus gravitated to one body in particular—Camila. Ning was right; it felt wrong to be leaving her behind, and yet we had no ability to take her with us. The image of her bloodied chest, her eyes open and head tilted to one side burned itself into my memory.

Annabelle turned to look at us and hissed in a voice not her own, "We must hurry. Our window is small."

She glided down the passageway at an alarming rate. The four of us had to break into a jog in order to keep up.

Guards appeared and only half-heartedly attempted to thwart us, but between Ning's blasts of ice, Chris's launched fireballs, and Annabelle's ability to call on Cody's telekinetic talents, they didn't stand much of a chance, and there was no further coordinated effort on the part of the facility.

At one passageway, several guards stumbled on to us, but Annabelle summoned up her sleep demon. Mora was quick, scampering up the wall and hanging from the ceiling, then digging into the surface with its fingers and toes. It stretched its mouth open to an unnatural circumference as a torrent of vile sand and grit was spewed out, covering the CMRD henchmen and instantly putting them all to sleep. If the Sandman visited every night to bring you sweet dreams, I can't imagine the nightmares induced by this creature.

As we entered the foyer, the one that held the security desk and the metal scanner I had passed through what seemed like a very long time ago, another small band of men had gathered, making a line across the front doors.

Ah, so the CMRD hasn't given up. Walking out those doors was never gonna be easy.

Cody's white smoke, seeming to emerge from underneath Annabelle's clothes, trickled down her body, pooled at her feet and then snaked across the floor towards them. Cody became corporeal within the vapours, but he simply stood there. He didn't appear as rotted as he had before his absorption into the horde. Perhaps being consumed by Annabelle's demons wasn't that bad. I could hold on to that hope.

Annabelle thrust each arm out to her side, mimicking a move I'd seen Cody do many times before. Guards flew in opposite directions, becoming pinned against the far walls in two clusters. Annabelle held them there, which cleared the way, and with no resistance, we headed towards the glass doors that led to the outside world. I had no idea what day of the week, or even what month it was, but looking outside, it was dark and snowy. Big snowflakes fell from the sky. It looked like it was going to be a cold escape. Our entire group could possibly fit into my car, but it would be a tight squeeze. That was if the beater of a vehicle was still in the parking lot—and even then, I didn't have my keys.

We were going to have to be creative to get away from here. Somewhere warm and safe.

Annabelle was already through the first set of doors when the *click-clack* of Miriam's heels sounded behind me.

I turned to look, and there she was, standing with more guards on each side of her. Her mouth was pursed, and her arms were folded across her chest. Chris and Ning had already trailed after our Arcane and were through the front doors, but Isaiah stayed by my side.

"You're not going to get far, James. Don't think you can just waltz out of here," Miriam said.

"I think that's exactly what we're doing. And one way or another, Miriam, I will find a way to bring this all down around your head. You tricked these kids, used them as a means to make money, and had no intention of helping them. You should be ashamed of yourself, but I don't think you're capable."

"You're all monsters," she said, her red-lipsticked lips turning into a frown.

"I think you're the monster." And with that, I turned and made a promise to myself right then and there that I would never walk into this facility again, and one way or another, Miriam would pay for everything she'd done.

I had just pushed the front doors open when I looked back and realized Isaiah wasn't trailing behind me. I panicked as I saw him standing in front of Miriam, several feet away but still within the CMRD walls. His body was tense and even though his hands were at his sides, a violent storm of lightning bolts sparked around each fist.

"Isaiah, don't do it," I warned him. "It's not worth it." But he didn't listen. I walked back into the foyer and stood behind him.

"Isaiah. Please, let's go," I said.

"Listen to him, boy. Leave now before you do something you'll regret." Miriam snapped.

The air suddenly became thick and heavy and smelled of ozone. Crackles and snaps were popping from all over the place as the static electricity built in the foyer.

"I know you think you're going to come after us. I know you want us dead. I'd never lower myself to be like you. Seeing how you've managed to come out of this unscathed, but managed to scar all of us, I think my parting gift to you is appropriate." Isaiah stated as he glared at Miriam.

Miriam turned to leave.

Isaiah extended one hand and clenched it into a fist. Miriam stopped dead, mid-step, "No, no. I'm not done. You'll be sticking around for this."

The room dimmed and the shadows in the corners grew long. A presence emerged from within the darkness at Isaiah's feet. It grew above his small stature and seemed to fill the room with oppression and fear. A tail sprouted from Isaiah's backside and lashed back and forth. The Asmodeus demon was presenting itself.

"Isaiah!" I said louder, trying to get through to him. He turned and smiled at me, his eyes had turned a luminescent ice blue. Massive horns appeared from his skull, which curled up and back from his head. With a mischievous grin, he winked at me, then turned towards Miriam and her henchmen.

"Isaiah, let me go!" Miriam yelled.

Words echoed through the hall.

Old words.

Ancient words.

Miriam's small crew swayed slightly back and forth, in time to the twitch of the demon's tail, like a metronome. Their eyes suddenly flashed sky blue in tandem with the beast's eyes, and then Isaiah turned and walked through the glass doors. I tagged closely along behind him, but my attention was focused on watching Miriam and her guards.

All the guns in the room turned towards her.

I couldn't believe what I saw. For the first time in my life, Miriam was afraid. I could feel the prickly emotion oozing from her.

Isaiah stopped, turned to me, leaned in, and pulled me close. His lips parted and, while standing on his tippy-toes, kissed me, gently but warmly. I shivered at his touch, it was exciting and rousing, yet vaguely familiar, because it wasn't Isaiah, it was his demon.

And then while we were in the middle of our kiss, he snapped his fingers.

The entire foyer of the CMRD lit up with bolts of electricity, sparking and arcing in every direction, until all the electricity converged on Miriam.

Little arcs of electricity flashed within her clothes, across her far-too-styled white up-do, and the inside of her cheeks lit up. Her eyes flashed ice blue as she jerked and twitched.

I pulled away from Isaiah, wanting to watch Miriam get what was coming to her. Isaiah nuzzled his beard into my neck as his inner beast let out a growl.

With her guards keeping her at bay and held at gunpoint within the foyer, each bolt of electricity missed the henchmen and, instead, headed straight for the old bitch. The electrocution continued. Miriam's eyes had rolled into the back of her head. Foam was forming at the corner of her mouth.

I glanced towards Isaiah. "Ah... before you—"

"Don't worry," he interrupted "They're not enough to kill her. Just enough to ensure she'll never forget she decided to fuck with the wrong people," Isaiah said between kisses on my cheek.

He leaned back and studied me, smiling, as his ice-blue eyes faded back into their luscious brown. The warmth coming off Isaiah's body was sensual. The smell was uniquely his, a mix of leather and sweat, and it hung heavy like musk between us. Dressed in only his tank top, loose-fitting jeans, and a baseball cap worn backwards, he produced enough heat to keep him warm in the dead of winter.

Isaiah grabbed my hand and led me out through the last set of doors of the CMRD. Chris, Annabelle, and Ning stood there, waiting for us.

"Okay, I'm bloody well freezing—we're out of this hellhole. Let's get far away from it. How do we get somewhere warm?" Annabelle said, her tiny arms crossed and folded, hugging herself as she tried to keep from shivering to death. Her teeth chattered in response to the falling snow.

Ning shrugged and Chris was half on fire. The elements clearly weren't bothering them.

Chris put an arm around Annabelle and used his elemental fire to warm her.

"It's a good question," Isaiah said. "Where do we go from here?"

"I need to get back to the city and find Shawna. I know that's not a priority for any of you, but I have to find her," I said.

"Well, I'm coming with you," Isaiah said. "Besides, my demon still hasn't got his side of the contract fulfilled yet, and I can tell you, he's getting restless." He winked and smiled lasciviously.

"I wish we could have brought Camila. She deserved that. She should have been able to get out," Ning said, dropping her head. It was almost a whisper. "I want to help you, James. You rescued us. The least we can do is help you find your sister. My Yuki-onna is going to insist on me finding her body, and when that happens, I will have to leave, but for now, I will stay with you."

"Ning, I never expected any of you to stay with me." I placed a hand on her shoulder, no empathic push, just a kind gesture implying that I understood. "I appreciate the offer, but you can go satisfy your contract if you need to."

"Not yet. She isn't demanding it, but eventually, I will have to go find *her*." Ning grimaced.

"I'll come, too, but I want to phone home. I need to let them know I'm okay," Chris said, and then he looked at Ning. "I want to come help you when you have to leave."

I wasn't sure, and I was so tired from our ordeal in getting out of the CMRD, but I thought, I sensed a little spark of...interest? Attraction? Was that in the cards for these two? Is that what I was sensing?

Ning nodded. "I would like that."

"Fire and Ice. Cool," said Isaiah with a genuine smile.

Annabelle rolled her eyes. "All right, well, that's great, but I'm still freezing to death. One thing demons don't do is keep you warm. Can we please get out of here? I'm all yours until Tonka comes to fetch me. I haven't got anywhere else to go, and it's not like I can go home. As much as I'd want to."

After hearing her say that last part, my heart hurt. I knew, despite her parents religious convictions, Annabelle still loved her mom and dad. She needed family. Perhaps she could find that within Tonka's coven.

I glanced around the parking lot, and there, buried in snow, was my old champagne Corolla.

I turned to Isaiah, "Think you can spark it into running?"

"You mean I get to hot-wire a car? Man, I haven't done that in ages!" He rubbed his hands together with excitement, sending off static discharges and little bursts of blue light. My eyebrows raised in genuine surprise.

Isaiah noticed my reaction and immediately reined in his excitement. "Yeah, okay, I might have done a few things in my past you don't know about."

"I bet. We'll chat about that later," I said.

We walked over to the car.

Chris placed his hands on the metal hood and heated the beast of a machine up, which melted the snow cover.

"Dammit, it's locked," I said.

"Ha, you know you could just teleport in there, but no problem. Least I can do for you." Isaiah flicked his finger, which unlocked the door. I rolled my eyes. He was right, of course. Isaiah took a seat on the driver's side and studied the dash for a moment, then placed his hands on the steering column.

Short little bursts of electricity erupted from hands. There was a sputter from the engine, a few grinding cranks, and then nothing.

"Hmm, I'm out of practice." Isaiah frowned, wrinkling his brow as he shook his hands out.

"It didn't exactly run well when I left it here," I confessed.

"Let's have another go, shall we?" Isaiah placed his hands back on the steering column and cranked up the bolts.

Just then, the doors from the CMRD burst open and a cluster of guards and a smoking Miriam emerged.

"Them!" She pointed in our direction as her henchmen raised weapons and aimed.

"Isaiah, it's now or never!" I yelled.

Isaiah's body clenched, jolting him forward, and an immense arc of electricity burst forth. Tiny sparks and little bolts danced throughout the metal in the car, but that's all it needed. The engine roared to life, and the belt under the hood screamed, complaining about its resurrection.

"Well done!" I complimented, not that Isaiah needed any encouragement. He was all smiles. "Shove over, I'm driving."

The rest jumped in.

"Let's go! So, first stop?" I asked my passengers as we hurtled out of the CMRD parking lot while gunshots flew around us but, amazingly, never hit the car. I looked in my rearview mirror. Annabelle sat in the middle of the back seat, her eyeballs completely white. Clearly she was doing demonic magic to keep us safe.

"I want real food," Isaiah said.

We agreed on a spot in the city, the southern edge, a diner I knew.

I glanced in the rearview mirror once more. This time watching the CMRD disappear into the distance.

Never again. I will get you, Miriam. Somehow. Some day.

Thirty-Four: Graduation Ceremony

IT WAS A long quiet drive back into the city. Thankfully, no one from the CMRD saw fit to follow us, but assurances on that were slim. We would have to watch ourselves over the next while. I didn't trust Miriam not to send out subversive Magicals to end us. After all, we were a black stain of failure for the CMRD. I was fairly certain she'd never attempt to abduct our motley band and haul us back. We weren't financially feasible. Hopefully, we had seen the last of her.

Regardless, I would be on guard for a long time to come.

I parked the car and everyone got out. Poor Annabelle was still shivering. She made a beeline for the restaurant doors.

"I'm so fucking cold," she grumbled. The black mist wafted out from behind her. That ought to set a few restaurant patrons on edge.

"Ah, money. Money is kind of an issue," I said, patting down my pants. I had no wallet. That had been left behind at the CMRD.

"Damn," Chris said. "Now what?"

Isaiah spun around, searching the vicinity.

"What are you doing?" I asked.

"Lookin' for a bank machine. Doesn't look like there's one here. Go on inside, get her warm." He nodded in Annabelle's direction. "I'll be back in a bit."

And then, like that, he was gone.

"Dammit," I said.

"What?" Chris gave me a sideways glance, as if to say what's your problem?

"I think I know what he's up to, and I don't like it."

"Don't care. I'm hungry. Let's go." Chris left me standing in the parking lot.

WE WERE SEATED by the hostess, a young girl, probably only a couple of years junior to Annabelle, but she treated us like we had the plague.

She dropped the menus on the table and said rather abruptly, "Kevin will be your waiter." She scurried away and then cornered a busboy on the other side of the restaurant, engaging him in a rather animated conversation, which was clearly about us.

We sat, scanned the menu and then ordered food when the server came and took our order. He mimicked the hostess's reaction. Clearly, we were making everyone uncomfortable. And when I sat back in my chair and looked around the table, it didn't take long to figure out why.

Annabelle looked like a Goth child with her Arcane mist flowing out the back of her. Occasional embers of fire erupted from the depths of Chris's dark skin, not to mention his eyes, which intermittently flashed bright amber. Ning's shocking white hair was nothing in comparison to the occasional patch of ice crystals that formed on the surface of her skin, only to disappear a few seconds later.

And then Isaiah teleported directly into the center of the restaurant.

Great. Okay, so, we're gonna have to have a chat about "fitting in."

Isaiah gave a plump plastic bag to Annabelle and then sat down. He dug into his loose jeans and pulled out a wad of cash and put it on the table.

"Dinner's on me!" He smiled.

"Okay." I turned towards him and whispered, "How?"

Annabelle squealed. "Oooh! Isaiah, this is perfect! Thank you." She pulled out a black hoodie that had a white skull decal plastered on the front. She slipped it on for additional warmth.

"Same way I started your car, but with a couple of bank machines." Isaiah smiled and winked at Annabelle. "Glad you like it! I remembered this store and knew there would be something there you'd like."

"Isaiah, that's stealing." I was a little angry. I mean, we had to have a way to get our feet steady out in the real world, but this wasn't the way to go about it.

"No, I paid for the hoodie." Isaiah scrunched up his eyebrows and looked a little sad.

I glared at him and then at the cash on the table.

Isaiah rolled his eyes. "Okay, look, I get it, but we have to eat, and I didn't take that much. There's only a couple hundred there."

I stared at him, "A couple of hundred?" I swiped the stack and counted. "More like six hundred."

"What do you want me to do? Take it back?"

"No," I hated this. He was right, but...this wasn't right. "Just, never again. Okay?"

Isaiah shook his head and frowned, then grabbed my hand and squeezed it. "Okay. I'm sorry. You're right. I won't do it again. What did you order for me? I'm starving."

I was looking forward to a fat cheeseburger and fries. I had ordered Isaiah the same thing. It didn't take long before our food arrived. I think the restaurant wanted us out as soon as possible.

"Oh my god, this is so good," Isaiah's words were muffled as he chomped down on the monster cheeseburger. Each of them were smiling and shovelling in their food. It had been a while since any of them had had a good greasy meal.

There wasn't much talking. We were too busy eating and the palpable sense of Camila's absence was still heavy. Not to mention the stares from everyone else in the restaurant that made our very presence awkward.

"So, now what?" Annabelle said, breaking the silence after we had finished eating. The busboy was taking away her plate and pushing his hand through the black mist behind her.

She noticed, and a face formed in the fog and snapped at the restaurant employee. That sent him scurrying.

"Well, no secret there." I ignored the busboy's actions. "I need to go back to my apartment and then start the search for my sister. That is not going to be fun, and given what Miriam has told me and shown me, it could also be dangerous." I wasn't looking forward to this. I should have just let Shawna go, but I couldn't. I had always been the one who cared for her. Admittedly, this might be the last time I was going to go out on a limb to try to reel her back in from the brink of disaster.

But last time or not, I still had to try.

"I need to call home, but..." Chris looked a little embarrassed.

"Dude, we need phones..." Isaiah said, interrupting Chris, and twisted his mouth into a frown. "I can't believe I forgot about that."

"Ning, do you still have yours?" I asked.

She shook her head.

"Well, I suppose that's okay. I can't imagine Miriam would have put a data plan on it anyway. It was more of a glorified alarm clock. Okay, well, let's go back to my apartment. We can get settled there and then figure out the other details. I'll warn you, though, my place is a studio and not in a

very nice part of town. It won't be comfortable, but we'll at least be warm."
I stood up from the table and the others joined me.

Isaiah paid the bill at the cash counter as I made my way to the rusted-out Corolla.

After everyone was piled in, I looked at Isaiah, "Okay, do your thing."

The engine was more forgiving this time and started up with only a couple of jolts from Isaiah's fingers.

"You're getting better," I said.

He smiled.

MY PLACE WAS in a seedy part of the downtown core, and from the suburbs, it was going to take at least an hour's drive to get there. I took the major routes. During the day, they would have been congested and clogged with commuters, but this late at night, the way would be clear. It was also the fastest.

We turned off the freeway, onto 101st Street when Chris yelled from the back seat.

"Jesus! Pull over, pull over!"

"We're almost there. What the hell is going on?"

Black mist enveloped the car, obscuring my view. I glanced at the rear-view mirror to see Annabelle in the middle of the back seat, eyes pure white, mist undulating and growing thick. Demon arms were unfolding from her back. The flesh was red and spotted with black clawed nails. One of the arms grasped my shoulder, its talons digging into my flesh.

"I see you..." Annabelle squeaked out in that airy high-pitched voice that would terrify anyone.

Annabelle sat up, constricted and jerky in her movements, while Isaiah tried to fan away the mist and clear the view of the windshield.

"Christ's sake, stop it. I can't see!" I said.

Annabelle placed her fingers over my eyes, completely blocking my vision.

"I see you..." she repeated.

I was completely surrounded by demon fog. Faces formed in front of me, then disappeared, and I could hear little clawed feet scampering around.

The mist parted to reveal my apartment building.

There were shadows of men hiding in various spots, which glowed a strange eerie red. One in a car across from the main entrance to the building. Another hiding in the alley between my building and the next. As I glanced up, there were people moving in the window of my apartment.

A voice that sounded like it could have been Annabelle whispered from behind me, "They wait for you..."

With a blink of my eyes I was back in the car and all hell was breaking loose. Isaiah had grabbed the wheel, Chris was yelling at Annabelle, and little flames were erupting from his skin. Ning was shrieking and clutching the back of my seat.

Annabelle came back as herself and the demon arms rescinded into her. "Oh my God, James!" She pointed.

The car was careening out of control, despite Isaiah's attempt to steer, my foot had pressed down on the accelerator. We were heading straight towards a lamp post.

I slammed on the brakes, yanked the steering wheel hard to one side. Then we hit a patch of ice...

The result was flipping the car.

Over and over and over.

The sound of smashing metal against concrete was overwhelming. The window on my side busted out. Little square shards of glass rained down on us like raindrops.

I'm still not sure if it was psychic skill or self-preservation, but I wrapped us up in a comfy telekinetic ball as the car rolled several times. There were several of the force fields that formed see-through pillowy security blankets. When I could see out a window, parts from the car flew off in various directions down the street, and we smashed into a couple of parked cars, which stopped the roll of the car. The vehicle bounced and rocked back and forth a few times until finally stopping to rest upside down on its hood.

"Everyone okay?" I asked.

"What the fuck, Annabelle?" Chris yelled.

"I'm sorry! I don't have any control over her. James, we *cannot* go to your apartment."

It took us a while to extricate ourselves from the badly crunched Corolla.

"If we're here when the police arrive, we'll be here all night," I said.

"So, let's go. Leave this. We don't really need it anyway," Isaiah said.

"Yeah, but if we can't go to James's apartment, where the hell do we go?" Chris asked.

"I don't care, just figure it out. I'm not standing out in the freezing night air." Annabelle's teeth chattered together.

"Um, I *might* know a guy who can help," Isaiah offered.

"Oh! Well, let's go see him!" Ning instantly perked up, pulling her white lock of hair behind her ear with her finger.

"No, that won't work," Isaiah said.

"Sorry?" I looked at him and squinted. "Why?"

"Let's just say I know this guy from my time on the streets, and he knows me but he doesn't take to strangers. Trust is a big issue. Let me go. I'm pretty sure he'll have a place we can crash for the night."

The others nodded and seemed fine with this plan, but in my gut, something told me there was more to this story than Isaiah was letting on.

I pulled him aside. "I don't like this. Please take me with you."

"James, it's okay. Trust me. But I can't take you. Daddy doesn't like unannounced visitors."

"Daddy?" I said, surprised.

"Yeah, his street name. Kinda sick. Just let me get this done." And with that, he was gone.

"OKAY, WELL, THIS is it," Isaiah said.

"Holy shit, man. This is huge!" Chris said, impressed. Ning was draped off his arm, staring up at the monstrous mansion that Isaiah had secured for us.

"Well, I told him there were five of us." Isaiah glanced towards Ning and Chris.

Ning rushed over and gave Isaiah one of her memorable and unrequested hugs.

Isaiah snickered.

"Okay, well, let's go in. The owners are foreign and never come here." Isaiah smiled and punched the numbers on the keypad. It beeped for each number entered and then the big black wrought-iron gate swung open, creaking as the mechanics worked their magic.

"What did you have to do to get this? I can't imagine this came 'for free,'" I said, still staring at the house.

"Yeah, well, let's just say I owe Daddy a favour or two," Isaiah said.

"Exactly what kind of favour?" I asked so just Isaiah would hear. The others were already waiting for us at the front door.

Isaiah dangled a ring of keys from his pinched fingers so they could see he had the way to get in.

"James, I don't do *those* kinds of favours anymore. Please trust me," Isaiah said.

"What do you mean 'anymore'?" I said, shocked.

"Dude, I lived on the streets for two years. Believe me, I did what I had to in order to survive," Isaiah said, a little angry, but I could tell he was embarrassed too.

"I'm sorry. I guess I..." I stumbled with my words.

"Wait. Are you jealous?" Isaiah canted his head to one side while he cocked an eyebrow. Ice blue flashed in his eyes.

"Well, maybe. A little. Geez, Isaiah." I instantly felt flushed. "I don't want my boyfriend doing *those* kinds of things. Okay?"

"Really?" A smile spread across Isaiah's face.

"Really, what?" I asked, suddenly feeling like I just said things I shouldn't have. The heat radiating off my face was becoming unbearable. I felt like such an idiot.

"You just called me your boyfriend. You mean that?" Isaiah's eyebrows disappeared underneath his baseball cap.

"Oh! Um...well, I ah."

Fuck, you idiot. Own this. Do it.

"Yeah, I do. I mean, we're not in the CMRD, right? So..." I shrugged stupidly.

Isaiah's smile turned into a bright beaming happy face as he closed the small distance between us and wrapped his arms around me, planting a kiss that was filled with silly giddiness.

"The demon will be happy about that. Let's go let the others in to the house."

IT TOOK A while before we had everyone settled in the house. Isaiah made a run to get some basic groceries. I pulled sheets off furniture, turned the thermostat up, and got the house running again.

It was late. And within minutes, the length of our day and the realization of what we had been through weighed heavily. The others made their way to bed, dead tired from exhaustion. Isaiah was putzing about in the kitchen, putting dishes away, in his customary tank top and a loose pair of sweatpants.

I came up behind him while he was drying off the last of the cutlery and slipped my hand up under his tank top, enjoying the sensation of his hairy stomach.

I kissed the back of his head. "I have to go."

"What, now?"

"Yeah. I need fresh clothes and there's a few things I need from my apartment." I squeezed him.

"But Annabelle's vision?" He shimmied around to stand face-to-face with me. His expression was plastered with concern and worry.

"Yeah, but that was hours ago. Surely if there had been anyone waiting for me, they'd be gone by now."

But Isaiah wasn't having any of it. "Nope. No way. If the CMRD is gonna come after you, then they'll have to take on all of us. Besides, I'm not letting you put yourself in harm's way. I just got me a boyfriend. I intend to keep you around a while." He wiggled his eyebrows.

I snorted out a laugh.

"Look, it's just a quick teleport in, grab some stuff, and then 'port right back out. I'll be in and out so fast, no one will ever know I was there." My hand stroked his back, trying to reassure him that this was okay.

"Nope. Not gonna happen. At least, not by yourself." He glanced at the dishes behind him. "So let's go bounce over to your place together, collect whatever you need, and come back here. I can help carry stuff."

"Well, there's not that much to get. A couple of things. My life was rather simple the last year or so. I'm pretty sure I can handle this myself."

Isaiah shrugged. "Maybe, maybe not. This is one time you don't get to be the teacher. Nope, it's settled. Let's go." Isaiah gave me a quick peck.

THE MOMENT WE hit my apartment and took our first breath, we were overcome with a stench so putrid we both gagged. It was pitch-black inside my apartment.

"What the hell, dude?" I couldn't see Isaiah's face, but I could hear him gagging.

"Oh, god, that is horrid." I tried breathing through my mouth, but that just left the scent on my tongue. It was so rotten I could taste it.

"Something must have spoiled in your fridge," Isaiah said.

As my eyes adjusted to the lack of light, shapes formed that weren't familiar. The air itself was not only rancid, but thick and close. The atmosphere felt seriously off. Wrong. A shiver ran down my shoulder blades.

"Isaiah, don't move and don't touch anything." I inched my way over to the wall and reached to flip on the light switch.

The moment I flicked it on, we were momentarily blinded by the harshness of the bare bulb glowing above us. But that dissipated, and then as my squinting receded, I felt the blood drain from my face. My hands turned instantly cold.

"Holy shit," Isaiah muttered.

Piled near the wall opposite my bed were several corpses. Their bodies were rotting and bloated. Flesh hung awkwardly. A pool of coagulated body fluids created a black circular stain on the floor. But it was the message written on the wall that hit me the hardest.

You left me.
I came.
Where were you?

"Shawna," I said very quietly, as if saying it any louder, the dead would hear.

"Oh, James, that's...that's not right." Isaiah grabbed my hand.

"Well, I guess Miriam was correct." It killed me to say that out loud. "She's obviously involved in Blood Magic."

The moment I realized that, I knew we were in trouble.

"Isaiah, why do you think my sister would have come in here, scrawled that message in blood, and left a pile of stinking, rotting bodies?" I already knew the answer.

"I have no—" Then his eyes turned bug-eyed. "She's set a trap. You wouldn't leave that behind unless it was for a spell."

"Exactly."

"What do we do?" Isaiah asked, fear anchored quickly, shaking his voice.

"We can't use any magic. None of our abilities. That might set off whatever devious spell she's left."

"Can we leave, please? This is way too creepy." Isaiah shivered.

"Yeah, I think that's best, but stay close to me," I instructed him, then squeezed his hand and started to make my way to the apartment door.

We had to get closer to the pile of bodies before we could get to the front door. There was no way around that.

A male, in his early twenties, probably about the same age as Isaiah, was lying on the top of the heap. Half his face had fallen off.

A mouse scampered out from underneath the pile of dead things. Just two more steps...

I let go of Isaiah, grabbed the doorknob, and with the other hand, twisted the deadbolt. The minute the bolt slid back, freeing the door, a crackling sound flared out from underneath my hand. Black veins of rot, laced with glints of red, spider webbed their way across the door, onto the walls and floor, and quickly spread.

"Shit!" I said loudly.

A heartbeat, that's all it took. A single moment in time for the spell to fire and then launch.

As the first threads of Blood Magic caressed the deceased bodies, they began to stir.

Isaiah and I stood there, slack-jawed and horrified.

On the mound of the dead, an arm twitched, a head turned, an eyelid popped open revealing a cloudy, yellowed orb.

The body that had been about Isaiah's age sprang up with alarming quickness. Before I could pull the door open, the rotting corpse scampered forward on all fours. A rotting hand pushed Isaiah out of the way as the cadaver lunged at me with its mouth open, chomping and snapping.

It all happened so fast.

I should have put up a force field.

I should have teleported us out of the apartment.

As the dead man's teeth clamped down on my wrist, Isaiah's beast made its presence known, and it wasn't happy. It brayed and bellowed, sending a shockwave of damage out from where Isaiah stood and pushed me up against the wall.

I smacked my head against the door with a sickening thud and saw stars. The room before me swayed.

The undead body, however, disintegrated. It turned to ashes. Whatever the Asmodeus demon did, its battle cry was enough to extinguish the Sanguimancy.

But it was too late.

With my vision still not right, I pulled my arm up to look at where I had been bitten. Isaiah came into my peripheral vision. I knew he was seeing what I was seeing. But his eyes were half ice blue and half brown. They were both watching.

The same veins of rot, black tinged with red, emanated out from the bite. I could feel the little branches like needles digging their way through the top layer of my skin. They spelled out words.

Now.
I.
Can.
Find.
You.

The spiderwebs of rot and words disappeared as fast as they formed, but the bite turned a nasty black colour, and from the center of it, a net of pitch poison ran through my flesh, scuttling through my skin, up my arm.

"Holy shit, James, it's already on your face!" Isaiah gasped. "James...James...dude, stay with me!"

Isaiah stared at me with huge ice-blue eyes. The shadows behind him had large curled horns.

My head swirled, my wrist ached.

Everything seemed way too hot all of a sudden.

A slick of sweat formed on my back.

"Oh god, Isaiah." A sharp pain shot through my arm and then my gut. I doubled over. Isaiah's hand was on my back, pressing my shirt and sticking it to my sweaty back. "I don't have to look for her. She's coming *for* me."

I threw up. Black vomit like tar poured out in front of me, splattering our shoes.

"Then let her come." Isaiah and his beast spoke at the same time. There was a malice hidden in the layers of his voice.

"I..." The room spun.

I'm sorry...

And then my vision tunnelled in.
All I saw was Isaiah's face.
So cute.
Everything faded to black.

The story continues in *Blood Rites and Sacrifice*, Inner Demons, Book Two.

About the Author

J.P. Jackson is an IT Analyst by day working in the health industry, but at night, when the monsters come out, he writes. Demons, shapeshifters, and a host of non-human entities converge around the computer as disturbing tales are shared and recorded.

Twitter: @Canuckbear88

Facebook: www.facebook.com/jpjacksonwrites

Tumblr (18+ only):www.canuckbear88.tumblr.com

Instagram: www.instagram.com/jp_jackson_writes

Blog: www.jpjacksonwrites.blogspot.ca

Other books by this author

Daimonion, Book One of the Apocalypse
'A Tended Garden' within *Into the Mystic, Volume One*
'Hood's Ride is Red' within *Once Upon a Rainbow, Volume One*

Also Available from NineStar Press

Connect with NineStar Press

Website: NineStarPress.com

Facebook: NineStarPress

Facebook Reader Group: NineStarNiche

Twitter: @ninestarpress

Tumblr: NineStarPress